Colorado Crossfire

Books by Stephen L. Thompson

The Crossfire Series

Colorado Crossfire
International Crossfire
Israeli Crossfire
Believer's Crossfire
Spirit Crossfire
Faith Crossfire
Chinese Crossfire
Texas Crossfire
Dark Crossfire
Island Crossfire
Jagged Crossfire
Violent Crossfire
Russian Crossfire
Nuclear Crossfire
End Times Crossfire
Revelation Crossfire
Gates of Hell Crossfire
Assassin's Crossfire
Albatross Crossfire
Global Crossfire

The SFO Series
Station Force One - Onset

Colorado Crossfire

God's Call to Combat

In the beginning God calls a young couple
into His service to battle the forces of darkness

Stephen L. Thompson

Colorado Crossfire

Published by
Stephen L. Thompson
Facebook.com/CrossfireNovelSeries

Unless otherwise noted, Scripture quotations are taken from the HOLY BIBLE, NEW INTERNATIONAL VERSION®. Copyright© 1973, 1978, 1984 by International Bible Society. Used by permission of Zondervan Publishing House. All rights reserved.

ISBN- 978-0-9850758-5-9

Published in the United States of America

Foreword

To my Christian readers –
The Crossfire series of action/adventure stories include depictions of violence which are unusual in Christian literature. It would be nice if there were no conflict or violence in our world. But we live in a time when evil is increasing instead of diminishing, when some men seem to be controlled by selfishness, madness, or evil forces. When the enemies of decent mankind are bent on subjugation of other men and women, righteous men and women must stand against evil. The yoke of oppression is not lifted by prayer alone. God is our shepherd and we are his sheep. As long as there are wolves about, God will use some of us as sheep dogs to defend the rest of us. These stories are about people like that and the forces they fight against. The stories describe violence because it occurs in the real world and it is active in the lives of all people whether they recognize it or not.

To my non-Christian readers –
The Crossfire series include depictions of spiritual warfare and spiritual activity with which the non-Christian may not be familiar. These stories describe the realms and activities of both God and Satan because they are real and active in the lives of all people whether they recognize it or not.

Stephen L. Thompson

NOTE: All characters, incidents, and venues described in this book are fictitious and entirely the product of the author's imagination and remain the property of the author. This book and all text are the copyrighted property of the author and may not be copied or reproduced in any form without express written permission by the author.

INTRODUCTION

Jack Malone looked up at the sky over Denver. The mile-high city in the Colorado Rockies was bright and sunny this afternoon. An occasional breeze gently wafted down out of the cool mountains. He could sense just a hint of the ice and snow still remaining on the mountain peaks which towered over the city to the west.

Those cool breezes tempered the warmth of the sun and made for a really pleasant day. Jack escorted his wife, Laura, across the street and into the fifty-year old men's fine clothing store on Court Place, one-half block off Colfax Avenue. Jack had always liked this store because it presented a subdued ambiance that spoke of traditional values and quality. He knew all the best lines were represented in a wide variety of styles for their selective customers. No detail was overlooked and the staff worked tirelessly to keep everything in the best taste for their clientèle.

Twenty minutes later he was standing next to the Brooks Brothers collection of custom men's suits. He handed Laura a suit jacket he liked so she could add to their purchases.

Jack looked up and saw his reflection. He stopped for a few seconds and studied his body in the full length mirror next to the racks. He felt that his 175 pound weight, which was spread over his six-foot, four-inch tall body, gave him a slender and contemporary look. His muscular build was courtesy of his daily workouts and strict dietary regimen. He was pleased with the way his blonde hair made a solid frame for his lean face. Laura had told him that his face was dominated by his intense gray-green eyes. Privately, he wasn't convinced his eyes were really intense as much as just very focused. Jack knew his eyes could quickly turn ice cold when something angered him. He had recently realized that he must be bothered on some deep level because lately too many things angered him. He preferred a peaceful, orderly environment without selfish and aggressive people trying to take advantage of everyone else. Unfortunately, that seemed to be occurring too much of the time anymore.

He noticed that he was looking for a reason to beat on somebody and that implied that he did not have good anger management. Worse than that, it meant that he had some unidentified issues that needed to be determined and resolved. Studying his image in the mirror he sighed lightly to himself.

While Laura had brought a calming effect to his life, his reactions were still less than compassionate towards other people. Laura told him he had an easy smile, and was friendly. His personal creed had always been to be courteous to people. At least the ones whom he felt deserved courtesy and to avoid ones that irritated him.

Shaking his head to rid his mind of those thoughts, Jack returned to selecting additions to his wardrobe. He knew that he looked good in almost anything he wore but he preferred to purchase only quality clothes. Clothing which smoothed out the solid muscle masses of his arms, legs, and chest appealed to him. He had learned that the proper clothing made him look more like a corporate president. Thinking back over the last few years, he knew his physique was the result of nineteen years of hard work and dedication to the Martial Arts. The fighting arts which he had mastered, somewhat, he was now teaching to students three evenings a week after work.

Glancing over at his wife he again admired this elegant looking young woman who radiated class yet didn't take herself too seriously. Jack liked the fact that she was as careful about her clothing choices as he was. This afternoon she was wearing a simple, light-green summer dress which toned down her bust line and hips while showing off her legs. In Jack's eyes the color of her outfit was very complimentary to her light tan skin tone. He had complimented her on how good the dress looked on her. This seemed to please her.

Over the first three years of their marriage Jack had noticed as Laura worked each day to keep her skin soft and beautiful. She was careful to keep her appearance fresh and elegant. In her matching necklace, bracelet, and earrings of gold she could have been a model. Laura was well educated and poised; but her jade-green eyes were always full of humor, or probably, mischief. This effectively concealed her intelligence and drive until she wanted to reveal them. He'd been caught off guard several times by that little habit after they had first met.

Glancing around the store, Jack noted how the elegant furnishings and displays in the store were complimented by the quiet classical music and by a delicate floral smell which mixed nicely with the odors of fine cloth and expensive leather.

Laura carefully hung the jacket on a hanger and placed it in the 'To Purchase' area while Jack straightened out the other jackets he had disarrayed while searching for the one he wanted.

All of his life, since elementary school, he had tried to keep things in order and leave a place in as good or better shape than he had found it. He felt it was a bit of a fetish he had learned from his grandmother on his dad's side. He remembered telling Laura how he liked the fact that his grandmother Helen would clean the house they were moving out of with as much effort as she did the one they were moving into. She taught Jack that how you left a thing was a reflection of your character. Jack realized that any form of clutter seemed to bother him on a sub-conscious level. Therefore, he tried to keep order without becoming totally obsessive about it.

Jack relaxed and realized that something was making him feel comfortable. He mentally chased the thought down to figure out what it was. It dawned on him that it was the smell in the men's store which reminded him of good times in his youth when his dad would take him to stores like this. It was a rich aroma that he had always associated with important and successful men.

That thought made Jack think back to the last time he had gone shopping with his dad. It sobered him when he realized it had been almost nine years ago.

So, the story begins.

CHAPTER ONE

Jack finally was able to stand still. He stared in the silence of the store at the two unconscious bodies lying on the floor in front of him. His memory flashed back over the last five minutes trying to rationalize why he had to do what he had just done.

----------------------- ****** -----------------------

He and his wife had been admiring a Brooks Brothers suit when suddenly, the front door to the men's store was shoved open and a middle-aged man ran hurriedly past them towards the back of the store. Jack subconsciously noted the obvious details; white male, about fifty, five-foot, ten inches, and light brown hair, dressed casually in nice clothes. He had an expression of fear on his face and behind his gold-rimmed glasses his eyes looked very scared.

Both front doors were suddenly slammed open again; this time crashing against their stops, as two men charged into the building. Glancing around the store they spotted the brown-haired man. Jack watched as they took separate paths and ran toward the back of the store in pursuit. One of the chasers was large and beefy and the other one small and wiry.

They quickly cornered the brown-haired man and closed in on him as he frantically looked for a way out. Without a word, or any form of preamble, the large man drove a fist into the victim's (as Jack now thought of him) stomach. The blow collapsed the slighter man to his knees on the floor in obvious pain.

The small man produced a long thin knife, grabbed the victim by his hair and yanked the kneeling man's head back and up. Looking into the man's eyes, the small man showed his victim the knife and asked him, "You know what we want; you know what we'll do. NOW, where is it?"

Jack had no trouble hearing them as they were close. When the winded man didn't answer, the small man looked at the larger man and said, "Hugo, I don't think he has anything to tell us. He's just another dead end, another real loser." Hugo looked doubtful and held up his left hand in a signal to wait. Leaning down, the large man grabbed the brown-haired man's face in his big right hand.

Squeezing the man's face brutally, the attacker shouted at him, "Tell us if you have the item we want." The brown-haired man wasn't able to say anything or even move his head. All he could do was look up at his abuser and blink his eyes. Sighing a large sigh, Hugo let the man's face go and said, "You're probably right Billy. He has nothing to tell us."

Billy smiled and with great passion he slammed the knife blade into the chest of the kneeling man. Jack felt anger building in him as the injured man coughed but didn't scream. Billy pulled the knife out and stabbed him again. Bright red blood flowed freely from the wounds, staining the kneeling man's brown shirt and leaking onto the floor as the victim fell onto his back.

The sales clerk, who had been going over to them, recoiled in horror at the sight of the brutal stabbing. He yelled at the two men to leave the man alone. The two attackers ignored the clerk as if he wasn't there. They stood there and watched the man bleed with a sadistic fascination on their faces.

The store manager was calling 9-1-1 to summon the police and medical help for the injured man.

Billy looked around at the five customers frozen in place throughout the store and shouted, "I think you had all better leave now." To emphasize his demand he then stepped back and kicked the moaning victim in the ribs. Although there was no sound of bones breaking loud enough to be heard where Jack stood, he estimated that at a couple were broken by the kick. Both men then proceeded to kick the prone man.

The clerk became so terrified that he passed out and fell to the floor behind one of the counters.

Jack could tell that Laura was thoroughly sickened and dismayed by the evil being done to the man. He also knew her instincts were telling her that she needed to be as far away as possible. But, even with the implied threat to their safety Jack admired the fact that she didn't want to abandon the poor man to his attackers. She turned to Jack. "What can we do?"

Jack saw the other customers hurrying toward the door and discretion urged him to get Laura out of the line of fire before the sadistic thugs took notice of them. He felt conflicting emotions wash over him. The first was fear of personal injury for Laura. The second was outrage that anyone could be so callous. The third was a growing anger and tenseness in his gut.

Jack knew at that point that he wasn't going to sneak out and leave the man to these animals. It violated his personal code of honor. He lived by his version of the Golden Rule and if that was him on the floor he would want someone to help him. He gently shoved Laura towards the door. "Go."

Jack took a deep breath and headed straight for the three men. Laura rushed quickly for the door. She was almost there when she stopped and turned to look back. The fear on her face was evident but Jack had to ignore her right then.

Channeling his anger into power as he walked quickly over to the little group, he kept his face calm. He also didn't waste time on threats or warnings. As he approached with an obvious intent to interfere, Hugo turned square toward him and raised his fists. Billy just grinned.

As he came up to Hugo, Jack watched his opponent's eyes. Hugo telegraphed the punch before he even moved. He swung a powerful right-hand, round-house at Jack's head.

Instead of taking the punch, Jack raised his left arm as a block and moved toward Hugo, inside the swing, and turned to his left. Jack allowed the force of the punch and his block to straighten out the arm. He continued to push the arm away as he swung his own right arm outside the man's elbow. Jack then strongly pushed outward with his left arm and snapped his right arm back towards himself. Hugo's right arm had become an unwilling lever which pivoted the wrong way, at his elbow joint. The crunch of the disintegrating joint was completely lost to Jack in the blast of pain Hugo screamed directly into Jack's right ear.

Jack continued his move by using his left hand and grasping the wrist of the damaged arm and quickly thrusting his right hand above Hugo's injured arm to his own left, past the wrist lock. Using full body torque and power, he then used the wrist lock to pull the big man's right arm east while he shot his right elbow straight west, back into the man's face.

This strike resulted in several instantaneous things. First being that Hugo quit screaming. Second, the big man's decimated right elbow joint completely disassembled since Hugo's right hand went one way and his right shoulder tried to follow his head in the other direction. Lastly, it gave Hugo a couple of choices. He could continue to scream about all the pain, and his overall discomfiture, or, he could just pass out.

Jack noted that Hugo's brain decided to shut down, thus avoiding all the pain because his eyes rolled upward in his head until there was only white showing. The big thug then collapsed to the floor as Jack released his savaged arm.

Jack counted on his last twelve years of martial arts training. He knew it gave him excellent speed and effective techniques. He sensed the adrenaline surge pulsing through his bloodstream which gave him extra power and speed. These two blows had been almost as fast as the single blow the big man had used on the victim.

Now, Jack homed in on Billy. The thin man simply stood there with his mouth open, not believing what he saw. Billy's eyes were bulging and he looked to be in shock. Jack stepped forward on his left foot and snap-kicked the knife-man in the jaw with his right foot.

This conveniently shut Billy's mouth, caused him to lose several teeth, drop the knife, and to stagger backward. Jack used this to his advantage by spinning around on the ball of his left foot. Then, he was facing the same direction and directly in front of Billy. Bending at the waist, Jack shifted his weight to his right foot and brought his left knee up towards his chest, then snapped his left foot backwards into the smaller man's rib cage.

The devastating mule-kick to the side of the chest repaid the thug for all the broken ribs he had given the victim, and then some. Jack watched as Billy flew backward into a sales counter. The bloody-mouthed thug should have joined Hugo out cold on the floor. But he sucked up the pain in his ribs and his face, and grabbed for a revolver. He pulled the gun out and started to swing it up to point it at Jack.

As the smaller man rebounded from the sales counter, Jack had seen the grab Billy was making and closed with him quickly. As the gun came up Jack grabbed Billy's right wrist in his left hand and pointed the pistol away from his body, then twisted Billy's right hand so that the palm, holding the gun, was facing upward. Jack then squatted down and spun to his left on the ball of his left foot, again coming around to the same direction Billy was facing. But this time, he was underneath the man's extended right arm. Jack pulled sharply down on the thug's wrist as he quickly rose to his full height.

Jack knew that the result would be similar to the "ax hand" destruction of Hugo's elbow, only cleaner. The thug's right arm was being pulled downward over the fulcrum of Jack's right shoulder. Billy's body provided the anchor on the other end.

At this point Jack knew only one of two things could occur. Either the elbow would resist being bent backward and Jack would flip Billy into the air over his shoulder or the elbow would shatter. It wasn't even close. The arm bent at right angles, backward to its normal direction.

Jack listened as the intense pain caused the thug to drop the gun and scream in a high falsetto. He released the man's right hand, and then Jack bent at the waist and reached between his own legs, grabbed the smaller man's pant legs, and yanked them forward. This suddenly pulled Billy's feet out from under him and he slammed his head into the edge of the sales counter behind him on his way to the floor. At this point, Billy went off to confer with his unconscious partner by passing out himself.

----------------------- ****** -----------------------

As he stood there, Jack felt a relief that the actual fighting was over.

CHAPTER 2

Jack looked up and smiled crookedly at Laura who was standing near the front door. Suddenly, that door was smashed open as a third man came rushing into the store. Jack saw the shotgun in this new thug's hands. It was coming up and being pointed toward him. Laura suddenly stuck out her left leg and tripped the shotgunner, who fell to the floor face first. As he fell, the shotgun went off.

The load of buckshot reduced a beautiful antique mirror on the wall at Jack's right to pea-sized rubble and pretty well deafened everyone in the store who was still conscious.

Anticipating what the new attacker would do next, Jack quickly stooped and picked up the revolver that Billy had dropped during the fight. As the shooter came to his feet and jacked a new shell into his shotgun he turned to blast the woman that tripped him, forgetting about Jack.

Even though Jack was twenty-five feet from the man, he dropped into a two-handed Weaver stance and aimed the short barrelled pistol. Seeing that Laura was out of his line of fire, he squeezed off two quick shots centered on the middle of the man's back.

The impact of the slugs knocked the man forward and caused him to again drop the shotgun. He fell to the floor, this time screaming from the pain.

Jack ran toward Laura as he saw her kick the shotgun behind a counter out of the guy's reach and back away from the irritated man. Jack's heart jumped into his throat not knowing for sure if that was the only weapon the man had. He kept the pistol aimed at the back of the man's head as he approached; slowing down as he saw the gunman had passed out. Rolling the man onto his back Jack yanked open the man's suit jacket. He found a pistol in a belt holster on the man's right side. Taking the gun out of the holster, Jack slid it over by the shotgun and well out of the man's reach if he came to.

Glancing around for any other potential threats Jack noticed that the store had fallen totally silent again. He then carefully put Billy's handgun on the ground next to the shotgun, turned to Laura, and took her into his arms as he tried to control his breathing and unwind from the unexpected action.

Laura hugged him back and clung to his chest for a minute, taking a few deep breaths she looked around Jack's left arm, and studied the man leaking blood on the floor. "Is he dead?" she asked.

Jack gently let her go and crouched down by the prone figure checking the man's neck he found a rapid but strong pulse. Realizing that the shot gunner was still alive he felt his stomach do a flip-flop as it dawned on him that he could have killed the man. That thought threatened to take Jack's mind in a direction he really didn't have time to go.

Jack noticed that he was again able to hear sounds. His hearing, deafened somewhat by the shotgun blast, returned enough to hear sirens, still a ways off, but closing quickly.

Jack quickly stood up and walked back through the store, checking to ensure that neither Hugo nor Billy would get up and attack them again. He did this by kicking each of them in their sides. But neither man seemed to notice the kicks.

Suddenly, Jack remembered the man who had been knifed. He walked over and squatted down beside the stabbing victim. Jack carefully looked the bleeding man over. He could tell that the wounds the man had sustained were very serious; he might even die from them. Yet, the man was awake and even trying to smile.

Jack saw that one of the knife wounds to the chest had probably punctured a lung because when the man tried to talk, a bright red froth filled his mouth. The man coughed up some blood and motioned for Jack to come closer. When Jack had leaned closer the man whispered, "Do you love Jesus?" Sensing the man's sincerity and desperate need, Jack gently lied and said, "Yes."

The man raised his head from the floor, put his left hand to his mouth and pulled out a key which was covered in blood. Staring at Jack closely he pressed the key into Jack's hand. Jack felt like he was being drawn into a whirlpool as the man said, "On your immortal soul, protect God's Holy

Treasure as I have, with your life if necessary. Do you promise?" Caught up in the moment and not really sure that he had an immortal soul, Jack said, "I promise."

The bleeding victim smiled gratefully and then his head slowly sank back onto the floor. Jack could sense the man was taking his last breaths. All worry and care had left his features and his eyes seemed to focus on something beyond Jack as he suddenly smiled broadly and confidently said, "Yes, Lord, here I am." Then his body lost its tension and his eyes became unfocused.

Jack knelt there a little stunned. This was the first person to ever die right before his eyes. But the thing that amazed him the most was the serene peace and even excitement on the man's face. He obviously did not just die into nothingness as Jack's understanding led him to believe was a person's lot.

Getting to his feet Jack carefully took out his handkerchief and wiped the blood off the key and his hand. Looking at the key, he thought about the last words the man had directed to him, "On your immortal soul..."

As he stood there, the men's store seemed to fade away and a chill ran over him. Jack thought that he could sense a dark, cold breeze rushing at him, blowing over an enormous, bottomless gulf of blackness that stretched endlessly below him. The feeling that he had just become involved in something far beyond his understanding was one he didn't like.

Looking once more at the peaceful smile on the face of the dead man, Jack took an overcoat from the rack and covered the man's body and then pulled it up over the man's face.

For the third time today, the front doors of the store were shoved open as two men entered the building with guns out. This time the men were Denver Policemen. Jack, while still unnoticed, slipped the key into his pants pocket. The first two police officers were joined by two more officers and a plain-clothes detective. Jack watched them as they secured the scene. The policemen collected the scattered weapons as the detective checked the three thugs and the body of the victim.

On the floor of the store the smaller of the two thugs, Billy Ortiz, regained consciousness. Two paramedics arrived and wrapped his ribs, packed cotton into his injured mouth, and immobilized his arm in a splint. Then they went to work on Hugo's arm and head.

As the paramedics placed Billy on a bright orange stretcher, the detective walked over and almost casually snapped a handcuff over Billy's left wrist and connected the other end to the stretcher. He then smirked at Billy's discomfort and proceeded to read Billy his Miranda rights.

Jack watched as they loaded Hugo onto a second stretcher. The big man was still unconscious but he was moaning. Jack walked back to Laura and saw the bullet wounds in the third thug being tended to by the paramedics.

CHAPTER THREE

Jack watched as the police took reports and pictures from everyone and of everything. They also interviewed the manager and the recently revived sales clerk. The lights had come on in the store automatically with the advent of late afternoon and the loss of sunlight. Jack noticed that the artificial lighting made the inside of the store a study in contrasts, blood and leather, teeth and Armani suits all over the place.

The detective asked Jack and Laura if they would accompany him to the manager's office. After they sat down the detective took his notebook out of his jacket pocket and produced a micro-recorder. He asked if they minded him recording their testimony.

Jack and Laura agreed to the recording. So the detective turned it on and referred to his notes. Looking up at Jack he asked, "What is your name?"

"Jack Malone." Asking for Jack's driver's license the detective copied down Jack's address and other data and dictated it into the record as he wrote it.

Looking up again he asked, "What is your occupation?"

"I'm the president of Technological Alternatives, a small research and development company located in south Littleton." Seeing the detective look up for more information he continued. "We develop and produce new technology in a variety of fields including the military, law enforcement, and the general public."

"How old are you Mr. Malone?"

"I'm twenty-eight as of June 2nd this year."

Jack watched as the man jotted down his description.

"Well, Mr. Malone, please tell me what happened here today.

As Jack related the entire sequence of events, he felt led not to disclose the key or the discussion he'd had with the dying man.

When the detective finished with Jack he went over everything again with Laura.

The detective pondered his notes and looked sharply at Jack. "You know, I wasn't always an overweight, middle-aged detective. I once served in the Army as an MP and was involved in a lot of fights and melees. What made you think you could take those two after you had just seen them knife a man to death?"

Jack smiled a cold smile at the policeman. "Because I'm a fourth degree black belt in four disciplines and I train or compete three days a week. They were just street thugs. I was sure my ability was sufficient to take them. Would you like me to demonstrate it for you?" Jack asked the question politely without any intent, but he watched as the cop chuckled a little, while looking at the two thugs on stretchers and decided that he probably didn't need a demonstration.

Jack was getting impatient by the time they were finally released with the standard warning, "Don't leave town without notifying us first."

As they left the store and walked into the fresh air of the Rocky Mountains, Jack felt as if he were coming out of a dry stale closet into a cool, refreshing mountain glade. Leaving the scene of the fighting brought relief for him.

The thought came to him that he owed his life to his wife's quick action. He stopped and hugged Laura. "I want you to know how fortunate I am to have a wife that would risk her life to save mine." He noticed the look on Laura's face. "You did know that guy you tripped wouldn't take it lightly that you did it?"

Laura laughed a nervous laugh. "To be honest, I didn't think past the point of keeping him from shooting you. It didn't dawn on me that he would turn on me. I guess that was not too smart, huh?"

Before Jack could answer, the store manager came out the front doors with a group of clothes in the store's branded bags. Seeing them standing there, he came over to shake their hands and handed them the clothing bags. "I believe that these are the clothes you picked out before the violence. Take them at no cost with my blessing. I also want to thank both of you for stopping the criminals. It was very brave of both of you. I was afraid to go near them. If you hadn't done what you did there is no telling what they would have done next." He smiled a big smile. "Your next trip to our store is totally on me. You remember that."

Jack and Laura thanked the man as the breeze picked up a bit and blew briskly down the street in front of the store. After saying goodbye they walked to their car and drove to one of their favorite downtown restaurants for an early dinner.

Jack looked seriously at Laura. "You know, I've probably broken several laws. I neglected to mention anything about the last conversation I had with Bill Martin."

Seeing the look of confusion on Laura's face he realized she had not heard that conversation. "The police said the victim's name was Bill Martin. Apparently he was an elder at a church in southeast Denver."

Jack stopped talking when the server came to their table. He waited while the man took their order and left. Then he continued, "I also failed to mention a key that the man gave me. I'm not certain why I didn't mention either one to the police. After all, aren't we supposed to trust the police? I probably should have explained everything to them and let them figure it out. But...I felt there was something about a dying man's last request and even if I'm not too sure where I stand in relationship to any God, I promised to protect the key and in the end, I wasn't able to violate a promise to him."

He took the key out of his pocket and turned it over in his hand, he said, "What do you suppose he meant by, "Protect God's Holy Treasure?"

Shaking her head in wonderment, Laura took the key and examined it. "It looks like a locker key. You know, like the ones they have in the bus stations and airports."

"And lockers in every bowling alley in town, too," Jack added with a frown.

Laura looked at him, "What do you think is in this supposed locker that is so important that a man would be willing die for it?"

Remembering the look of peace on the late Mr. Martin's face as he died, Jack smiled wryly, "I have no idea. I should probably turn it over to his church. Whatever it is will probably have more meaning there."

Watching Jack's eyes carefully, Laura asked him, "Are you just going to give them the key or do you think you should see whatever it is that he entrusted to you?"

Laura handed the key back. Jack clipped it onto his key ring so he wouldn't lose it. She asked, "Do you think your Sensei could help us find out if this is a locker key and where the locker could be? After all, he was a Denver policeman for twenty years and has probably had to do this before."

"Good point" said Jack. "But, Sensei will probably think the whole thing is about Western religion and therefore a complete waste of time."

Laura got very serious, "Jack Malone, that man died to safeguard this key and he entrusted it to you." She glanced around and leaned over and said more quietly. "Jim Grady will not think it is a waste of time. I don't know him as well as you do, but I do know that he is sensitive about honor, and giving your life up in a matter of honor is deadly serious." She paused for a minute and took a sip of her tea.

As Jack thought about the entire ugly process that had placed this key into his possession, he realized that there was more to his refusal to discuss the key or the man's last words with the police.

Laura put down her cup and waited while the waiter refilled their water glasses. "If you do try to find out what it is, what are you going to do with whatever you find in the locker, assuming you will find something or that you find the right locker?"

He reviewed the events and realized he had, in fact, 'felt' led by something beyond himself, to lie to the injured man and keep secret his key and last statements.

He smiled, "This time I made a judgment call and I feel that there is more to this matter than I understand right now. Therefore, I agree with you that we should look into this 'treasure' before we turn it over to anyone, including the police."

Jack was beginning to feel more like his normal self. He again felt pride in his abilities and that made him sure about himself. Realizing what she had just done, he again appreciated his wife's ability to settle him down.

Jack carefully respected his wife's thoughtful silence and looked around at the restaurant. It was an upscale diner that had great food and good service. The decor was in muted yellows and tans with 1950s memorabilia which was considered very retro.

Their food came and they ate quietly. After Jack paid for their meal, they left the restaurant and went to find the Sensei. Jack enjoyed the beautifully crisp early Rocky

Mountain evening and they knew they would probably find the martial arts master at his dojo, (school).

Thirty minutes later they were in the Sensei's comfortably cluttered office. The gray haired man was cordial and glad to see them. Jack again watched in amazement as the Sensei moved through what looked like clutter that was stacked everywhere. Yet he somehow knew where to find anything he was looking for at the time.

Jim Grady was a big bear of a man. He sat still as he quietly listened to Jack and Laura as they related everything that had happened. He didn't even frown when Jack told him about omitting information to the police about the key.

After they were done, the gray-haired man got up and poured himself a cup of the same tea he had offered them when they first came into his office at the dojo. Jack had always liked the beautiful white surface of the set which was tastefully decorated in delicate red roses. He remembered that Jim Grady had explained that the tea service had come back to the United States with him when he had returned as a young black belt from Asia.

Making up his mind in his usual fashion, the heavily-muscled man turned smoothly to Jack. "You know of course, that the reason this Bill Martin was tortured and killed was probably for that key?" He peered over his half glasses at the two of them. "The fact that he had it hidden in his mouth also indicates that he knew what they were after, but rather than trying to save himself, he saved the key."

Jim got up and went into the study portion of his office, pushed several books aside, and pulled a large volume from the shelf. Taking the key from Jack, he slowly opened the book to a section near the back and flipped several pages. Running his finger down the listing he located the number which matched the number on the key. Using the cross reference he turned to another section and read for a moment.

Closing the book, he turned to the computer on his desk and clicked through several icons on the screen. He then typed for a few minutes, waiting several times for responses. He finally found the information he wanted. He tapped his finger on the screen, "Bingo!" He looked over the monitor to the anxiously waiting couple and smiled. "The key opens a locker located in the Greyhound Bus Terminal in downtown Aurora."

Jack did not like enigmas and he started to stand up. "Great, let's go see what is in it and get this resolved."

Before he had fully gotten to his feet, the Sensei made a small motion with the ring and small finger of his left hand. Jack had learned long ago what that gesture meant, "sit down and shut up." So, he sat down and shut up.

Jim Grady was serious when he continued. "Before you rush right out to that locker, you might want to lose the policemen following you."

Jack smiled and shook his head, "Watching us? Why would they want to watch us?"

Jim smiled, "Standard police practice. They don't know why this man Martin was killed. The only people known in this case who are at large are you two. Your coming here is a normal reaction. If you go to the bus depot and pick up a package, they will be very curious as to what it is and if it could be connected to the killing. There would be a lot of sticky questions for you to answer. Right now, at this point, you can plead amnesia or simple confusion. You forgot about the key in all the hassle. But, if you pick up a package from a locker using the key you 'forgot' to tell them about, then you would have given the police, and most likely the district attorney, probable cause concerning your involvement in Bill Martin's murder."

The small clock in the office chimed eight while Jack thought quickly, "Probable cause for what? I was defending him, I even stopped the two men who attacked him and shot a third attacker."

"Yes, you did. All good and commendable actions, and I believe you. But then I know you and know what you are like. The police don't know much about you. They would have to assume a profit motive on your part since you concealed vital information and evidence, filed a false police report concerning that evidence, and apparently, decided all along that you were going to possess whatever is in that locker."

Jack didn't like where this was going. He could be getting both himself and Laura in some serious trouble. "Okay, I'll just go down to the police station and give them the key and tell them I forgot about it originally."

Frank Grady steepled his fingers under his chin. "Two things are wrong with that decision. First, they aren't going to just forgive and forget. They will naturally assume if you didn't tell them about this, there may be other things you're hiding from them, like, your possible involvement in the murder to start with. Second, and possibly more important, you are very intelligent and you didn't tell them about the key in the first place. Probably for a very good reason, even though you may not know what that reason is or be able to articulate it right now. Second guesses are almost always wrong."

Jack thought about this for several minutes, weighing his options, and calming himself from the flaring anger at himself that his action had caused them. "Okay, I'll tell you what. Come outside with me to our car. I have something we want to give to you. If we don't have the police watching us then that will suggest that it will be all right for me to go and tell them about the key. On the other hand, if they are out there, then we'll have to resort to plan B."

The Sensei crunched his eyebrows together, smiled and asked with a knowing roll of his eyes, "Plan B? What, pray tell, is plan B?"

Jack smiled, "I don't have the foggiest idea, but I'm working on it."

All three of them went out to the 2014 white Cadillac ITS-V. The evening had turned a shadowy dark, as night descended on Denver. Jack disarmed the alarm and opened the passenger door. Reaching in, he opened the glove box and withdrew the package he had Laura wrap for the Sensei's upcoming birthday. He handed the package to his Sensei with a respectful bow.

Jim Grady carefully took the wrapping off of the package and opened the box. Inside he found the latest in formidable edged weapons from Cold Steel, the latest version of their master Tanto line, an extremely beautiful, and very deadly knife in matte black. This was an impressive birthday gift, especially several days early.

The Sensei unsheathed the knife and held it up in the cool Colorado night air. The black matte surface made the knife seem to disappear completely. The flowing lines belied its function and presented a dreadful beauty as they shifted into and out of sight.

He sheathed the blade and gave Jack a hug, an honor he very seldom gave to anyone but his wife. Murmuring so quietly Jack almost couldn't hear him, the Sensei said, "Thank you from the bottom of my heart for this beautiful, beautiful gift." He then casually informed Jack about the Chevy behind the white Ford truck, half a block up the street. Stepping back, he again bowed to Jack, who returned the bow.

As Jack locked his car, he glanced up the street at the designated car and there were two men in the front seat. One of them was training binoculars on him right then and there. Jack also noticed the black wall tires and the small airfoil antenna on the trunk of the beige four-door sedan. "Ahh, man!" thought Jack. The car may have been undercover, but it screamed "POLICE."

Back inside the dojo, Jim suggested that they simply act normal for the next few days. The Sensei smiled at Jack, "If you are unexceptional for seventy-two hours, the police can't justify the cost of twenty-four hour surveillance on either you or Laura."

CHAPTER FOUR

Two weeks later Jack still hadn't investigated the locker, not sure, yet, if they were still being watched. The events of the fight at the store had faded from an active concern to a somewhat ugly memory that he didn't know if it was wise to revive. Laura was back to her old self and he didn't want to upset her again.

Jack noted that this day had started with one of those incredibly beautiful Colorado spring mornings. The sun was warm while the breeze from the snow capped mountains flowed caressingly over the skin like a cool liquid. The air was sparkling clean, fresh, and invigorating. The sunlight, dappled by new leaves dancing in the breeze alternately darkened and gleamed in passing. Infinite promise was everywhere. He was glad the notorious 'brown cloud' of smog had blown off toward the north and the snow-crested mountains in the west looked so close you could almost touch them.

But, there was always something to take one out of the mood. The early morning traffic was light due to a partially-observed holiday and Jack was trying to keep his mounting temper under control. For the last three blocks he had been attempting to get into the right lane. The Ford Taurus in the right lane had deliberately stayed alongside him for those last three blocks.

Jack eyed the Ford and noted the SHO insignia that indicating this model had over 280 horsepower. If the guy had any sense he'd leave Jack's Cadillac ITS-V with its 6.2L SC V8 with 556 horsepower alone. Anyway, Jack had signaled and was also attempting to lag back and let the other car get ahead of him all to no avail. He wasn't about to risk getting into an accident racing the idiot in downtown traffic. His darkening mood was interrupted by a pressure on his right leg.

Laura had placed her left hand on his right thigh to get his attention. A small smile lifted the corners of her mouth as she said, "Think we can get around this character and turn right at the next corner?"

Jack recognized that his wife was worried about his being upset and he sought to reassure her by calmly replying, "No problem, he's about to let us over" He decided to accommodate the jerk but, not the way he expected.

Jack hoped he had proven to Laura in their three years of marriage that he didn't make positive statements unless he was sure he could back them up.

Jack watched as she sat back and waited to see what was about to unfold. He saw her glance at the digital readout of the dashboard clock. Jack knew that they had enough time before her first meeting that they could go around several blocks if they had to. He watched as she looked over at the other car and saw the young guy driving the car smile at her. The way she snapped her head back to the front told Jack that she was startled to realize that the idiot was messing with them just to attract her attention.

As the light changed to green, Jack accelerated quickly across the intersection. He knew that the guy in the Ford was obviously eager to race. He had to know that the 556-horsepower V8 engine made the luxury car fast, but, he apparently thought that he could beat them if he could get Jack to race him.

When the Cadillac surged forward, the guy mashed the gas to the floor and Jack heard a scream from the car's tires. Coming hard off the line the jerk had a big grin on his face as he shot by the right side of their car. That was before he realized he had been had. By the time he got off the gas Jack had slowed and pulled in behind the Ford.

Seeing the irritated look on the guy's face in the Ford's rear view mirror Jack smiled broadly at him, and made a quick right turn onto 16th Street. As soon as he had resolved the problem Jack forgot about it. He literally dropped the entire event from his mind.

He thought about how Laura had adopted his weekly routines of exercise, rock and cliff climbing, and frequent bike riding in the mountains during the warm days. She seemed to really enjoy the mountain bike riding. Jack was reminded every time they rode that it was on mountain bikes that they first ran into each other, literally. His thoughts flew back to that important time in their lives.

------------------------------*****-------------------------

His wife had been Laura Templeton then. Jack had met her on the mountains of Colorado where they were biking some of the same trails above the scenic city of Boulder. Her first introduction to him was when they ran into each other at an intersection while changing trails. She was coming downhill on a transition trail that crossed his trail and then ran uphill again. He was coming down a steep incline about to transition onto a major bike path. He had seen the impending collision and dropped his bike to the ground, opting out for a quick run up a rock wall to lose speed. Laura had tried to stop but struck Jack's bike which had flipped into her path. As her bike flipped she went airborne over the handlebars. Jack remembered being glad she was wearing protective pads and a helmet. She had managed to complete an acceptable tuck and roll that kept her from being really hurt although she did receive some bruises and abrasions. Later he learned that it was probably her college training in acrobatics that had saved her from any serious injury.

Jack had helped her up and after ascertaining that she was okay, they went over and examined their bikes. Both bikes were damaged beyond use with bent wheels and possibly a bent frame on his bike. Jack had commented that the rental people were not going to be happy. They carried their bikes down to their cars.

Jack offered to buy her dinner to make up for spoiling her ride. Laura had cautiously accepted.

She told him later that she felt a real tingle getting ready for their "date". They went to dinner at a nice restaurant and then enjoyed a pleasant evening at a musical in the city.

Afterward, he took her to her hotel, thanked her for a great time, excused himself, and left to go back to his apartment.

Apparently Laura was impressed by his gallant behavior. He remembered her arranging it so that they saw a lot of each other during her time off from her business meetings.

Jack had been impressed with Laura and her gentle ways. He didn't intentionally go easy on her during their exercise and play times but, he was sure she had found the relationship required her to be quick of mind, and demanded that she have a great deal of physical agility to keep up with him.

He told her early on that he really liked her because she was a beautiful woman of honest charm, sophistication, and that she had an understated strength and grit. He thought about her a lot and realized at that time he was infatuated with her.

Jack thought back to the events after she returned to California. He made sure that they kept in touch by phone and email for three months. He decided to go to Los Angeles for a three day business conference and ended up spending four weeks with her. They worked well together on every level and they had both enjoyed the time which he now agreed with her was a courtship.

He had avoided any overt or aggressive intimacy because of his sensitivity to her emotional needs. He sensed that she wasn't in the relationship just for the physical side. He knew he was falling in love with Laura Templeton and like most couples in their mid-twenties; they were physically attracted to each other.

He was relieved when she explained to him that her upbringing did not condone premarital sex. He admired her for that and controlled his hormones and emotions. He understood that it would ruin everything if he insisted.

During his third week in L.A., her rather aggressive style of management reached an impasse with the staid management in her company and she suddenly found herself unemployed. Over the next two days they spent time discussing her possibilities between walks on the beach and swimming in the ocean.

Jack was aware that her college education, direct business experience and sideline experience qualified her for many different jobs. Of course, jobs weren't that easy to find in the economic times that existed then. Jack told her that he could offer her a job with his company, but that it would probably destroy their relationship or cause personnel problems in the company, because he would definitely favor her.

On the third day after she was fired, they were wading in the ocean at Torrance Beach near the cliffs. Jack had been really thinking about their future. He remembered that he had been unusually somber and quiet all morning. He realized how much a part of his world she had become and how important it was to keep her with him. He knew her financial situation was weighing on her and this was aggravated by her having no future prospects at the moment. Jack had insisted that he pay for everything while he was with her, including her monthly rent.

Making up his mind, he gently pulled her to him and hugged her. Then he proposed a completely different concept which had required some real courage. She told him later that she had been silently hoping he would finally get around to asking her to marry him but did not want to broach the subject herself. She also told him that he had certainly taken his time.

He had picked her up, sat her on a rock wall, got down on one knee in the sand, asked her if she would marry him and spend the rest of their lives together. She jumped down off the wall, and kissed him. She said, "Yes" with a smile that lit up the whole beachfront. They packed up her stuff and returned to Denver. After finding a nice ring for Laura, Jack made arrangements for her to meet his family. Laura had two brothers; her mom had passed away some years ago, and she made it clear she wasn't interested in introducing anybody to her dad.

They were married three weeks later. Laura had been attending a Church of Christ Church and they decided to have the ceremony at the local church in Denver. He remembered with a smile that she wanted a simple ceremony and the church would only allow so much pomp and ceremony anyway. Still, he made sure it had all been all that she could ever have wanted.

While the church itself wasn't elaborate, Jack had the building beautifully decorated by an expert in wedding arrangements. Laura told him later that she had loved the hundreds of pink and white balloons tied with chrome and satin ribbons that reflected the interior lights and the sunlight and gave the whole affair a dream-like ambiance.

Jack smiled to himself as he remembered insisting that the reception be held at one of the largest hotels in Denver. There were over two hundred people in attendance. Jack told Laura that only six were relatives and the rest were distant family, company personnel, press, and professional party attendees that found some way to get an invitation. Laura's brothers were her only family attending the wedding.

Jack also recalled that Laura had been really excited when she had been talking to Connie Thornton, a teacher and counselor from her high school in California. Laura told Jack that she really wanted Connie to be able to come to their wedding.

After spending some time on the phone with Connie, Laura had discussed it with him and asked him if he would help her to attend the wedding. He purchased her round-trip ticket from California and paid for her entire trip. Jack also covered the cost for Laura's brothers to attend as they were financially unable to do it.

They spent their honeymoon in Hawaii. That was two of the most wonderful weeks that Jack had ever had and he would never forget them. The days were warm, tropical, and full of fun, while the nights were sweet, exotic and full of love.

Jack had found a nice home in southeast Denver in a fairly exclusive gated community and they began the process of learning to live with each other. Laura found a progressive investment company in downtown Denver and joined the Financial Department as a Financial Analyst. As was her way, she worked very hard for two years. Hard enough that she was promoted to an important position as Junior Vice President.

Laura had been raised a Catholic by her mother. But, she told Jack that she had stopped going to church when she left for college. Laura had also shared with Jack that she hadn't felt any real connection with the Lord until she started attending the Church of Christ like the one where they had gotten married. She continued attending on Sundays and Jack would go with her but hadn't really felt like getting involved.

Settling into the normal routines of a married couple, they had agreed that they didn't want to have children until they, themselves, were ready. Jack knew that first he and Laura had to learn to live with each other.

Two months after they were married, the sale of his second product allowed them to live in style and to make choices based on desire rather than funds. Jack remembered getting the impression at that time that Laura had began to imagine what having a child would be like. She had discussed the idea with him as a future concept, but not yet.

Jack felt that she wanted him to herself for a while longer. Babies would also take away her ability to fully compete with the unencumbered co-workers in her company.

Jack had made sure that both he and Laura took time each year, regardless of how hectic their work was, to go skiing several times each winter and to go sailing or four-wheeling in the summer. Jack's old friends and the new friends they had made as a couple kept their lives full of activity.

Jack shook his head as he remembered them going through the bumps and hassles that all married people go though. He and Laura had learned to accommodate each other and not demand their own way after some heated arguments and hurt feelings.

One time a woman interested in his money tried to drive them apart with rumors and suggestions that she and Jack were having an affair and gave some very credible information and dates that he couldn't deny because he had been gone at those times.

Foolishly, he was angry when Laura confronted him with the accusations. He denied the entire thing. When she wouldn't believe him, he left in anger and spent the night in a hotel. But, he hadn't spent the time brooding, instead he started tracking down the dates and locations of his supposed affair.

After he was armed with enough evidence, he went home to convince his wife he hadn't been running around. Apparently, by that time she had cooled down enough to realize he hadn't shown any real signs of dissatisfaction or unrest as a real two-timer would have. Laura had come to the conclusion that she had jumped too quickly. When he came in with a full head of steam to convince her he was innocent, she had already reached that conclusion and asked him to forgive her.

Jack remembered smiling because Laura didn't hate the woman that started the flap but definitely didn't want her to continue with the nonsense. She tried to help her by offering to come over and discuss the problem, but the other woman quit her job and moved away from Denver to avoid running into either one of them.

Jack had continued to work at his martial arts. His mastery of the combative arts was another thing that made him special to her. He told her that his dad had introduced him to the activity as a young boy and he had grown up loving the arts.

Jack learned that in the years before he was born, his father had attended the Jui Jitsu School while he lived in Denver. When Jack was eight years old his dad took him to the martial arts school and enrolled him in a Judo class for children. At that time, this particular class was being taught by the owner of the school, Sensei Jim Grady.

Jack remembered telling Laura that he had taken to the Judo school like water running downhill. He soon found that he had a natural sense for the physical rhythms and patterns that make up the art, and he found relevance in the underlying philosophies that form the real basis for the martial arts. Jack felt he was able to combine the Eastern philosophy of the martial arts with his scientific background and make them work together.

When they had first come to Denver, Jack had introduced Laura to Jim Grady. Jack was pleased that she was impressed by his courtly manner and self assurance.

The Sensei had told Laura he was proud of Jack and gave her some of Jack's history at the school. Jack had developed into a graceful and competent combatant in the sparring sessions called Kaumate. Jack remembered that the Sensei had told him that he was impressed by Jack's sense of honor, both in the martial arts sessions and rest of his life. They had become close as teacher and student with mutual respect for each other.

By the time Jack had graduated from Colorado University he had become a second level instructor known as 'second degree' black belt in Karate and Jui Jitsu. He had reached a similar level in both Kung Fu and Ninja training, even though they didn't award belts as rankings like the other arts. Since then he had moved up to the level of fourth degree black belt in each art and spent three evenings a week teaching students at the school, which was called a "Dojo". Sensei Grady told Laura that he was grooming Jack to help run the school when he retired.

Jack had always liked to study and had earned a major degree in International Business and Finance with a minor degree in Japanese Language at the Boulder campus of Colorado University. He was now fluent in three languages;

English, Japanese, and Chinese. He was working on learning Russian and knew some Spanish. His language skills and the two separate years he spent in China since college had helped him immensely in his negotiations with overseas companies after he formed his own company.

In those early days, Jack had used his training in management and finance to multiply a $450,000 investment into a $28 million dollar business which he owned in partnership with Bob Wexler. Bob was a really funny older man that Laura had taken a liking to as soon as she had met him. Both men were proud that they had accomplished a five hundred per cent growth of their company in the last five years.

Everything seemed so positive about their lives that it sometimes seemed unreal. Jack realized that it was human nature to remember the good things and forget the not-so-good things. There had been tough times for Jack as a teenager even though he hadn't been a real "rebel". He also knew Laura's past was dark enough that she didn't want to think about it let alone talk about it.

----------------------- ****** -----------------------

Jack's mind came back to the present as they turned into the driveway of her company.

Slowing to a halt in front of the twenty-story building Laura's investment firm used as a headquarters, Jack put the car in "park", leaned over and kissed his wife on the lips. She responded and put her hand behind his head on his neck and pulled his face to her for a longer kiss.

His green eyes sparkled as he smiled. "Are you sure you want to go to work today?" The happy, dreamy-look left her face as she held her chin up and imitated a Southern drawl. "Darlin, someone's got to keep this company on its toes, and that someone is me." She smiled at him as she opened the door and got out of the car.

Walking towards the building she turned and waved before going inside.

For the tenth time that morning, Jack thought how lucky he was to have a woman like this in love with him.

After she disappeared into the building, he checked the traffic and headed south to his own company.

CHAPTER FIVE

Laura watched as the car left the driveway and smiled to herself as she turned to the bank of elevators in the back of the reception area. Her thoughts ran a normal pattern of gratefulness. "Thank you again, God, for putting such a wonderful man in my life."

She continued to think about Jack on the ride upstairs. Oh, sure, he has his faults, like the fact that he is too picky about neatness and clothes. Like the fact that he occasionally looks at the negatives more than the positives, especially when dealing with other people. He didn't seem to find any faults with her though, and she was going to keep it that way.

As she reached the 15th floor where her executive office had a nice panoramic view of the mountains, she focused on the meeting that was about to take place. She recalled that she had set the agenda for the meeting last Friday and she intended to see that it was followed. She was upset that her last two meetings had resulted in endless debates and nit-picking by another junior officer. While probably meaning his best, he was acting like a horse's rear.

As the elevator opened onto the reception room she casually surveyed the area. The reception area was done in a Southwestern motif that she thought was a bit gaudy, although she liked that the soft carpeting and wall hangings were all matched in Indian designs and colors. There was quiet background music playing and the lighting was arranged to complement the filtered sunlight coming through the tinted windows along two walls of the area. A jarring note for her was that as she exited the elevator she recognized the horse's rear immediately.

Laura thought again that Len Craxis was an odd looking sight. He stood about six foot three, was rail thin and bald on top. He had a healthy fringe of hair around his head which he had accented by allowing a full mustache and Van Dyke to grow out in matching salt and pepper coloration. The jarring note was the shininess of his bald head. Sometimes the glare was enough to make her blink. She noted that today he was dressed in a conservative three-piece dark blue suit with tiny gray pin-stripes running vertically throughout. As normal, he had picked out a tie that clashed horribly with the suit, his complexion, his hair, the walls, or almost anything else you could see. He wore a set of gold wire frame glasses over his watery blue eyes which hid an extremely agile mind. Laura thought it unfortunate that the agility quite frequently went everywhere but to the point.

She shook her head slightly when considering Len. She knew he held a doctorate from Berkeley and an attitude reminiscent of the sixty's counterculture groups. The degree he held was in Applied Linguistics and how the man loved to talk. He could talk for hours on any subject, important or trivial. Usually his dissertations were mind-numbing and unwanted by the recipient.

"Thank God he's married." she thought. Just the thought of him hitting on her was enough to make her shiver. "Besides, he's old enough to be my father." The thought of her father made her like being around Len even less.

As she walked up she heard Len expounding at great length on an obscure African rodent to the secretary. Laura stopped at the desk. Mary was happy to see her and held out her messages while asking Len to excuse her for a moment.

He seemed to realize that there were only a few minutes left until the eight o'clock meeting and excused himself, rodent forgotten, and made a dash to the coffee machine.

Mary rolled her eyes and drawled in her best Texas accent, "My word...but that man can carry on forever."

Looking at her messages Laura smiled and nodded. It wouldn't do to have one company officer cutting down another, regardless of how much truth there was to the accusation. She remembered the adage, "One doesn't wash the management's linen in public."

Laura had always enjoyed dealing with the little receptionist. She was an efficient worker and had a good heart. Laura smiled at her, "Don't worry Mary, I'll take him off your hands for the next couple of hours." Mary grinned and acted like she was wiping the sweat off her brow. "Thanks, I owe you."

Laura went into her office and noticed the phone voicemail light was blinking on her phone/intercom. Usually, during business hours the calls were automatically routed to Mary to reduce the client's irritation at having to talk to a machine. Whoever left this call had dialed around the normal number and reached the phone mail directly or Mary had patched it through to her voice mail. She punched the codes into her machine using the speakerphone arrangement so that she could continue preparations for her meeting.

Surprisingly the date was this morning and the time was less than two minutes before she reached her office. Thinking quickly, she picked up the handset in time to hear Jack tell her that he missed her and he loved her and that he hoped her meeting went all right, and that he loved her, and that he couldn't wait to get his hands on her again, and that he loved her.

Glad that she had prevented everyone nearby from hearing him she smiled and thought, "Men in love were certainly sappy," which was great. She erased the message, turning out the light and replaced the handset. The warm feeling his message had generated in her with his call from his cell phone geared her up for her meeting the way nothing else could have. "Probably just like he expected it to do," she thought.

Mary was waving her right hand in Laura's direction and pointing to the conference room with her other hand. Laura looked at the clock. One minute of eight. "Time for the grand entrance and the fist of steel", she thought, practicing her glower in the mirror on her desk.

As she walked into the conference room she noted that they were all there, Len, Mr. Brighton, and a host of other company notables, each with a personal agenda that had little to do with what this meeting was all about. She deliberately walked slowly to her chair near the head of the table. She knew her makeup was good, that her hair was in place and the very feminine yet business-like five hundred dollar outfit she was wearing raised the heartbeats on the almost exclusively male group. Her figure was full and firm, thanks primarily to the hours of exercise she forced herself to do every week. Of course, still being in her twenties didn't hurt either. She noticed several hastily averted glances following her to her seat. "Good", she thought, "Let them recognize me on several levels at once, keeps them off balance. Show me a man who is responding to his hormones and I'll show you a man whose mind isn't focused on his argument."

Mr. Brighton, the owner of the company, smiled at the assembly and opened the meeting. "You all know why we are here today," he intoned in his deep baritone. "Ms. Malone has brought us together again to attempt to resolve the delay on the Dilby investment. This investment opportunity represents one of two possible futures for this company today. If we agree to invest the five and one-half million dollars they want, we can expect a return of two to three times our investment, or so say their people. We are poised on the brink of losing this opportunity unless we decide today what we are going to do." he exclaimed, startling some of the members by slamming his hand flat onto the table surface.

The owner sat back and looked around the table at each person gathered there. He looked at Len Craxis. "Len has a bad feeling about the ability of this account to do anything except waste our investment." He then looked at Laura. "Ms Malone has become our youngest officer by being accurate in every decision of any merit she has worked on since she arrived over two years ago. None of the rest of you can make that statement. But, she has never bet on such a large investment as this one to date. Therefore, I want a decision, a unanimous decision." He paused to glare at everyone again to make his point. "By ten o'clock this morning. Go or no-go, let's do it. Len, you're up first. But, let me make it perfectly clear that you have exactly ten minutes to make your statement, at which time you will stop talking, period. Understand?"

Len nodded his head to the left with a small dip of the corners of his mouth, as to say, "If YOU say so boss." He didn't stand up to address the group. He merely kicked his mouth into gear and let the words roll. Laura had heard everything he said, it was old news, the bad feeling about Dilby's accounting procedures of the past, their unwillingness to cooperate, etc., etc., etc. When Mr. Brighton's hand went up in the air, he clamped his mouth shut in mid-word and sat silent. This was unusual, so much so, that no one else said anything for several seconds waiting for the inevitable continuing flood of words.

Mr. Brighton pointed at Laura and said, "Ten minutes and then we will discuss for one hour and vote."

Laura stood and said, "Thank you Mr. Brighton." She favored him with a smile. "I think we can resolve this matter more quickly than that." She turned and addressed the rest of the group. Her voice was clear and distinct, yet, not loud. Her speaking voice had been trained in debate at UCLA and she was justifiably proud of her vocal delivery. "Correct me if I am wrong, but the crux of this indecision is the fear that the Dilby personnel will not utilize the investment correctly, possibly hiding the waste or misuse from our audits, and eventually going broke at our expense. Does that sum up the problem?" she asked looking directly at Len Craxis. He pursed his lips, which looked like two white worms squirming in a gray grass lawn, and nodded his agreement with the assessment.

"Well then, to eliminate that concern, I spent most of Saturday in a meeting with the management team of Dilby and we came to an agreement which should reassure us of compliance." Every eye was glued to her at the moment, except for Len who had somehow managed to fix her with one eye while keeping the other one on Mr. Brighton somewhat in the fashion of a lizard. The silence held with no break while Laura fished a sheath of papers out of her portfolio with a flourish. "Dilby has signed this agreement which stipulates that we will have one of our people on his management team with veto power on any decision to spend more than ten thousand dollars."

With that statement she handed the paper to Mr. Brighton and sat down.

Fifteen minutes later she was back in her office watching Len try to convince anyone who would listen that he really felt that it would be a good investment but that someone had to play devil's advocate to 'balance' out the decision process.

Mr. Brighton mumbled something about 'horse manure' as he stopped in her doorway. He seemed somber considering the events that had just taken place. "It looks like I'm going to have to find another junior financial officer," he said. Laura's heart rose into her throat. Perhaps she had overstrained her authority by hammering out that concession with Dilby. "Rats", she thought. She didn't want to lose this job after all the long hours and innovative work she had to put out to get to this position.

Mr. Brighton shook his head and added, "And this time I want one without a Ph.D. in Applied Linguistics." Laura was so relieved that she laughed. He laughed with her and complemented her on her incentive to make something positive happen to resolve the deadlock. The Dilby deal would go through because of her resourcefulness and he promised her a sizable bonus after the signing took place tomorrow. Her phone rang. She thanked him for his support and answered the phone.

The day went quickly. Laura managed enough time to grab a quick salad with some fruit for lunch before she got trapped on a three-way conference for two hours. By four-thirty she was more than ready to go home and leave the in-fighting until tomorrow. The shop called and told her that her Dodge Avenger was finished and yes, they would have it at the front door to her office by four-thirty.

Getting thumbs up from two of her peers on the way to the elevator did a lot to buoy up her spirits for the trip home.

CHAPTER SIX

After leaving Laura a voicemail, Jack drove south on Broadway under the Interstate Highway and past the old Gates Rubber plant location. Selecting an icon on his cell phone, he dialed his office. Using the hands-free microphone and speaker which were embedded in the headliner of the Cadillac he talked with the plant manager. "Hi Bob, how are things going today on our project?" Bob Wexler chuckled a bit, "Everything is going as planned and we're actually somewhat ahead of schedule."

Bob continued, "I do have one concern which is bothering me though. One of the plant personnel is causing considerable disruption on the assembly lines by talking up the need for a union. Several workers have come to me and asked me to either respond to the statements being made or to consider allowing a union to organize. My quandary is caused by the fact that the agitator is well liked and, up until recently, one of the best line workers we have employed."

Jack thought for a few seconds. "I'll look into the situation when I get there." Jack broke the connection. As he was approaching Bellevue Avenue, a sharp, warning tone caused him to quickly slow down. The cars behind him suddenly had to slow down too. Some drivers were irritated seeing Jack's Cadillac stop at a green light. Jack saw the driver in the Lexus directly behind him swerve into the left lane and accelerate pass him toward the intersection.

Suddenly, the driver of the Lexus slammed on his brakes and came to a quick halt thanks to the ABS braking system on his $85,000 Japanese-designed luxury car. Jack watched as the lady passenger who apparently was not wearing her safety belt found herself compacted on top of the dash, mashed against the windshield with a bird's eye view of the ambulance that rocketed through the intersection from right to left, lights flashing and siren wailing.

Jack shook his head at the possible injury to the woman. The warning tone that alerted him about the approaching ambulance was the result of his first project. A much needed device when driving such a well insulated car.

The Wexler Siren Monitor had been a project that his father had been involved with for the past twenty years, prior to Jack's offer to fund the pilot production in a company he had only envisioned at the time.

Jack considered TA's siren monitor which was produced by a large manufacturer located in Colorado Springs, Colorado. The device was a miniature, self-contained, two-piece unit which was mounted on the inside and outside of the windshield. The inside unit held the electronics and the outside unit contained the sensor to listen for sirens outside of the carefully insulated interior of the vehicle. The outer unit was powered by a small amorphous silicon solar panel and triggered the inside alarm mechanism through a coded, infrared signal passed through the glass. The solar panel charged up capacitors for operations during brief periods of darkness such as tunnels and shadows.

The inside unit was also powered by a solar panel which received its solar energy through a Lexan window in the body of the outer unit. For operation during night or long periods of limited sunlight, the backup power source was the car's battery which powered the inside unit and lit a long-life bulb. The bulb faced the outer unit through the windshield and powered the outer unit through an inwardly facing solar cell.

Held to the windshield by special glue, the entire assembly was so small it was unobtrusive. Mounted outside the sweep of the windshield wipers in the upper left hand corner of the windshield, it was only noticed when it sounded a warning of an approaching emergency vehicle running Code 3, which meant sirens and lights.

Jack recalled that his father, uncle, and other associates had attempted to get funding to develop the device for years. Appeals to the National Highway Safety Administration had fallen on the deaf ears of administrators who politically funded far more important projects. Projects such as the multi-million dollar study to determine the sexual habits of the microbes which existed on the sides of the road to eat up worn-off rubber from tires of passing cars.

Everyone they contacted were enthusiastic about the promise of the device but, were never were able to come through with actual funding.

After college, Jack remembered that it seemed like fate when he had met Bob Wexler at a financial seminar for start-up businesses. Bob had years of experience in setting up and running a plant, but little management knowledge about how to finance or run a business.

Due to the massive resizing done by many companies after the 9/11 terrorist attacks in September of 2001, and the financial crises of the first decade of this century, Bob had lost his job and was replaced by a younger man with much smaller salary needs.

Jack smiled at the memory of how he and Bob had hit it off and devised a plan to create the company they both now ran. Bob had access to $450,000 which he had saved up from his stock options with his previous company and offered to use that as their seed money. Bob's investment had been rewarded by getting his original money back ten times over in the last three years.

Jack had approached an investment group with his plans for a research and development company for his father's siren monitor as their first project. His thorough detailing and conservative planning was a match for the investment group and they added ten and one-half million dollars to the start-up venture. As it is said, "The rest was history." Some contacts Jack had with an old buddy from college who was in the media allowed Jack's new product to become known and within four months of the first production unit sale, General Motors purchased the patent and rights to manufacture from Jack's company, Technological Alternatives, for thirty million dollars plus a small royalty on each unit sold on each licensed unit produced by anyone. Their company was off and running.

Driving by the Lexus Jack really felt sorry that the woman had been hurt, but then he thought, "Maybe she would learn to wear her seat belt after this." Jack knew that the man driving the car enjoyed the silent ride so much he didn't realize the danger it put him in from police cars in hot pursuit or ambulances and rescue squads speeding to help people. Fire trucks were usually more noticeable because of the use of the "Super Horn", which unfortunately could cause damage to nearby pedestrians due to the volume of sound it generated.

Jack drove by the various auto dealers which make up a goodly portion of the Englewood suburb on South Broadway and noticed the signs marketing the new Siren Monitor on the GM lots. The other vehicle manufacturers would have to adopt it to stay up with the GM products. Eventually the royalty would exceed the thirty million GM had paid up front. He knew that there were over three hundred and fifty million cars, trucks, and motorcycles already on the registration rolls that could get GM's aftermarket version, and the fact that each one was a potential purchaser of the Siren Monitor didn't hurt. That didn't even include the ten or twelve million new cars sold each year.

Jack carefully checked the on-coming traffic and then turned east on County Line Road off of Broadway near the Littleton Medical Center. The Medical Center was a branch of Swedish Hospital and quite convenient to all the businesses in the area. As he headed away from the mountains Jack again appreciated the beauty of the Colorado countryside in the morning.

As he crested the hill he had a wide view of the Denver sprawl. Small white cumulus clouds floated over the area in a light blue sky full of sunshine. As a skier Jack knew how fast the weather could change in the mountains and while he was really enjoying the morning weather, he wouldn't be surprised if the conditions were completely different by that afternoon.

Parking near the entrance in his marked spot he took his light gray suit jacket off of the hanger behind his seat and put it on. Checking his overall appearance in the side glass, he triggered the car alarm and walked across the concrete to the front door. Emblazoned over the entrance was the TA logo and in smaller letters the name of the company done in a tasteful light green color.

Jack felt the initial bite of the air conditioning as he came through the front door, but by the time he reached his office it felt good, cool and dry. Jack smiled as he thought, "It was fortunate for everyone that the equipment and computers required the same refreshing atmosphere that they preferred."

Settling in at his desk, Jack reviewed the progress on their new project. This was another one of his father's designs. Jack had been able to secure a military contract for production after demonstrating a prototype to the Air Force. This was an advanced weather reconnaissance unit which was almost entirely solid-state and could be air dropped in battle zones if necessary to provide precise information on the prevalent weather conditions.

The unit used the NSA technique of 'timed burst transmission' to send in hourly reports. This kept the data secret on time, and required very little power. The deployment and accuracy of many of the modern sophisticated weapons, especially laser-guided missiles and bombs, depended upon predicting certain weather conditions such as smoke, fog, and temperature inversions.

The use of the "Wrecon" as his dad had nicknamed the system would allow the Air Force to save many of the multi-million dollar weapons presently wasted because the target was obscured when the weapon was fired. Jack expected to negotiate a lucrative sub-contract for manufacturing with the Colorado Springs firm to make the Wrecon in quantity for the Air Force if the unit could pass the government standards inspection.

Calling his head of research, Russ Conners, Jack inquired into the next two projects under development. "Good morning, Russ, how are the 'Pointer' and 'Star' doing today?" The references were to two more of his father's projects, an inexpensive personal locator beacon and an active home defense system.

Russ' answers were encouraging, as were the plant production figures, and operation costs for the last month. Jack finished signing the necessary forms and other business. Unlocking a file cabinet, Jack noticed the key he had gotten from Bill Martin. That seemed like a year ago. The police had apparently stopped following him after several days of normal activity, but Jack wasn't sure he wanted to revive the events of that day just yet.

Finished with the morning paperwork Jack looked around his office. As President, Jack's office was tastefully done and of a good size. But he hadn't followed the route of other CEOs that made their office a statement of power and wealth. The other officials in his company had similar offices and furniture.

Jack knew that a leader led by example, not by status. Still the quiet chrome and wood tones were modern, classy, and comfortable. The majority of the lighting was indirect which added to the comfortable feeling.

Jack turned his attention to the problem bothering Bob Wexler. The employee in question was Don Kolby, whose file was lying on Jack's desk. Thumbing through Don's personnel information and merit reviews Jack found the two year background history of a diligent, intelligent, hard working technician, and production line worker. His merit reviews were outstanding with commendations from his managers. Nothing in his file showed any inclination towards rabble-rousing or dissatisfaction with his job. In fact, he had one of the better paid positions with the company. Out of one hundred fifty-seven employees, engineers, supervisors, and other personnel working at TA, Don Kolby's record had been one of the best.

Having paid heed to Bob Wexler's experience and work knowledge, Jack had provided an excellent benefits package with medical, dental, vision, and maternity coverage. The salaries for the employees exceeded the local average by almost thirty percent, and the working environment was deliberately designed to promote harmony and safety. The dining area served good, healthy food and was modeled on the success of such programs as that at the Woodward Governor Plant in Fort Collins. The company paid for the labor, the space, and the utilities for the dining area. All the employees had to pay for was the bulk cost of the food. This meant that you could get a roasted chicken lunch with a couple of vegetables, drink and desert for just over two dollars.

Jack had made sure that the middle management supervisors and line supervisors had been trained off-site in quality and effective management and were rated by their employees every quarter. The quarterly merit reviews kept each employee in close contact with their manager and they knew exactly where they stood as to performance. They were awarded serious prizes for innovative procedures and concepts and even had private personal or family counseling available off-site, but paid for by the company. All this cost was more than repaid by the quality and output of the people working there.

The star of the benefits package was the profit sharing options. Stock in the company and or financial rewards allowed each of the employees to share in the success or failure of the company in a personal way. Jack could not understand why someone would attempt to start a union here. The only result would be a loss in profits and benefits for all of the employees.

In keeping with Ross Perot's teachings on competitive management with the Japanese and others, Jack had kept the upper management salaries within a range not much higher than the employees. Their main source of compensation was additional stock options based entirely upon their job performance, backed up by hard data and their outstanding contributions to the company above and beyond their normal duties. "No," he thought, a union makes no sense." He picked up the phone and called Bob Wexler. "Bob? Will you please bring Don Kolby into my office?"

Five minutes later, a portly, middle-aged man with sparse hair and a ruddy complexion knocked on the door and entered Jack's office. "Please sit down, Don," Jack said, indicating the chair across from his desk. After the man had seated himself, Jack smiled and asked him, "Do you know why I asked to see you?" The man wouldn't meet his gaze.

He shifted in his seat and replied "Yeah, I gotta idea."

Jack waited; a ploy that usually caused his opponent to indicate the direction of his intent.

When no further comments were forthcoming, Jack reached over and flipped a switch on the panel to the left of his desk. He assumed a stoic face and told his visitor, "I have just activated a video and sound recorder to record the remainder of our conversation, is that all right?"

Don looked around apprehensively attempting to locate the camera without success. Then he slumped back into his chair. "Yes sir, I don't mind", he replied in a flat voice. What Jack didn't tell him was that he had been on camera since he had walked into the office. A twenty-four hour recording was kept, in sequence, for two weeks. This "backup" allowed Jack to recall any details that had been forgotten or overlooked during business meetings as well as serving as an excellent security tool. The three Sony color video cameras, which were less than an inch in diameter and less than three inches long, were easily concealable.

Jack was puzzled. According to his records, this man was cheerful, outgoing, and friendly. Either he had suffered a major stroke, lifestyle change, or the records were dead wrong. He was inclined to believe the records.

"All right, Don," Jack said, as he steepled his fingers in front of his mouth. "Explain to me why you think the company needs a union."

The pain that flashed across his eyes told Jack that the man wasn't behind the idea completely, and in fact, had divided loyalties. He obviously was under a great deal of pressure. So much pressure that he couldn't handle this confrontation. His mumbled protestations were nothing but smoke and mirrors. Jack felt he had to do something, to offer something, so that this man could unburden himself of the embarrassment he was suffering. Jack could sense an unspoken scream for help.

Jack got up and walked around to the other side of the desk and sat in the other chair, thereby making himself appear on the same level and importance as his employee. Softly, he asked with obvious concern, "What's the matter Don? There's nothing so bad it can't be worked out if we try." While this was a tried and true psychological technique for getting a person to open up, Jack really did feel for the guy and wanted to help him. This had now become important on a personal level as well as an attempt to save a loyal and productive worker.

Don hung his head and said, "Will you really help me?" The worker rolled his eyes up towards the ceiling and let his head drop back onto the top of the seat back. "Can you help me? I'm desperate!" The last word was almost a shout and definitely a plea for help. Jack crossed his legs and let his hands rest quietly in his lap. He told the miserable man, "I want to help you Don, but you've got to tell me what the problem is."

Don stuck his chin out and compressed his lips for a second as he considered the dangers involved in his decision to talk. Realizing that he was at the end of his rope he made the decision. Jack could see it in Kolby's eyes as he straightened up in his chair and looked directly at his boss. Jack was jarred by the look and realized that the determination mixed with desperation was very similar to the look on the face of the man who had died in the clothing store. Then like a dam breaking, the words rushed out in a torrent of confession. "I have a beautiful family Mr. Malone, two little girls and a wife that any man would be proud to have. I got a nice home and some money saved up for a boat. Last week two men came up to me while I was raking the front yard. They were union organizers they said, but, I don't think so. They asked me to pass out some pamphlets and spread the word at work that they were offering a great deal if everyone would join in a union to protect their rights."

The employee looked acutely embarrassed at this point but didn't break his eye contact with Jack. "We don't need no protection for our rights here Mr. Malone, you guys treat us real good. A whole lot better than the other jobs I've had. Anyway, I told them not only no, but hell no! That's when they got mean and told me that I would do what they asked or they would see that my family met with a terrible accident. They described how my little girls could get an early education in the ways to please a man. They told me they knew where my kids went to school and where my wife worked and even told me when we went to bed at night."

Don Colby paused to take a deep breath. "They scared me, but I wasn't going to give in, until they went back to the car and brought out a blood-soaked bundle and laid it on the lawn. It was my neighbor's dog. It had been run over and was real mangled. These guys thought it was my dog and wanted to show me how vicious they could be. The fact that they didn't care whose dog they killed convinced me more than that poor, dead animal that they meant what they said. They'd hurt or kill my family without a care. For them it was nothing personal, just business. So I agreed to do what they asked. I don't want my family hurt more than I don't want to lose my job Mr. Malone, but if you fire me, then maybe they will leave me alone and I won't have to hurt my friends and your company anymore." He had thought the matter through to this conclusion, which was the only way he could see to get himself out of a terrible situation.

Jack thought the whole situation out for a couple minutes. He remembered when he was a little boy and a bully in the third grade gave him a similar choice. He'd taken a beating or two before the bully realized that the blond-haired kid wasn't going to be intimidated. Looking at Don Colby he knew that this was the same thing, only real life and death were going to be the results.

Then he rose and went to his phone to call Bob Wexler into his office. As a business partner and second-largest stock holder in TA, Bob's business advice had always been a great asset to Jack. Bob's desire to continue working and run the plant as supervisor worked well with Jack's ability to handle the paperwork which Bob never liked. Together they had a working arrangement which gave them both what they wanted and made for an efficiently run operation. Bob's advice in this situation could be invaluable.

Jack ordered coffee for all three men after inquiring how they wanted their drinks. He then summed up Don's situation to Bob and asked for recommendations. Bob was livid. "Call the police; they can't get away with things like this." he stated. "No way are we going to give into scum bags like that."

Don shook his head and pointed his finger at Bob. "You weren't there to see these guys and the evil in their eyes. They mean business and I don't think the cops will be able to keep them from hurting my family. In fact, they said they had the cops on their side and would know if I blew the whistle. I'm pretty sure they do too, because they were real confident about it." Don was obviously very afraid that the result of this meeting would be the death of his family. Jack silently agreed with his beleaguered employee and asked him a relevant question. "What did you mean when you said that they introduced themselves as union organizers but you didn't think that was so?"

Don nodded his head in agreement. "Well sir, several things, first, they didn't really have any idea what a union does for the workers, and they also thought that they were Union Stewards. Hey, I've been in a union and Stewards never dirty their hands recruiting. These guys were supposed to be Recruiters but they never tried to talk up the advantages for the workers. Then there was their clothes, they were dressed in real expensive suits and had lots of real expensive jewelry on them, especially the watches. I remember those gold Rolex watches. They were not union people. They were hoods and that makes them bad news for me. Anyway, as I was carrying the dog away like they told me to, I overheard the little one tell the other guy to call 'Jack' and tell him that everything was cool."

Jack figured that the 'Jack' they were talking about probably wasn't him and then considered what he had heard about organized crime. His information came from reading, television, college, and particularly what his Sensei had detailed to him about such activities locally in Denver.

While Bob and Don were discussing the ugly confrontation, Jack recalled the recent meeting he had with Jim Grady concerning Jack and Laura's unintentional involvement in the local crime scene.

CHAPTER SEVEN

---------------------- ****** ----------------------

As he worked out, Jack envisioned Sensei Grady's Dojo. It was an interesting building. It resembled a two-story cinder block building with a domed roof over the largest part of the building. The eastern third of the building was a flat-roofed single story structure with the main entrance down several steps from the street. It didn't have the look of glitz or fancy construction for a reason. The instructor and students had built it themselves over twenty-five years ago. But inside the building was a forty-foot square exercise/combat area that was constructed to the standards of the Asian Martial Arts arenas.

Jack appreciated the layout of the Dojo. There were tiered benches on two walls. With those two exceptions the entire floor surface, except for a small walking area around the mat structure, was covered by rice Tutami mats nine inches thick. The mats were three feet wide by five feet long and were removable for cleaning, a cleaning process which was accomplished on a weekly basis by the students. The Tutami mats were supported and held in place by an edged oak flooring one-inch thick. This surface was, in turn, supported by cantilevered oak boards on edge. The oak boards were then fastened to the final surface, eighteen inches below the first flooring. The structure was designed to give, rather than have the bodies of the participants give when they hit it. Each component in the flooring moved marginally to absorb the shock when a person dropped or was thrown onto it.

The one-story portion contained the entrance, the office, the dressing rooms, and Mr. Grady's private office, which was run by Mrs. Grady. She was an Asian-American native who maintained a firm, but pleasant relationship with the black belt teachers and the students. She ensured the cleanliness and order in the Dojo. No one, not even the Sensei debated her on maintenance of the Dojo. So, it was a constantly pleasant and airy place to study the Martial Arts.

One Thursday, after classes were over, Jack had been working on a particularly tough Kata when he was interrupted by an obnoxious and arrogant young man with a black belt around his Gi. The Gi is the traditional canvas uniform worn by Judo players and other martial artists. The black belt without additional adornment in the form of one or more stripes is an indication that the person wearing the belt has reached a level of proficiency of instructor rather than just a student. All serious marital artists were forever students, learning continually and attempting to better their technique or abilities.

Jack stopped his technique and stared at the newcomer. "Can I have your name please?" Jack asked politely. The answer came back with an attitude. "Yeah, my name's Tony Johnson." Jack was slightly irritated because Mr. Johnson had violated the Dojo protocol three times by the time he faced Jack on the mat surface. First, he had neglected to remove the thick gold chain around his neck which could harm him or anyone he competed against. Second, he had neglected to honor the Dojo or Jack by bowing to both as he stepped onto the surface. Lastly, he had rudely interrupted Jack's workout without a sufficient reason. Needless to say this confrontation did not start off on the best footing.

Jack extended his hand to the newcomer and asked, "Can I help you?" which, as far as Jack was concerned, was courteous and proper considering Tony's actions so far. Tony had a full head of black hair which was spiky and held in place by something resembling varnish. His prominent nose and thin lips gave him a brooding, pensive look.

Tony put his hands on his hips and challenged Jack to a session of Kaumate.

Jack hadn't liked the guy since he had approached him and wasn't interested in working out with him, so he told him, "No, thanks." Jack turned away from the brash young man and started to leave the mat surface to prevent a hassle. Out of habit, Jack kept an eye on the guy in the mirrors surrounding the mat area. When Jack saw Tony rotate to his left and flick a side kick at the back of his head, he threw himself down and to his left, out of the way of the kick. Jack executed a forward shoulder roll over his left shoulder on the mat surface which allowed him to come back up to his feet and rotate to face his attacker.

The man turned to face Jack who was now on his left side. "Okay wiseguy", he mumbled, the anger showing in his attitude. Tony immediately launched a quick series of punches and kicks and threw in a spinning back heel kick in an effort to engage Jack.

As Jack ducked and swayed away from his opponent's attacks he realized that there was no way to resolve this peacefully. He channeled his mounting anger towards the clumsy attacker into an icy calm of focused energy. A feeling similar to the one he had felt in the men's store came over him. When Tony attempted a front snap kick to the groin with his left foot, Jack saw the entire movement as if in slow motion.

Jack stepped forward on his right foot, inside the kick and used a Jui Jitsu technique which consisted of reaching between Tony's arms while his leg was still moving upward behind Jack. The rigid edge of Jack's hands struck both sides of Tony's neck with devastating force. At the same time, Jack pivoted on his left foot as his right leg swept under Tony and removed the only leg he had to stand on.

Jack was very aware that he was able to break two-by-fours with the knife edge of either hand. He had perfected his technique over the years. He also knew he could have just as easily snapped Tony's neck. But not being inherently vicious or working out of emotion, he pulled the blow sufficiently to prevent death. But, because he was unhappy about the unprovoked attack, he put a bit more than enough focused energy into the blow, rendering Tony unconscious. The pest was going to have a severe headache and neckache for quite a while after his nap.

Jack was turning to leave even before Tony's body had fallen to the mat. He was fully aware that his untalented opponent had decided to sleep for a while. He could tell by the satisfactory way the light went out in Tony's eyes as they preceded to roll up into his head after the blow.

He bowed off the mat and went to find Jim Grady. He didn't have far to look. The older man was standing in the shadows at the front of the Dojo's mat area. The Sensei moved forward and bowed his head to Jack. His voice was strong despite his fifty-plus years of age. "You did what you had to do, Jack. He forced you to defend yourself, and I commend you for the restraint you exercised in not damaging him further." The Sensei paused looking distastefully at the fallen man.

"Now please leave before he awakens and let me deal with him. I know his kind and the world he lives in very well." Jim placed his hand on Jack's arm, "I would like you to attend me tonight at the Golden Dragon. There are some things you need to know which could take some time in the telling." The Sensei stepped back and teacher and student again bowed to each other as a sign of respect.

As he walked towards the dressing room, Jack looked at the prone body lying on the mat and had the distinct impression he would have been better off never meeting the man. This was the second time in a month that he had had to enter into actual combat and it did not indicate a healthy trend. He taught respect for others and it concerned him that he had experienced a thrill of satisfaction when he had put the fool down. Jack still wondered about his right to hurt other people no matter how much they deserved it.

He undressed and showered quickly. Putting on his street clothes to leave he remembered that Sensei had not specified a time for the meeting at the restaurant. Walking softly back to the mat area he heard a slapping noise and talking. Easing up to one of the entry ways to the mat area he was careful not to allow his reflection to show in any of the mirrors.

Glancing in briefly, Jack saw his Sensei shake the recumbent man into a ragged state of awareness. The way that Jim was handling the man showed his lack of respect for the actions of this man. Jack realized that he had seen many TV cops use this type of rough, 'take-out-the-trash' style. Jack could understand this since Jim Grady had been a Denver policeman for twenty years until he retired recently. He would automatically drop back into a police persona when he needed to.

Jim was holding Tony Johnson as the punk tried to knock the Sensei's hands off, but couldn't. Finally, the words Jim was saying appeared to get through.

Jack was amazed as he watched Jim Grady hold the street punk's head off the mat and glare at him. Jim's words were clear to Jack as he stood in the shadows.

"How dare you stink up my place with yourself? Don Miland owes me big time and you have just earned yourself a one-way trip to an alley off Larimore." Jack knew that this was Jim's reference to a common dumping ground for dead mob bodies, usually brutally tortured.

Jim started to yank the young man up, off of the mat. Tony cried, "Please, please don't kill me! Look, I'll leave and I promise I will never mention this happened to anyone. Look, I made a mistake. I didn't know this place was yours."

Jack was taken aback slightly. He was pretty sure, as scared as Tony was, he probably didn't suspect how really close he was to leaving this world at that moment. The Sensei continued to glare at Tony for a full twenty seconds.

Jack watched as Jim finally nodded his head. He released the man's Gi and pointed to the dressing room. As the thoroughly beaten Tony was limping for the dressing room Jack heard the Sensei say, "If you ever mention this to anyone, or even think about picking on any of my people, I will see that you, your entire family, and even your invalid aunt in Omaha are killed, several times." The information seemed to frighten Tony even more. He fumbled the car keys out of his pocket, caught up his clothes and ran from the building still in his Gi.

Jim Grady stood at a window and watched the Corvette tear up the street towards Broadway. Without turning, he smiled as he said, "Did you like my performance?"

Jack wasn't surprised that the master knew he was still there. The man seemed to know everything. Watching his teacher turn from the window he replied, "It was a work of art that you seem to know quite well. Do you really have an acquaintance with this gangster?"

Jim grinned as he said, "Sure I do, I busted Don Miland when he was a punk, eight or nine times if I remember right. This was back in the 90's while I was a patrolman. Of course nothing ever stuck because he had expensive lawyers to keep him out of jail. But I daresay he would remember me if my name came up. After the third or fourth arrest, I wasn't very gentle with him when I arrested him."

Jack asked, "Aren't you afraid that the guy that just left will talk to this "Miland" character and then come back for revenge when he finds out that you don't have some big "in" with the mob?"

"No." Jim sat down and shook his head. "Tony Johnson, or as he is known on the street, "Tone, the Bone" is a fifth-rate street punk with no solid connection with Don Miland. Tony will never say anything about this incident because he would lose stature, or face, with the other members of the mob. There are about fifteen members in Don Miland's employment right now." Jim shook his head and smiled ruefully as he talked about the gang. "Tony never will amount to anything because he's sly, but not smart. The only reason he is a street boss is because he is more vicious than anyone he has met so far. One day that will change and Tony will be filling cat food cans."

Jim walked into his office, sat down, and reached over, unlocked, and opened the large left drawer in his desk. Taking out a thick sheaf of papers he looked through them and pulled one out. It was an official police mug shot and dossier on Tony Johnson.

Jack raised an eyebrow at this. Jim Grady held up the stack of mug shots and said, "I like to keep up on the activities of the scum of the day. I still have contacts on the force since I retired last year." Retrieving Tony's file he replaced the papers and stood up. "See you at eight o'clock at my table."

As he left the Dojo, Jack was quite sure that his teacher did a lot more than just "keep up on" the crime scene in Denver. All the late night meetings he had seen going on in Jim Grady's office now seemed to make sense. Many of the men and women he had seen coming and going to the Dojo had an official presence and the lean solid bodies that fit police personnel. He wondered just how active a role his friend and teacher still played in the police department.

----------------------- ✶✶✶✶✶ -----------------------

CHAPTER EIGHT

The steamy vapors from the hot tub gleamed on the tile walls of the sauna. The subdued lighting was reflected off the water in the tub, causing reflections to sparkle throughout the room. The air in the room was exchanged and filtered every two minutes along with a mild pine scent via the air handling system. The low music in the background set a slow mellow mood, as it played Mantovani selections from movie theme songs. The luxurious furnishings complemented the quality decor of the entire room.

Carol Nolan, alias Dixie Tuccine, knew that Joe Miland thought everything in the room said class in capital letters. He had purchased it that way and had apparently decided lately that it was a little too stuffy for his taste.

Carol had read the man's file. He liked beer better than champagne, rock and roll better than the instrumentals that were playing now, and lust better than romance. But, since she, as the lady of the moment, thought it was wonderful, it could stay for a while.

Carol watched as a touch of irritation flickered into being in his eyes. The Colorado Bureau of Investigation operative figured that this little romance wouldn't last three months. The data in his file showed that Joe Miland made sure that he did not invest his emotions in any woman's hands. He had been terribly hurt and discarded by the only woman that ever gave any real meaning to his life. History showed that no woman would ever have his heart again. Carol went over his history while he was relaxing in the hot tub next to her. Joe's real name was just plain Joseph Miland. He didn't have a middle name because he was the illegitimate child of a rich rancher from Amarillo, Texas, and a hooker who had come through that hot dusty town for a few days some thirty five years ago.

The records indicated that the street walker's original idea was to give birth to the rancher's son, so she could force him to give her money. It was an age-old scam that was used everywhere in the world.

The Psychiatrists that compiled the files on Miland figured that the hooker knew it was the rancher's child because she had been in jail in Ft. Worth for two months before she was released. Detectives had determined that the rancher was the first and only man she had been with since she had come to town. She was arrested on a soliciting charge right after he had left and spent the next month in jail.

She worked a normal job as a waitress for the next eight months and the child was born in a hospital. She had the hospital provide her with the baby's DNA type. Upon investigation, the detectives had learned that one of the friends she had made during the winter worked at the hospital and had copied the rancher's DNA information for her. Not a criminal charge but sufficient to get the woman clerk fired.

The files showed that a friend of the rancher had told detectives that the woman made her announcement at a restaurant the rancher frequented. The rancher's friend had laughed, as he related that dumbfounded would pretty well describe the rancher's reaction when faced with an unexpected son and a clever street walker. She knew he couldn't afford a scandal. The rancher had paid her twenty thousand dollars but said that he promised her that she was as good as dead if she ever came back to Amarillo or bothered him again. She left town that afternoon with little Joe, on a plane to Dallas.

Unfortunately she wasn't really very smart concerning money. Less than four months later she was back walking the streets.

The next five years the woman and Joe lived in Dallas. Interviews showed that he was tended to by a ragtag group of unsavory types while his mother plied her trade.

She got an offer to move up to call girl status and apparently that meant more to her than the emotional ties she had to little Joe. She handed him to another girl, and walked out of his life forever.

The Psychiatrists suggested that the next few months were a struggle for him. But, he had inherited an excellent brain from his father and was actually very bright. Along with his intelligence he got the genes for a large, powerful body. Living in the worst part of society he somehow managed to survive by becoming cunning. This childhood caused him to grow into an exceptionally cruel and selfish man.

He lacked formal schooling but he nevertheless intuitively knew how to make people listen to him. The file showed that he prospered by catering to the baser needs of people. He worked it so that other people handled the actual contacts with his customers.

His history showed that he quickly became a leader in prostitution down in the really seedy area of Dallas, off Harry Hines Blvd.

Eventually, Joe overstepped his capabilities. He had a friend of the Chief of Police killed for leaning on his organization. He fled Dallas before the Police found him. There was always big money and an open market available in his line of work in Denver.

The secret to his success was simple, applied violence and control. He was given the street name of "Don" Miland after he organized three different groups of prostitutes into an efficient organization. It seemed that he was the last one standing after a 'white flag' meeting he had held with his other two competitors.

Denver Police reported that Joe generously gave himself eighty percent of his employee's earnings. Every now and then he would select someone who had snubbed him or angered him in some way and performed public evil on them so that all would know he was the boss. Carol's boss had told her that Joe really got high on making other people suffer. They cited that at one time he had a man who had tried to cheat him tied onto the front of a truck and then let the truck roll down a hill towards a deserted building. He used a video camera to record the guy's facial expressions and his screaming all the way to the wall. He sent copies to the other crime bosses in Denver and labeled it "Joe's way to squash the competition."

Still, Joe was just a violent, small time street boss and destined to do little and die young. Unexpectedly, Don Miland's reputation had suddenly blossomed. The low-life, the vile, the cruel, and the criminal-minded suddenly turned their business dealings with hookers, dope, protection, and/or anything illegal over to Joe.

The bosses, who had been the source of the city's human misery, mysteriously didn't want anything to do with Joe and conceded their losses to him without a whimper. Some did complain, even to the Police. But, those people rapidly lost everything they had built up and eventually they disappeared never to be heard from again. Also, not surprisingly, Joe inherited whatever they lost. This was when the CBI decided they needed to keep tabs on Joe "Don" Miland.

Joe apparently used his new found riches, power, and control to debase himself and those around him in every way.

Carol was very aware that Joe was financially, emotionally, and physically a pain junkie and he needed constantly bigger and bigger pain reactions from those he hurt. The doctors felt that this constant escalation could only lead to eventual dissatisfaction and probably self-destruction.

Now apparently, Joe was taking the gang in new directions. Carol heard him telling one of his thugs, "It's either diversification or cross-polluting, at least I think that is what the company big wigs call it."

The strident ring of the phone distracted her thoughts. Joe snapped his fingers at Dixie Tuccine. Carol immediately climbed out of the hot tub, left the room, and closed the door.

She walked down the hall to the dressing room next door to the sauna. Stepping inside she closed the bathroom door and locked it. She sat on the closed top of the toilet and picked up her handbag. She had left it there before going to the hot tub. She opened the large tote and took out her hair dryer. One of the smaller units on the market, it would still push out enough hot air to dry a woman's wet hair if given the chance.

However, this one would have to struggle to finish the job because the small motor in the casing was smaller than normal. The primary function of this motor was to make realistic dryer noises. The reason the unit was so under-powered was because it also housed a miniaturized radio receiver and micro recorder which were powered by two batteries in the handle. Plugging the unit in the wall outlet, she pushed the earplug speaker into her ear and tuned into the conversation being taped by the recorder. Carol had found the time to put a miniaturized tap on the phone line into Miland's house. This way she could hear both sides of the conversation.

Joe listened to Carlo, his number one enforcer. Carlo was updating his Don on his latest project. "Boss, we've got this Kolby guy doing everything we wanted at TA. He almost lost his lunch when we laid his flattened doggie in front of him. And guess what, the best part is that we didn't even run over the mutt. We just found it by accident and Sammy remembered seeing it in the guy's front yard the day before."

Joe asked. "Has he got the troops at TA worked up yet? My partner and I want to put pressure on the guy who owns this little high-tech firm as quickly as possible."

Carlo was quick to brag about his effectiveness to his boss. "Oh yeah, according to our snitch in there, lots of people have been asking the plant manager to hold a vote for a union. We'll probably be running the place by this time next month."

Joe wasn't overly impressed. He had heard this type of optimistic garbage from Carlo before. "Well then, you had better give your guy a couple more days to stir things up and then you pay a call on the owners this Thursday, while the heat is still on. Got it?" Carlo agreed. Joe thought for a minute and then told his man, "Give the owners the usual options and when they give in and sign the contract, we'll ease them out and use the company in our own special way." Carlo asked about when he needed to report and then hung up the phone.

Joe hung up his phone, climbed out of the hot tub and dried himself off. He knew that the real reason for pressuring this Jack Malone character wasn't to get his little company. This was a direct order, not a request, but an order, from his invisible partner. This Malone guy had something that his partner wanted and Joe was going to see that he coughed it up. Going out into the hall, he heard the sound of the hair dryer in the next room. As he walked down the hall, he began shaking his head over the amount of work a woman had to do to look pretty. He continued walking on down the hall to his bedroom for a shower.

In the bathroom, Carol finished toweling most of the water out of her hair and used the weak flow of warm air from the multi-talented hair dryer to finish the job. She wondered who the heck 'TA' was, who this 'partner' was and what Joe Miland wanted with control of the company? No matter, she would report to her control tonight, give them the tape, and let them make what they could out of the conversation.

CHAPTER NINE

Jack Malone punched in the number for his personnel manager, Sharon Wallace, and asked her to step into his office. After the door had closed behind her Jack glanced over at the stylish 'bug box' on his desk. It was dark.

Jack liked the small, innocent-looking 'bug box' which was one of his Uncle Larry's personal inventions. The microprocessor-controlled unit used several wired and wireless sensors to detect any active transmitting devices within the room, including any that a person in the room might have brought in. It was also connected to an intricate lattice of wiring throughout the walls, floor, ceiling, windows, and doors of the office. The electronic and focused audio interference it generated resisted any attempts to use a "spike mike" or resonant speaker type of eavesdropping on the office.

The windows were built with triple panes to prevent listening by using a laser beam to sense the sound waves in the room through the movement of the glass. The foil in the outer pane reduced outward light transmission by more than half to prevent telescopic lip readers. The middle pane was also a half-inch of bulletproof Lexan just for safety's sake. Jack's father and uncle had helped design this office and tended to be a little paranoid as far as Jack was concerned.

Since none of the LED's on the 'bug box' was lit, Jack was assured that what he was going to say would stay in the room. He sat back in his chair and stirred the papers on his desk with the fingers of his left hand. The only sound was the sigh of the air conditioning and the breathing of the assembled cast. Jack reconsidered all the facts and endeavored to come up with a plausible plan that could serve all of them. After a few minutes, all the pieces fit in his imagination.

"All right, here's what we will do." He looked at Sharon, "Just between us in this room, Don Kolby is going on immediate leave-of-absence with full pay until I terminate that leave. Sharon, I want you to get the contract company to pay Don on a weekly basis. They don't need to know anything except his social security number and his direct deposit account."

"As far as anyone else is concerned, and that means '*anyone*' outside this room, including your friends and trusted co-workers, and everyone else on your staff, this meeting never happened and Don's LOA and pay doesn't exist on paper or electronic form. You handle it privately without record." Jack then got up, walked around his desk, and leaned against it, giving Sharon full understanding of the importance of this directive. Now that the plan took shape he was intent on getting it to work before something happened to Don's family.

Jack continued, "Other than ourselves, the story is that Don is being terminated immediately for disrupting the work area and insubordination. I want the paperwork to reflect that, I want your people in personnel to think that, and I want the unemployment people, the insurance people, even the employment agency people to think that."

Sharon nodded, "Yes Sir, I'll see to it right away." She turned and left the room.

Bob stared at Jack with surprise and puzzlement on his face. "What's the matter? I can understand putting that story to the outside, but we can trust the people inside our own company can't we?"

Jack looked at Don and shook his head. "Can we? Not with Don and his family's lives on the line. I know he won't say anything, and I know we won't say anything other than the fact that he was fired. But I believe that the type of people that threatened him will make good on those threats if there is any hint that he hasn't been ousted from the plant. Otherwise, that would mean to them that he was defying them. There can only be one result then. Can you say that someone in this company hasn't already been coerced into spying on us or hasn't been bought off to do the same thing or worse?"

Bob had been in Viet Nam and it rattled him to think like that again. He shook his head, "I'm sorry Don, I didn't think..."

Don took a big breath and said, "That's all right, Mr. Wexler. I want to really thank you Mr. Malone. I'll tell my wife the truth when the kids aren't around, but no one else."

Jack thought for a second before he spoke, "Take her to a noisy part of the mall to tell her and keep your mouth covered so no one can read your lips. You never know who's listening to your private conversations at home or on your phone. Now, when I tell you, walk out of here like you are mad as the devil. Don't talk to anyone and go home and get upset with your neighbors. Oh. Don't forget to file for unemployment compensation and act like you are looking for a job."

Jack stared at the man for a few seconds. He was reflecting relief and concern at the same time. Jack, as President of TA added, "You are one of our best workers Don. I want you to know that this is a paid vacation which won't get charged to you. I want you back as soon as this blows over. Until then, hang in there and realize that we are pulling for you. Call Sharon if you need to get in touch. Give her a line about how you want to 'discuss' your termination with me." Jack smiled and shook the man's hand. Then Jack turned to his plant manager.

"Bob, get one of the security guards up here to escort Don to his locker to pick up his personal things and then to the parking lot. Explain to the guard that Don has been terminated and that he is not to talk to or bother anyone."

The guard was summoned, given his instructions and left with a protesting Don. Bob went out to perform damage control in the plant. Jack speculated on how long it would be before the gang made him the same offer with his company as the bargaining chip.

Jack wondered privately if perhaps his father's tendencies for combat-like precautions were hereditary after all. No, he thought, it's probably the conversation he had with his Sensei after the fight with the street punk in the Dojo that made him take precautions.

He had always regarded his father's occasional comments about the violent world just below the surface of the everyday world as part fantasy, part sensationalism, and mostly made up. Until Jim had laid it out for him last Thursday night, he hadn't really thought about several things. Jack realized he hadn't thought about his father's comments in the light of his dad's experience. First, his dad had been in weapons control in the military. Second, his dad had worked in armed and unarmed security for years. Third, his dad had also attended Sensei Grady's Martial Arts school for years. Lastly, his dad had also been taught by Sensei Grady, a man who had been a Denver policeman for almost two decades. Jack decided he had better pay more attention to his dad's information.

CHAPTER TEN

Jack thought back to the previous Thursday night.

---------------------- ****** ----------------------

During the early evening on the night after his run-in with Tony Johnson at the Dojo, Jack had met his teacher at the Golden Dragon Restaurant on South Broadway Avenue in the Littleton suburbs.

The cool cloudy night had promised rain, and big drops had just started falling as Jack ran to the entrance. The ornate stone dragons and tigers guarding the entrance had fierce expressions. But the interior was warm and discretely lit. Jack noted that the threat of rain had cut down the normally heavy evening crowd. The reputation of the Golden Dragon was one of delicious oriental cuisine and a particularly excellent selection of rice wines.

Bowing to the owner/manager who had become a good friend over the last few years, Jack talked to him in Cantonese about the business and his family. He excused himself and then threaded his way between tables and patrons over to Jim Grady's table. He was glad to have a chance to practice his Oriental language with a native of China who had decided to make America his home. Jack was also very glad the man had brought the best of the Oriental cooking with him.

Two young Asian people were sitting at the table talking to the quiet-looking, unassuming older man who was nodding his head and making an occasional comment. When Jack walked up to the table he was introduced to Charley and Linda Wu. They greeted him with bows and polite greetings. They then went to sit at another table so that the two men could talk in private.

Jack raised his eyebrows at the unexpected duo. Jim Grady smiled at Jack. "Those two young people may be able to help us in the near future." Jim Grady's remarks were made to Jack while the Sensei was gazing somewhere in the far distance. Jack held his tongue knowing he would be enlightened when it was time and no amount of urging would make it sooner. His teacher focused on him and said, "Let us order dinner, and then I have a story to tell you."

After they had enjoyed four delicious courses and were enjoying their tea, Jim nodded his head as he began his tale. "About twenty-five years ago, I had just returned from Japan to the United States. I knew about the Tongs and about the Japanese mob, the "Yakusa." I had seen them at work many times. Back then, even they had an honor of sorts. You didn't talk to outsiders, you didn't inform, you stuck with your fellow gang members regardless of the risk, and other macho things like that."

He paused to sip his tea while he looked at his student with interest. "I then came home and started this school. To make ends meet at first, I needed more income. That's when I decided to become a policeman. In the last twenty years I have learned more about the American crime scene than any sane person would want to learn. There is a seething world of evil violence living right next door to the safe, sane world most of us inhabit."

"Every once in a while it spills over into our safe world and everyone gets a shock. Yet, after a short while, the normal people go back to pretending that the event was an aberration. They feel that almost everyone is decent and believes in the same values that they do at home and in most cases they are right."

"In the last few decades, the crazy violent world has been moving in on the safe sane world, pushed by tough financial times, boredom, inequality, and massive amounts of money available through illegal drug sales." He looked at Jack and sighed. "I wish that I could make the world a safe place for you and your family, but the facts are, I can't. No one can, not even you. Oh, you might get by for the majority of your life without attracting a mugger, a rapist, a break-in artist, or a pusher. But lately, the odds have multiplied so that you will more than likely run into a crazy with a gun, who is on drugs, or is a tanked up nut, who thinks he is a race car driver on a public street. Still, those are the normal odds we all face every day."

Jim let his face take on a very somber cast. "Tony Johnson is a minor member of a much worse brand of sharks. Joe Miland is their leader and made himself a 'Don' copying the Mafia leaders. He runs a collection of violent, immoral men who prey on innocents and each other. If they want something bad enough they will take it." Jim stopped talking and took a sip of his tea while his eyes scanned the room.

He continued his 'lesson' for Jack's benefit. "This particular gang has pushed its way to the top of the fast riser category of the Organized Crime Task Force lists." Joe's organization was founded about four years ago. Joe Miland, who uses the alias "Don Miland", is an import from the Dallas, Texas area. The police down there became incensed when he killed a good friend of the Chief of Police. To add salt to the wound, the officer he killed was the Chief's son-in-law. Until recently, Joe was just another petty crime boss. He has suddenly managed to parlay a series of big drug deals and other sick activities into a large fortune and power base. There doesn't seem to be any good reason for his sudden climb to success in these chosen fields."

"There is evidence that Don Miland is now being backed by an unknown partner who has real pull in the criminal world. This is only supposition because of observed items and overheard comments. There's no actual person that the police can pin down as Joe's partner. Deals fall into Joe's lap and other competitors hand him territory and deals which were theirs that they would have normally killed for without a second thought. Miland doesn't, or didn't, warrant such consideration. Therefore, there has to be another, more powerful, player in his group. But, thorough investigations by all levels of state and federal forces haven't been able to unearth who that might be."

"The general public thinks that the police have got these criminals under control. Nothing could be farther from the truth. They are bigger, stronger, and better armed than they were two years ago. They are getting nastier, too. The tactics they are using are pushing out the Colombian, Oriental, and South American drug cartels."

"This particular group has done some things that are so vile the Colombians can't stomach it. That's really, really bad. Two and a half years ago, a Colombian posse member invaded one of their houses of pleasure and ripped off a bunch of money and jewels from the 'customers'. Don Miland had that guy and eight others in his 'posse' hideously tortured and then, while they were still alive, stacked them up and set fire to them with gasoline. Miland video taped the whole thing and sent it to several other gangs. They got the message. They leave Don Miland's operations strictly alone.

Jim sat back and shook his head. "These people will stop at nothing even if it was too costly to them in terms of power or money. When something threatens to expose them to public view, political retaliation through the police, or is grossly unwise financially, they attack it regardless of the costs. A normal criminal group would try to avoid or downplay the situation. Not this bunch. They do totally unreasonable things and still come out on top." He drank some tea, and poured them both some more from the pot on the table. He was obviously upset by the evil done by Don Miland's group. Jim casually indicated three men enjoying a meal in a booth by the back wall. "See those three men?"

Jack casually looked over like he was looking for a waiter. "Yes, are they part of Don Miland's gang?"

"Yes, they are, right down to their patent leather shoes." Jim replied.

Jim sighed, "Many of the street troops are men who aren't much more than human failures with fancy clothes and jewelry. They get their kicks by causing pain, grief, and death just so that they can enjoy the feeling of power it gives them over others. The financial angle is not always their guiding criteria. There is a rumor that Miland has bought one or more cops and has them on his payroll. That could be why he operates with impunity. Some think that his 'partner' might even be an official high up in the law enforcement world."

"Either through stupidity or ego they will spend thousands of dollars to settle a score with someone who probably didn't do anything on purpose in the first place. They can also kill someone at no cost to themselves or they're compensated by the money in the person's wallet or purse. They just don't have any compassion or concern about other people."

The Sensei looked closely at Jack, "You met your first members of Don Miland's little group at the men's store several weeks ago. You met another one today. It's a pattern that doesn't look good. I don't believe Tony will be the last one you'll meet." The Sensei paused and looked at his student for a few seconds.

Jack knew that his teacher wanted something from him at that point. Many years of working under his training made this a natural thing and Jack thought about the last few statements Jim had made. The inference was actually simple, brutally nasty, but simple. Jack nodded his head, "Yeah, I see now, the first was an accidental run-in, but the second time they came looking for me. That means they know who I am, what I am, and where I am. That's dangerous for Laura and me, not to mention the school."

The Sensei nodded, "Remember, the first time is an accident, the second a possible coincidence, the third time is enemy action."

Jack smiled back, "Remember Sensei, there is no Hebrew word for coincidence." Sensei Grady rolled his eyes and smiled back. "I really doubt that any of Don Miland's people are from Israel."

Jack indicated the young couple at the other table who were in deep conversation with each other. "Why did you say they could help us in the near future?"

The Sensei smiled, "Those two youngsters have just been selected as house servants for the local mansion that Don Miland owns. The reason they were picked was because they had good credentials as servants, were inexpensive, and they don't speak English."

Jack frowned, "They greeted me in excellent English."

Jim nodded, "All right, let me rephrase that. They don't speak English to anyone except those they trust implicitly, which includes me and you by extension. Okay?"

Jack casually looked the couple over. The man was a typically compact Asian in his late twenties with a definite 'sports' build. He wasn't bulked up like a weight lifter but solid muscle masses with little fat. He would be a serious competitor if his knowledge of Martial Arts was thorough. Somehow Jack felt that it would be.

The woman was typical of many Oriental women. Her age could have been in her twenties or even up into her forties. She was a classic Asian beauty with a more pronounced bust line than most of her sisters in Asia. Jack asked his teacher, "What do they do that qualifies them to spy on Don Miland?"

Sensei Grady smiled a small smile. "They were both top agents in the Asian Ministry of Internal Affairs. That means they are the equivalent to both the FBI and CIA combined."

Jack whistled softly. "Wow. What ever brought them to the U.S? Can we trust them?"

Jim nodded slowly to the questions. "We can trust them because they found Jesus, converted to Christianity, and left China before they were executed. The FBI has cleared them and they have become American citizens. Neither of them is allowed to enter the security services of the U.S. which was all right with them. They had some rough times after they found Christ. They fled for their lives. They also provided the FBI with a great deal of new information, much of which has been verified by the way, about the internal affairs in their old country."

Jack sat rapt as the conversation went well into the next morning with Jim detailing the local operation of Don Miland's gang and some of their tactics and recent atrocities. The excursion at the men's store was another bizarre operation on Don Miland's part. It didn't really make any sense. Of course, they hadn't counted on meeting Jack. This confirmed for Jack that the man he beat today was a scout for revenge.

Jack decided he needed to get some clarity. When he mentioned the scout concept to Jim it caused his teacher to pause and consider the situation. Eventually he shook his head, "No, I don't think so. It doesn't make any sense. But then, nothing Joe's people have done lately makes a whole lot of sense. You did embarrass him and eliminated several of his hirelings, who know, maybe."

Jim continued, "Normally, I doubt that Tony would have been brave enough to take you on, alone, in my Dojo after what you did to the other men at the store. Therefore he was probably operating under orders. You need to exercise caution though. It is possible you may be right in that they are interested in finding you and getting even, but I sense that they have a more sinister reason. What that reason is, remains unknown."

Jack drove home with the sinking feeling that he was a lot wiser but, as with any innocence lost, sad that the world wasn't such a nice place to his eyes anymore. Even at that hour of the morning he spotted the black Lincoln that he suspected a pimp drove, parked by the curb. The black man driving the car was talking to two young girls with short skirts and high heels that didn't look like they were out of high school yet. According to the information he had learned tonight the odds were good they were still under eighteen.

CHAPTER ELEVEN

Since that talk, Jack had noticed many of the signs of gang-related crimes that are right out in the open. That was if you knew what to look for, and where to look. His Sensei had given him a crash course in identifying the bad guys. Still, things were going well and he did not want to worry Laura, remembering how the incident at the men's store had upset her. So he didn't mention his talk with Jim or the signs of trouble he saw on the streets.

Jack resolved his problems by himself, seeking no help. He decided that he needed to research the key and the mysterious 'Holy package' that Bill Martin had presented him. It left him in the middle of something with which he wasn't too thrilled about. Dying people could be very inconsiderate, Jack thought, humorously.

As Jack drove home the evening after Ron Kolby had left the company, he came to the conclusion that his Sensei was right. If Don Miland had his eyes fixed on him, then he and Laura could have real trouble.

If this 'Don' discovered that Jack Malone had been given a key by the man they killed, Jack would have more trouble than he'd ever dreamed was possible in his life. He just wasn't sure what he could, or should, do about it. He would let things slide while he searched for answers. But, he wanted to be prepared to get Laura out of the line of fire if it came to that.

Jack drove up the driveway to their home and noticed that the gardening crew had been there. They had done a reasonably good job of cutting and trimming the yard except for the area around the hedges. They simply couldn't understand the concept of a trimmed border. He wished, for the twentieth time, that he had time to do it himself, but he was needed elsewhere and couldn't handle everything at once.

The weather had cooled somewhat, as it tends to do early in the spring in the high country, and partial cloud cover had floated out over the Denver basin from the mountains. Jack noticed that Laura had reclaimed her shiny black Turbo Stealth from the clutches of the dealer where it had gone for warranty work. He enjoyed driving the sporty little car around town on occasion, but liked his Cadillac much better.

He glanced at the far end of the three-car garage as he walked up the front walk and could see the Range Rover looking forlorn and lonely. They hadn't had much chance to go up in the mountains since Laura's job had become so hectic. They probably wouldn't get much chance while the threat of gang violence hung over their heads and the mystery of the dying man's key remained unsolved.

That thought made him stop and look at his house in a different light. Instead of being gateways of warmth and sunlight, the large windows on the ground and second floors at the front of the house loomed as potential targets for drive-by shootings. The ornate front door seemed flimsy and the general layout of the shrubbery around the house actually lent itself to unseen assault rather than an effective defense.

Shaking his head in a physical effort to throw off these ugly thoughts, Jack opened the front door and walked into the foyer. Laura came out of the kitchen with an apron on over a pretty two-piece outfit while he was looking through the mail. As normal, she had placed it on the eighteenth century English writing desk sitting in the front hall so that he could see it as soon as he came in.

She was all smiles, "And how was your day?" Without a pause she continued, "I bet it can't hold a candle to how interesting my day was." She slid her left arm under his coat and around his slim waist and hugged him to her. He caught her up in his arms and returned the hug, and threw in a few kisses for good measure. He whispered in her ear, "You look exceptionally pretty tonight, Mrs. Malone." She purred and smiled up at him. "Dinner is almost ready, Mr. Malone." She grinned and headed back to the kitchen. "Come on and eat, I want to tell you what happened at work today. After that we can throw the dishes into the dishwasher and relax."

During dinner, he listened distractedly as she described her victory in the conference room ending with the promise of a bonus and the hassle she had in the grocery store trying to find just the right food for tonight's dinner. He let questions about his day slide by without any real discussion.

Later that evening she snuggled up to him enjoying the closeness before they fell asleep.

Jack was sure Laura had noticed his distracted attitude. She was probably wondering about his sudden preoccupation and quiet wakefulness at this point of the night. Validation of that thought came as she slowly caressed his arm and asked him, "What's the matter?"

Jack made a decision to tell her because their relationship was based on honesty. So, he didn't try to deny his preoccupation or give her a song and dance. Instead he related the events surrounding Don Kolby and the probable gang involvement.

By the time he was finished giving her the gist of the talk between him and Jim Grady, they were both wide awake sitting at the kitchen table having toast and coffee. For the first time he put into words the worries he had about the mayhem at the store, the punk at the Dojo, and the apparent union take-over attempt at TA all being the work of this one gang.

He then told her what the possible dangers were that he foresaw for them in the near future. She was endangered by just being married to him. Until he brought the concept to their doorstep, it hadn't seemed real, more like a TV story which they could turn off if they wanted to. Now it loomed large in their future.

CHAPTER TWELVE

As Laura listened to Jack tell her about the possible danger to them both, from somewhere deep inside her a sudden chill ran down her spine. The more she thought about all the things that had happened, the more the fear tightened the knot that had suddenly formed in her stomach. She thought that this was too much like the time she remembered being frightened as a child.

Her father had been a dandy and a charmer who, while being a great salesman, was frequently drunk, was a habitual liar, and cheated on his wife. He acted friendly, especially to anyone who could be of benefit to him but in reality he treated everybody else, men, women, and especially her mom, shabbily.

When she was fourteen years old she had begun to develop the curves of womanhood that she was proud of today. One weekend her father and a drinking buddy were drinking at their house while her mom was out of town visiting her sister for the weekend. The buddy decided he wanted to put his hands all over Laura. When she tried to stop him he slapped her in the face. Her father just sat there and told her to stop being such a baby. After all, the guy was his friend and she was making him look bad by acting so poorly. After being hit, and hearing her father's words, the abandonment was almost too much. She had pushed and shoved but the man was too big and strong for her.

Fortunately, the man had been drinking for hours and passed out before he could do anything. She pushed his heavy, smelly body away from hers and crawled out of the room. Her dad just continued to drink and watch football on the television.

At that point her whole world had crashed down around her. She was so afraid and there was no one to help her. The man she had looked to for protection and possibly some fatherly love had become the enemy. She sat in the corner of her bedroom with the door locked and cried for hours.

She was terrified that her dad would open the door to let the man in and there was nowhere to run. She remembered realizing that her father probably never had cared what happened to her. She hated him and damned him to hell. She was afraid to come out of her room and she went through a terrible time on a downward spiral for days after that evening.

When she did leave the house she hated to go back. Her grades continued to worsen until one day she met Mrs. Thornton as she was sneaking out of the school building. Connie Thornton was a guidance counselor at her school and caught her skipping classes that day. Mrs. Thornton listened to her excuses for not wanting to go to class and asked Laura to come into her office and talk to her.

Connie Thornton had come through the ordeal of child abuse by an abusive father herself and, with help, had managed to make her life healthy again. Understanding the depression that such abuse can cause, she had made a career out of trying to help young people caught in the same trap. Later, Laura realized that she had been exhibiting all the signs of child abuse and it wasn't hard for the woman to figure out what was going on in her life.

After talking to her, Connie realized the enormity of Laura's situation. She arranged to have Laura attend three sessions a week with her on a one-to-one basis. Although it had taken most of the school year, they worked through the anger, the guilt, and even the shame that her father had caused her. Laura had always felt blessed because Connie had been there immediately after the event and helped her before it totally destroyed her self-image and she got in trouble by acting out her anger.

She had been deeply hurt and betrayed, and in turn, had avoided her father completely. Now she faced him with the understanding that he was an alcoholic who was out of control. She had taken control of her life with Connie's help and found help at Alanon meetings, but she still had to live at home. When her dad brought home another 'drinking buddy' she quietly slipped out of the house and called Connie for advice. It was a Saturday and they went to the movies and had dinner at a nice restaurant. Connie suggested that she call her mother, who was out of town again.

Laura knew her mother would be of no help. She had seen her mother cave into anything her dad wanted to do. Her mom never had been a forceful or assertive woman. She had tended to let her husband make the plans and decisions for the family and she overlooked his excesses the way she thought a dutiful wife should. She gave a great deal of love to her children but considered a husband as a necessary force in the family circle regardless of how he treated her.

Connie let Laura spend the rest of the weekend with her and her family. Connie's husband, Grant, was everything her father wasn't and none of what he was. Connie's kids liked Laura and their daughter Jane who was only a year younger spent hours with Laura trying on makeup and styling their hair. These family-friendly activities were new for Laura.

When she went home on Sunday evening she found her dad asleep, or more likely, passed out in the living room in front of the television. He obviously had never missed her. After that she spent more and more time away from home, with Connie or some of Laura's decent student friends, the ones she called her 'inner circle'. These were girls that had affectionate families and caring parents. They lived in comfortable homes or apartments and enjoyed having Laura around. She had always insisted on pulling her own weight when she stayed with anyone. She would do housework such as dishes, or vacuuming, or walking the family dog. One time she helped a friend and her mother paint their entire house. It took two weeks of constant work during the summer and her dad never mentioned that she hadn't been at home. Laura remembered that this was the way she was able to make it through high school. She was with some of the people so much she figured they claimed her on their tax returns as a dependent.

Her mother died suddenly of a viral infection while Laura was away at her first year of college on scholarship. Laura had taken care of the arrangements and stood there with her brothers while they buried their mom. Laura's father could not come to the funeral because he had an important golf game with his friends scheduled at the same time.

Later that year, while Laura was away at school, her older brother had joined the army and the younger one had quit school, got an apartment, and worked as a mechanic. She knew they left to get away from their dad and the situation at home. With her brothers gone, there was nothing left at home for her. Laura took a trip home and moved all of her things and some of her mom's stuff out of the house that day and never looked back. But, she never forgot the fear of being so alone and defenseless that first night.

Now, here it was again. That same feeling that there was no safe place for her in the world. Deep down inside a heat started to build. She wasn't a teenage girl who depended on somebody else for her protection. She wasn't a child without resources and determination anymore and she darn well wasn't going to hide in the corner and be scared. She was going to handle the situation, whatever came. She knew she needed to provide a steady anchor for Jack when he got mad. He would get mad if someone threatened his family or his work and there was no telling the amount of damage he would do. "Pity the poor devil that makes Jack mad", Laura thought. Regardless, she couldn't fold up this time, her husband needed her. SHE needed her , and they would both need her thinking clearly.

She stood up and walked around the table and bent over and kissed him on the cheek. "Let's take a run to burn up some of this tension honey." With that she headed upstairs to change into her running clothes.

After Laura was gone, Jack wondered if he would ever figure her out. "Run?" He thought that didn't compute. He looked at his watch: it was eleven o'clock at night. Then he grinned, "That's right, let's show us we aren't afraid." He bounded up the stairs after his wife.

Fifty minutes later they walked the last five minutes of the distance to let their hearts slow down to a normal level. Jack was pleased that the run had been uneventful, giving them a sense of balance to the frightening thoughts that they had been discussing an hour before.

After his shower Jack activated the recessed box labeled "Milady's BathBot" and watched as the mechanical arm swung out and started to use its ultrasonic head to inspect, clean, and wash down the tub and the walls of the shower stall. Another one of his dad's brainstorms. Jack sighed; he hadn't gotten in on this one. Now, every motel and hotel in the world wanted the units. "Oh well", he thought, he had enough on his plate as it was.

He was bedded down and beginning to relax when the telephone rang. The clock on the bedside table read one-thirty a.m. He picked up the phone and said "Hello?" His dad's voice was clear even though he was calling from over a thousand miles away. "Jack, I got a call from Bob Wexler this evening and then I talked to Jim about twenty minutes ago. Can your Uncle Larry and I be of any help?"

Jack thought about the offer. His dad and his uncle had developed the NovaStar home defense system that he was building at his plant. They were certainly defensive minded. They could provide a lot of support for both him and Laura. He didn't want to expose his relatives to the dangers but he was quite sure they were aware of the odds if they had talked to Jim Grady. Jack realized the enormity of the problem facing him. He decided, uncharacteristically, that this was no time to be independent at his own cost. "Sure Dad, we'd be glad to have some help, of course",

Hedging his bets, Jack added, "You know that this could all blow over and you'd be wasting your time coming up here."

His dad laughed, "That would be great if so, but it's all right either way son. We have to be up there in Denver for the demonstration of the NovaStar system this month anyway. It should be fun to spend some time out there with you kids. We'll see you sometime Monday morning."

After hanging up, Jack explained the conversation to Laura and openly wondered exactly what his older relatives considered fun. Then he and Laura tried to get some sleep before the six a.m. Tuesday morning alarm.

CHAPTER THIRTEEN

Joe Miland sat behind his massive desk brooding with anger and thought dark thoughts. He had received another phone call from his partner and it didn't go well. He looked at the crew assembled in his office. On his left was Carlo Ritter, a leg-breaker and enforcer. Carlo was attempting to move up to a better position of power in the operation. Ambitious, dependable, and he really liked to hurt people. Underbosses in the organization needed to think before they acted, regardless of their emotions. Thinking was not Carlo's strong suit.

Next to Carlo was Johnny Casner, a really mean little snake. His partner was on his left, the ever ready 'Big' Joe Scarborough. This one was a borderline crazy who made a lot of trips over that border on a job.

The other three guys were men who served as needed and didn't open their mouths. Typical muscle that tended to end up as cannon fodder, but they didn't have much of a choice. Joe remembered his hope that maybe he'd get picked to be a sub-boss a couple of years ago. He smiled inside as he remembered that he had made his own opportunity by eliminating his boss after he got hired onto a crew in Denver. After that, no one argued with him about being the boss. He used to have to keep a sharp eye on his men so that they didn't use the same method to move up. But, since he signed on with his new partner, nobody but nobody, threatened him.

Joe told them to settle down and then lit a cigar. After a few puffs he looked at each man in turn and began outlining his phony design for the takeover of the Technological Alternatives Company. "I have plans for this company. Plans you guys don't need to know about, but, plans that are real important. I want each of you to realize how important these plans are to me."

The Don paused for effect. "If I get control of this company, I will be the top boss of Denver, and maybe a whole lot more. If I climb the ladder, you guys go right up with me, see?" He watched their faces and wondered if they were buying any of this bull. His partner was adamant about getting their hands on this Malone character and grilling him about the box. His whole gang had been hunting for it for the past three months. Joe thought, "Of course, they didn't know that, they just take orders."

"Now I'm gonna want each of you to do your part to 'encourage' the owners of this little company to see things my way. First, Carlo and I are going to pay the owners a visit, this morning. The rest of you guys come with us and act like the muscle you are. Now, no rough stuff, just a show of force to let them know we can back up our demands."

"Big Joe, get the cars. The rest of you guys go out in the hall and wait. Do something, I don't know. Check your guns and ties or something. Carlo and I have to discuss tactics before we go out there."

After the rest of the group left the room, Carlo frowned and asked, "What is so important about this little company that you are going to go out there personally, Boss? I mean, you know, you told me to drop in on this character. Now you're going to go, I don't get it."

Joe stared at his enforcer like one would look at a particularly aggressive pet, one that was not overly bright but dangerous when laughed at. "Well, Einstein, I've got my reasons. Remember, we need to get this Malone guy to come to us after this meeting. Otherwise, I don't give a hoot about his company, got it?"

Joe carefully watched Carlo for any sign of understanding."Why don't we want his company?" Carlo asked. Joe counted to ten inside his head. "Because my partner wants to grill this Malone guy, now, do you get it?" Carlo nodded his head up and down with a big grin, not sure he understood but not stupid enough to ask his boss the same question for a third time.

They spent the next ten minutes going over the dog and pony show they were going to pull on the unsuspecting company president. Then they joined their men and formed a two car parade.

Joe was pleased with the mansion in which he, as the 'Don', lived. The main house was all alone on an isolated ten acres south of Denver in the rolling hills northwest of Castle Rock, Colorado, off Outer Marker Road.

They exited through the electrically controlled gates and in three minutes were merging with the north-bound traffic from Colorado Springs on Interstate 25. Exiting I-25 they turned westbound on I-470 which runs towards the mountains south of Littleton and the Denver Tech Center. They pulled off of the Interstate and turned onto westbound County Line Road. A few minutes later they were stopped at the gate to the Technological Alternative's company parking lot.

The guard took a careful look at them and got on the phone to the head office. "Mr. Malone? I got two carloads of some tough looking guys down here wanting to get into the plant site. You said to alert you if anything out of the ordinary came up." Jack decided to have the guard inquire as to their business. When the answer came back that they wanted to speak with the owners on an important matter, Jack thought for a bit. "Tell them that I am out of the plant right now but if they will come back after lunch time, I will see them then, say, two o'clock."

The guard passed the message on and the convoy swung around and headed back towards the mansion with Joe upset that the meeting hadn't been arranged in advance. He took out his irritation on Carlo. "You told me that guy was there every morning all day, every day, didn't you?"

Carlo flinched, "Yeah, Boss, but I guess even he has to go out sometime." The logical answer was no help to anybody. Joe took out his cell phone and called Johnny Casner in the other car. "You guys double back and watch the plant. Carlo says this guy drives a new white Caddy four-door. When you see him you call me, got it?" The other car slowed and turned left as Don Miland's car continued back to their base.

CHAPTER FOURTEEN

After a quick conference with Bob Wexler, Jack punched in the phone number and tried unsuccessfully to reach Jim Grady. He then dialed the local office of the FBI and asked to speak to special agent Rhodes. Jack remembered Gary Rhodes as an intelligent man who also happened to be a top-notch agent for the Bureau and was stationed in the Denver office.

Jack had forgotten he'd met Gary at a conference six months ago. He couldn't understand why the man popped into his head at this time. He thought back and remembered striking up a conversation with him concerning the actual possibility of terrorists based in Denver. What he got was polite chatter which had no content. This made Jack think he was being given the run-around. He subsequently made a phone call to the local FBI Resident Agent in Charge. Two days later he got a phone call from Agent Rhodes and an apology, along with an explanation.

"Mr. Malone? Gary Rhodes. I apologize for the seeming misdirection. Many people attempt to learn what the Bureau knows by interrogating the agents. They want the information for every reason from simple curiosity to criminal intent. No agent discusses active cases or even unpublished information unless they are authorized. I wanted time to check you out before discussing anything about local terrorists with you."

Gary told Jack he had received a clean record from the Bureau, the local police, and the CBI. Then Agent Rhodes gave Jack what he could. The picture wasn't very well defined because they only had vague hints and rumors to work with at this time. After all the time spent there had been little helpful information.

This time Agent Rhodes answered Jack's call immediately. "Hello, Mr. Malone, what can I do for you?"

Jack related the problem he had with Don Kolby and the fact that he was going to be called on at two o'clock by a gang of rough-looking guys probably from the same or a similar group. "What can I do if they make me an offer I can't refuse?" Jack asked with an oblique reference to the Godfather movies.

Gary Rhodes laughed. "Don't worry! They usually don't get that serious at first, if this really is a visit from the mob. Don't you think you had better hear what they say before you accuse them of anything? You know, they might just be a bunch of aggressive IBM salesmen looking for new business." The fact that the agent was minimizing the situation made Jack stop and wonder if he was becoming paranoid. Jack told the Agent, "Okay, I'll see them and find out what they want. Just in case they are the bad guys, should I call you again?"

Gary said, "Sure, give me a call if they turn out to be, he paused to pick the right phrase, what you think they are. In fact, I'll give you my cell phone number in case I'm out of the office." He proceeded to give Jack the number and said good-bye.

Jack was pondering what other steps he could take when the phone rang. It was Jim Grady. "Jack, I understand that you were trying to reach me earlier. Is there something I can do for you?" Jack breathed a sigh of relief. "Yes Jim. I wonder if you have a minute to give me some pointers about some guests I am going to have this afternoon?"

Jack went ahead and explained their first approach and the meeting scheduled that afternoon. Jim told him to not agree to anything if they were the mob, but not to disagree either. "Just tell them you need to think about it for a day or so. Then we can determine what they want and what we will do about it.

Jack felt better after he hung up. Jim's calm, sensible approach and support was encouraging. He put the matter aside until that afternoon and concentrated on the rest of Thursday morning's workload.

It was almost lunch time when the guard at the gate called him again. "Mr. Malone, I've been watching a car parked at the back of the gas station across the street most of the morning. I'm pretty sure it was one of the two cars that came to the gate this morning with all the tough guys. Do you want me to have the police check them out?"

Jack asked the guard, "What would they check them for, loitering?" The guard answered "Yeah, suspicion that they have been casing the gas station."

Jack thought about the situation and said, "Why don't you call the gas station and get them worried enough to call the cops? Just in case they are bad guys and can find out who called the cops, we don't want them to know it was us, okay?" The guard agreed and hung up. Jack thought about it for a few more seconds and then got up and went to the closet at the back of office. Taking a pair of 10 x 40 binoculars out of a case he went to the panoramic window overlooking the front of the plant and locked them in on the gas station across the street.

The guard looked up the station number in the phone book and called the girl at the self-service Conoco. He pretended he was a concerned citizen who had just bought gas there. "Ma'am, I think you should be worried about the tough looking guys sitting at the back of your gas station. They could be sizing you up for robbery."

Six minutes later against a beautiful mountain backdrop, Jack watched as a Littleton Police car pulled into the gas station lot and cruised to the back of the lot where the big black car was sitting.

Sergeant Sam Joiner punched in the license number of the big black car on his NCIC computer and waited for a 'wants and warrants' response.

When the response came back negative, he called in the stop to headquarters. He didn't like the looks of the dark-windowed luxury car or the two men he could see through the front window. They hadn't made a move to get out of the car or roll down a window to see what he wanted, even though his patrol car was pointed directly at their left front fender and he was obviously interested in them. Feeling uneasy about the setup made him ask for backup. "Base, I've got a suspect vehicle backed into the rear of the Conoco on County Line Road across from the Technological Alternatives plant. I'd like some backup." Headquarters put out a call for a backup. Sam sat there and waited while he watched the occupants of the suspect car.

A few minutes later a two man team pulled into the other side of the gas station. Sam was surprised to see a Colorado Highway Patrol car rather than another Littleton Police car. Recognizing one of the State Patrolmen, Sam switched to TAC3 on his radio and talked low-power to the State Car. "Hi, Bill, how come I rate support from State?"

The driver in the State car picked up the microphone. "We heard your call Sam, and since we were in the area and available, Mario and I thought we'd check out the action. Do you want to chat with these bozos, or do you want us to do it?"

The Littleton officer said, "Just keep your eyes open, these guys look like hard cases to me." He hung the microphone back on the dash and swung himself out of the car. Undoing the thumb-break snap on his holster he approached the driver's door of the long black Lincoln with his hand on his gun's grip. As he got near, the window slid down noiselessly and a swarthy face stared up at him.

"Yes officer, what can I do for you?" No surprise, no worry, just casual businesslike chatter. Sam leaned down to look at the other three men in the car. He asked, "Could I see your driver's license and proof of insurance."

One of the big guys in the back said, "Look Officer, do you know who...." At which point the driver held up his hand. He turned around and looked at the offending torpedo. "The boss would be real upset if you were to announce to the world his business. Understand?"

The guy in the back seat fell quiet and the driver dug out the paperwork and handed it to Sam.

After looking at the license, the officer went back to his squad car to run the license through the computer. When it came back with two outstanding murder warrants it was at such odds with the guy's behavior he ran it again and asked for details. The warrants were issued by Illinois and had just been made available to the Colorado Criminal Computer Database. Sam looked at the almost friendly face in the driver's window watching him. Sam thought, "Obviously Johnny Casner does not know that his out-of-state crimes are now known locally."

While Sam was doing his computer checks Johnny was beginning to worry. It didn't usually take this long to get him a clean bill of health. He casually pulled his pistol out of its shoulder holster and told the other guys to be ready just in case.

The two Highway Patrolmen had been watching the black Lincoln and had seen the subtle movement which could only mean one thing. Before Sam could call them to tell them about the warrants, he saw them pull their squad car directly in front of the Lincoln and both men bailed out the cruiser's doors.

Mario crouched behind the front fender of the squad car and had the shotgun leveled at the Lincoln while Bill used the microphone to activate the loudspeaker on top of the patrol car. "You men in front place your hands on the dash and don't move. You two in back roll down your windows and extend your hands out the windows, empty."

The sudden sound of the loudspeaker caused the other people using the gas station to dive for cover or leave the area with all haste.

Johnny said, "Screw this!" He started the car and slammed it into the patrol car. The patrolman with the shotgun fired directly into the windshield. The shot ricocheted harmlessly off the bulletproof glass leaving only a small star pattern where it struck, although the buckshot continued on and tore a two-foot hole in the gas station overhead.

Both patrolmen were thrown backwards by the violent collision. Sam had gotten out of his cruiser while the other officers hailed the Lincoln. He crouched behind his door at the sound of the Lincoln's engine starting and yelled into his microphone for more backup.

When the Lincoln jumped forward into the highway patrol car and the other officer fired the shotgun, Sam saw the pellets bounce off the windshield of the armored vehicle. So as the big car forced its way past the patrol car it had crumpled, Sam saw his chance and unloaded his 9mm automatic into the left front tire of the four door sedan. The tire was foam filled and bullet resistant but one of the rounds found the steering system and fractured the tie-rod bushing housing. The suddenly freed left front wheel decided to go a different direction than the rest of the car. This made the big car swerve to the left and it ran violently into an old Ford pickup truck to Sam's left. Sam saw the collision slam the men in the back seat into the front seat and smacked the front passenger's head against the windshield hard enough to knock him unconscious.

Before Johnny or the other two men in back could get themselves sorted out, Sam had reached the car and yanked on the driver's door latch. To his amazement, the door opened. Sam shoved his freshly reloaded automatic against the side of Johnny's head and yelled, "Okay, dirt bags. Drop your weapons and raise your hands, now!"

Sam saw the two men in the back angling to get a shot at him, but the driver knew he wouldn't survive a shootout. He dropped his pistol and raised his hands. The other two looked at each other as if deciding whether to shoot it out with the Littleton cop even if Johnny was in the way. The front seat passenger stayed unconscious and ignored everything.

Suddenly, one of the two Highway Patrolmen pulled open the opposite rear door on the car and stuck his shotgun into the rear seat area. Sam knew that looking into the sewer pipe-sized hole in the end of the 12-gauge shotgun, both of the men in the back seat could see an extremely short future. They dropped their Uzis and put their hands on top of their heads.

Two more Littleton Police cars roared into the gas station with lights blazing and sirens howling and slid to a halt near the Lincoln. Sam and the new officers frisked and handcuffed all four men. Sam read them their rights but noticed that the front seat passenger was still out of it.

Sam's report summed up the action. All in all, the police found on the four men, or stashed in the car, four fully-automatic Israeli 9mm Uzis, four various caliber pistols, six knives, and one set of brass knuckles. An ambulance came and Mario, who had been banged up somewhat in the collision went with the unconscious suspect to the Littleton Medical Center at County Line and Broadway. Sam sent the other three to the Littleton jail charged with a variety of criminal activities.

Sam worked at getting his heart to slow down as a fleet of tow trucks arrived in response to the police request. After finishing the paperwork Sam let them leave, towing the Lincoln to the impound lot, the highway patrol car to the repair shop, and what was left of the old Ford pickup, to the wrecking yard.

Sam sat writing up his report and wondered why Johnny Casner, a suspect in two murders and a heavily armed team were sitting in the gas station.

CHAPTER FIFTEEN

The security guard at the front gate was excited when he called Jack. "Mr. Malone, you should have seen the results of that phone call. Those guys shot it out with the cops and lost big time. There were five squad cars, a chopper, two ambulances, and three tow trucks involved in that mess. And, I was right about the car, I got a good look at it as they towed it off. It was one of the two cars here this morning."

Having watched the whole show Jack quietly smiled a grim smile. "I had a feeling that might be the case. Thanks a lot. You've done a good job. Keep your eyes open though, I still expect the other car to be back here at two pm."

After he hung up the phone and sat back in his chair he thought about calling Agent Rhodes again. But, he didn't because the impression he had gotten from the agent indicated he would have to be fighting tooth and nail before the FBI would consider his problem big enough to get involved in. So, he took a minute to write a note to give the security guard a bonus for his good work.

Jack wondered if push came to shove if he would have to add to his list by killing a human being. It just wasn't normal for a person in his lifestyle to have to make that type of decision. If they tried to harm Laura or Jim, he probably would. But, the question still remained. Jack knew that he was now considered 'blooded' as far as actual street combat went, but he still had an internal argument concerning the propriety of the taking of a human life. Jack thought back to battle in the store and the face of the recently dead Bill Martin. Jack shook his head, he also had enough sense to realize that wondering and worrying about it would solve nothing. So he put it aside until such time as it became necessary to find out.

A few miles south of Jack's company, Joe Miland was mad enough to irrationally hurt anybody in close vicinity to the telephone. He shouted during the conversation with his lawyer. "He did what? Why? Look! You go down there and get that turkey out, and have him come here so I can kill the little idiot myself!"

Joe slammed down the phone and picked up his desk chair and threw it into the wall of his office on the first floor of his mansion. The chair smashed through the wall hard enough that one of the really expensive paintings fell from the wall and smashed against the floor, scattering glass in all directions.

Carlo Ritter slammed through the door with his pistol up and looking for something to shoot. This took quite a bit of the wind out of Joe's sails because he knew that Carlo was as stupid as he was vicious and could shoot him for lack of a better target. He crouched behind his desk and yelled, "Carlo, put that away!" Joe peered out from behind his desk and was relieved to see the intense expression on Carlo's face loosen up and the fact that he had lowered his pistol so that it now aimed at the floor.

Carlo put the gun away in his holster and went over to the shambles that was left of the wall. "I'm sorry, Boss. I thought you had trouble in here. That's the only reason I came in with my gun out. I didn't want whoever you were fighting with to get the drop on me too."

Realizing that Carlo didn't mean to imply that he, Joe, would be an easy mark, Joe shook his head and said, "Thanks Carlo, I was just letting off some steam. That idiot Johnny Casner got himself and all three of the boys with him thrown in jail. Not just for a traffic violation either. They have been charged with a crap load of charges like; murder, assaulting a peace officer, willful reckless driving, possession of automatic weapons without a license, attempting to elude a peace officer, and God knows how many other dumb things he could do all at one time." Joe was building another head of steam. "I don't know why I ever gave that little snake a job in the first place. All he's ever done is given me grief."

Carlo took his boss' question literally. "Boss, you hired him because he was the best hit man available when you wanted to take out Tino Martin. Remember?" Joe stared back at his henchman and wondered why he had ever hired him either.

"Get the car, Carlo. We got to go see that punk at that Techno Alternates place. I guess we don't need four more guys just to talk to the character, right?" Joe rubbed his hand across his face. "And get somebody in here to clean up this mess, one of those chink kids. Use that hand sign crap you got to tell them to do a good job."

Carlo nodded and hurried to comply with Joe's wishes. A few minutes later Charley Wu came in the room with a small broom and a trash can. He smiled inanely, bowed several times to Joe and hurried over to the picture and chair lying on the floor. Stooping down he carefully placed the broken glass into the trash can and hung the picture back on the wall. Miraculously, the painting itself had not been damaged. The heavy frame had protected it and the glass had all blown outward away from the picture. Charley continued to pick up the pieces of glass and sweep up the area.

The chair, likewise, had not sustained any damage. Unfortunately the same could not be said about the wall paneling itself. A large section would have to be replaced. Charley picked up a piece of the paneling and examined it. Shrugging, he placed it in his pocket and returned the chair to Joe's desk. Picking up the trash can he bowed to Joe and left the room.

Carlo returned to get Joe, "Okay, Boss, the car is ready out front." He looked at Joe who was staring at the damaged wall. "What's the matter, Boss?"

Joe shook his head. "That gook kid just stole a piece of my wall!"

Carlo looked at the damage to the wall, "Boss, I don't think that is what he did."

Joe yelled, "What'd you mean, you don't think so? I just told you I saw him take it."

Carlo took on the look of a patient parent, an act which made Joe try to remember where his gun was. "No sir, I don't mean you didn't see him take a piece of the wall, I mean that he didn't steal it. I told him to clean up in here. To him that means he has to fix the wall, too. He probably took it as a sample to get some new paneling."

Mollified, Joe backed down and quit looking for any loose object large enough with which to brain his henchman. Joe could just hear the sarcasm in his partner's voice as he told him about the antics of his men. "Let's go!" he said, and they pushed out of the room and through the front hall to the driveway.

Charley Wu's intelligent mind was concerned as he watched them drive away and then he smiled. Sensing the approach of somebody, he adopted the silly peasant boy look and turned around. It was his wife, Linda, looking equally silly in the black pajamas she had to wear as her 'servant's outfit'. Her outfit differed from his only in the diamond shaped opening below her throat through which a generous portion of her chest was revealed. One of the reasons Joe had hired them was because Linda was very well built for an Oriental. Charlie thought to himself, "Pity the poor man who tries to get fresh with her."

Linda looked out and watched the black car leave the driveway. She looked at Charley and raised one eyebrow with a questioning look on her face. Speaking Cantonese so that none of the other people in the mansion could decipher their comments she asked him, "What was that great crashing I heard?"

Charley tipped his head at the departed car and replied in the same dialect. "The number one wacko pig was in a real snit. Don't know why, but he smashed a big hole in his study wall. I've got to replace the panel immediately, before he returns. I hope you still have that 'ear' in the car." Charlie was referring to a listening device he wanted that would gather information quietly and only broadcast it to a listening receiver when it was triggered by a radio signal.

She nodded and went off to prepare an afternoon snack for some of the men still in the building.

Charley left and after stopping at his car for the listening device, took a small truck to go to the Handy Dan lumber yard on County Line Road.

CHAPTER SIXTEEN

Joe had calmed down when, precisely at ten minutes before two in the afternoon, his Lincoln Town Car pulled up to the main gate of Technological Alternatives. Carlo told the guard that Joe Miland had a meeting with the President of the company for two o'clock. While they waited for the guard to get permission to let them in, Joe looked the place over. The company was housed in two buildings. The front building was a two level administration building with the name over the door and lots of pretty flowers strategically placed around the building to give it an inviting look.

In contrast, the second building was much larger and more functional. Joe figured it was probably about fifty thousand square feet in floor space. It was obviously an engineering and manufacturing facility and the double chain-link fence topped by coils of razor wire didn't entice one to have a closer look unless they were invited.

Invited to review the property is exactly what Joe expected to be in the next hour. His powerful partner had outlined everything and how he was to handle it. Joe's job was to lure Jack Malone to a remote location, where his partner would interrogate the young man. After Joe had accomplished his task of getting Malone to the remote location, he had been promised a treat better than anything he had experienced to date. He felt a big burst of excitement. It was like getting a Christmas present three months after the holiday. None of his partner's promises had ever failed to come through. No one had seen fit to reject his partner's offers in the past either. They knew they could get dead that way.

The guard came out and wrote down their license plate number and went back to the guard shack. He triggered the gate release and the ten-foot long chain-link portal swung open. Carlo let the big car sweep up the drive to the administration building and stopped directly in front of the main entrance. He got out and went around to the passenger door and opened it for Joe. After shutting the door Carlo hurried around and moved the car to a parking place and came back to go in with the boss. They left the other two guys to wait in the car until they needed them.

Joe waited calmly and then he and Carlo walked up the steps and into the lobby of the building. Carlo was precisely one step behind and one step to the right. No one was there to meet them so they walked over to the receptionist and announced themselves. She checked her schedule and carefully penciled in the time and visitor's names. Then she smiled and said, "Mr. Malone and his staff will see you in just a moment gentlemen. Would you please wear these visitor badges and have a seat for a moment until someone comes to escort you?"

Carlo laid his badge back onto the girl's desk and quietly told her, "We don't need any badges lady, and we aren't waiting. Which way is the boss' office?" He had leaned over until his face was inches away from the receptionist's face.

Instead of cringing and complying, the girl stared him in the eye and waved her hand back and forth under her nose. "Whee hoo, what did you have for lunch? I'll bet you could kill a fly at three feet with that breath."

Caught completely off guard, Carlo stood there dumbfounded. Joe decided to take control of the rapidly deteriorating situation.

"He had a nice Mexican pizza for lunch, Miss. Would it be too much trouble to have someone lead us to the President's office? I have a very busy schedule this afternoon and it would be a big help if you could expedite this visit."

Making a small face at Carlo, she turned to Joe and smiled sweetly. "Certainly Sir, if you and your friend will put on your badges I will get someone right away.

She turned to use the phone and Joe clipped his badge onto his suit pocket. Reluctantly, Carlo reached over and picked up his badge and put it on. A few minutes later a young man came and led the gangsters through a door and up a flight of stairs. The stairs were quality redwood, buffed to a high luster and capped with brass edges which had small rubber strips to prevent slips. The staircase was in a darkened hall and highlighted by floodlights every three steps. It made for a showy, fanciful entrance. Joe nodded his head, "I like this place," he thought, "It has pizzazz."

The upstairs hallway was carpeted in a dark forest-green colored, plush pile that your feet sunk into as you walked on it. There were people using the hall but the acoustically designed wall panels and the carpeting drank up the sounds so well that there was almost no background noise. The young man led them to a large oak door and opened it up. He stood there until they had entered and then closed the door and left.

Jack and Bob were sitting at the conference room table and both stood to shake hands with Joe and Carlo.

As they had rehearsed, Carlo immediately attempted to take control of the meeting. Looking at the two names on the corporate business cards he had picked up at the front desk, he said, "Mr. Malone, Mr. Wexler, Don Miland has looked over your business and decided that he would like to invest a substantial sum in it. I recommend that you accept this sum and Don Miland as a silent partner. You will find that this action will greatly improve your chances of success," he smiled broadly, "especially in the near future." He then promptly sat down and stared at the company owners.

Jack and Bob looked at each other. Jack indicated that Bob respond with a nod of his head.

Bob cleared his throat and looked at Joe, ignoring Carlo completely. "Mr. Miland?, I doubt if you know our business, and if you did, you would recognize the fact that we have created an R&D company that is very successful in producing new products. We have a five-star rating with anyone who counts and more money in the bank than we can apply to the business right now. I appreciate an offer like yours, but we really are not interested in taking on any partners." Bob then sat down.

Without rising Joe smiled coldly at Bob Wexler. "Let's take the gloves off here, Bob. I can make things easy for this company or I can make things hard. It's your choice."

Bob stared back at the stocky man. Bob Wexler was not a pushover, but then he recognized the threat implied in the last comments and the power the man represented. "Mr. Miland....

Joe interrupted, "Call me Joe."

Bob cleared his throat again. "Joe. I don't want to cause hard feelings, but we are not interested in your offer. If you want to go out of your way to make things tough for TA then

I guess you're going to have to do it that way." Bob sat back and looked at Joe.

Joe scratched his cheek and looked at the two owners. The young one hadn't said a word yet. Keeping his gaze on Jack, Joe thought "That's where the power lies." Addressing Jack directly he said, "Mr. Malone, I think your partner is being stubborn to the point of absurdity, don't you? He hasn't even asked me how much my offer is yet."

Jack stared at Joe. "Joe, would you give us a couple of days to consider your offer? I may be able to convince my partner to listen to you."

Joe saw the concession as a definite hint of weakness. Smiling, he opened his hands in a gesture of welcoming. "Well, Jack, I normally would like to give you guys more time, but this is a dog-eat-dog world and there are other sharks out there." Joe badly mixed his metaphors attempting to indicate the danger of the situation.

Joe's intentions were very mindful of his partner's wishes and he decided to move these guys into line. "I think we really ought to talk turkey right now." He slapped his hand onto the tabletop as emphasis.

The light in Jack's green eyes suddenly turned ice cold. Joe had a premonition that things had gone to pot. Still quietly, but with much greater force he said, "Then Bob gave you our answer. We are not interested in your deal regardless of the amount you want to invest." Jack leaned forward onto the tabletop. "I don't like your pushy and supercilious attitude, so please leave."

Joe wasn't sure what 'supercilious' meant but he was pretty sure he had been insulted by this young whelp and he needed to make him learn a lesson not to insult a man of his power. "Carlo, hurt the man so he speaks with the proper respect to me," he said, pointing at Jack.

Carlo was glad the play acting was over and he could do what he liked to do. He got up and came around the table toward Jack. Joe knew Carlo wasn't going to really hurt him, just slap him around until he learned a little humility. Jack rose from his seat as Carlo came at him. Carlo reached out to grab his shirt front in his big, beefy left hand. He had told Joe before, that this was just so when he was slapping the guy back and forth he didn't fly away.

Joe flinched because, suddenly, Carlo was airborne with nothing but a wall and a carpet as a landing pad. Joe hoped he'd hit the carpet rather than the wall but Carlo's trajectory wasn't right for that maneuver and he managed to do a face plant into the wall before he dropped to the carpet.

Joe knew Carlo, and this wasn't going to stop him. Even though his nose was bloody and the little finger on his left hand was bent in a funny direction, it didn't really slow Carlo down too much. He got to his feet and approached Jack more carefully this time.

Joe hoped that maybe this time he would hurt the guy some.

Carlo waded into Jack swinging a hay maker left that connected with nothing but thin air. Joe saw the young president drop to one knee under Carlo's left cross and deliver a straight punch to Carlo's groin with enough power that the seat of Carlo's pants puffed out even as the wind flew out of his mouth.

Joe groaned in sympathy for Carlo. He watched as Jack then smoothly rose up to his left and kicked to the outside of Carlo's right knee which snapped with an audible pop. Joe watched as Jack finished the ailing hood off with a punch to the left temple.

All of this happened in less than five seconds. Joe had started to rise when Carlo came at Jack the second time. By the time he had stood up, Carlo was a useless bag of clothing on the floor.

Jack looked at Joe with a small grin. To Joe, this was something the canary probably sees on the cat's face just before it is eaten.

Joe backed up and held out his left hand. "Don't do anything you'll regret buddy," he said, continuing to back up. Jack advanced toward him and held out his right arm and pointed at the door. "Get out! I'll have this" he pointed back at Carlo's inert body, "delivered to the front door in a few minutes. Don't plan on coming back again. I'll give you two minutes after he's delivered to get off the property before I call the police."

Joe turned and walked to the door. Pausing he turned back and said, "You've just made the biggest mistake in what's left of your short life, jerk!" He quickly opened the door and went out. He tried to slam the door but the pneumatic hinges prevented anything but a gentle 'snick'. Storming over the soft carpeting and down the elegant staircase, he walked out into the brightly lit lobby. As he passed, he ripped the visitor's badge off and threw it at the young woman manning the receptionist desk.

She reached up and deftly caught the badge as it came towards her and smiled at Joe, "Thank, you sir." she said, "You have a nice day."

Joe was totally ticked off now. He couldn't even embarrass a young girl at this place. Not to mention that karate killing machine they had as a president, he thought as he slammed out the main entrance. Jack had definitely scared him. For which the young man would pay dearly.

Joe knew he had totally blown his assignment to get the Malone kid to his partner. He was more than a little concerned about the reaction he was going to get. Joe felt certain that it would be a bad, bad phone call. He decided to blame it all on Carlo.

Joe walked over to his car and got in the driver's seat. Starting the car with a spare key from the ashtray he burned rubber spinning the car in a circle and pulled it up to the front door. A minute later two big, burly guards came out the front door with an unconscious Carlo by the armpits. They loaded him into the back seat of the Lincoln with the other two thugs. Joe roared out of the driveway and past the guard at the gate, who already had the gate open on the outbound lanes.

Thinking black thoughts of revenge Joe drove back to his mansion with murder foremost on his mind. "That should make Mr. Power Partner happy. I know it will make me happy." He glared at the two men in the back seat holding Carlo. He could also see that they knew better than to ask questions.

CHAPTER SEVENTEEN

Joe pulled into the driveway leaning on the horn of the Lincoln. Several of his men came out to see what the disturbance was all about. Joe stopped the car and got out. "A couple of you guys help the two guys in the back get Carlo out of the back seat and watch what you're doing. He's unconscious and I think his right leg is broke." He stormed into the place and headed for his desk. He yelled over his shoulder as he entered the building, "Get him a doctor, out here. Do it NOW!"

Dropping into his chair he pulled a cigar out of the bottom drawer and snipped the end off. He then got it started and drawing well. Collecting his thoughts while he was fooling with the stogie, Joe picked up the telephone receiver and punched in the code for his partner.

The phone rang and rang. Nobody answered. Joe hung up, puzzled. He thought, "That's the first time that he hasn't been there to answer the phone."

The in-house intercom buzzed and made him jump. "Wow", he thought, "Just thinking about this guy has got me nervous." He punched the button and shouted, "What?"

Joe instantly recognized his partner's voice. The words were chilling. "Joe, you failed me. I told you that I wanted Jack Malone where I could talk to him without interruption. I think you need closer supervision, so, I have taken the liberty of setting up an office in your basement in what used to be your billiards room. I don't want anyone to disturb me unless I ask them to come in here. You can control your men at least that well, can't you? I should say, the few men that aren't in jail for doing really stupid things?"

Joe's mind was reeling as he thought furiously, "How did he get into my house without the boys seeing him? Crap! He's right in my house. How did he know about the shoot-out and the cops?" He knew he had no grounds to demand anything with this guy. So he said, "Hey, okay, now we can work better together and really get things done." At the same time he thought, "Now I might have a chance to take this guy out with no one being the wiser."

Joe recalled that when he had agreed to the partnership he had tried to get a name out of his partner all he got was 'Mr. D'. The guy was sly and a real professional at hiding his identity. So, to smooth over the problems he had been having with Jack Malone, he decided to give Mr. D. the royal treatment. "How about I come down and we visit for a few minutes to set things right?"

Joe thought he detected a touch of graveyard ice in the humor he could sense in his partner's voice. "Sure Joe, come on down, just do it alone."

"Sure thing", said Joe, Thinking that he now would have a chance to meet the guy who had accelerated his empire so well. Joe got up and went down to the finished recreation room at the bottom of the stairs. Going over to the door of his one-time billiards room, he knocked. "Come in", came from behind the door.

Joe opened the door and stepped into the room. The partner kept the lighting really low. It was so dark it was hard to see anything.

Joe made out the dark form of the man sitting in a chair which was backlit by a red light toward one side of the room but couldn't make out any facial features. "Hi, there", said Joe, "why don't you crank up the candle power in here?"

The man's voice came out much lower and more powerful than it did on the telephone. "I happen to like the dark, Joe. Sit down."

This had not been an invitation, it had been an order and it carried such power that Joe didn't even think about debating it with the guy. He just found a chair and sat down. He tried again, "what would you like me to do about this Malone character?"

The raw blast of evil hatred that washed over him made Joe quail in his shoes. His mind reverted to a simple being in total fear and the only sounds he could make were little mewing sounds. The hate and anger seemed to be tangible things and it was if they flew around the room and hammered at him.

In the small part of his mind that was still functioning Joe suddenly realized that his partner wasn't remotely human. He realized he was talking to evil itself, a demon. It occurred to Joe he could now understood the nickname, Mr.

D. No wonder every low-life and criminal gave Joe free rein to do what he wanted.

But none of that mattered right then.

Joe was totally terrified by the shadow that sat across the room from him. The terror was so complete he lost control of his bodily functions and soiled himself.

The demon changed his approach to an oily pitch for Joe's ego. "I'm sorry, Joe. I get really upset when my requests are not met. You understand, don't you?"

The demon gave Joe an out. "I realize that you are doing the best you can with the type of help you can get. I want you to know I appreciate your efforts and want to continue with our partnership as before, but, with a clearer understanding of what I want to achieve. Is that all right with you?"

Joe's terror had subsided considerably when he realized that he wasn't in any immediate danger and in fact, had apparently impressed Satan's henchman with his efforts. "Yeah, well, sure. We can work things out. Exactly what is it you want me to do?"

The dark form, which Joe could now see wasn't proportioned properly, shifted and blurred somewhat and made a short statement. "I am trying to acquire a small box that my Master has been after for many years. The last person who had the box in question was Bill Martin who your over-zealous thugs killed. I have reason to believe that he may have passed the secret of the box's location on to Jack Malone. If you can get him alone, and, in pain, I think I can convince him to give me whatever information he learned from Bill Martin. I will leave it to you to get him in condition to talk to me and that doesn't mean dead. Now, go away."

Joe was only too glad to oblige. He got up hurriedly and left the billiards room and closed the door. The shiver that went down his back told him that he could easily be in more trouble than he ever thought was possible. Maybe he could get on the demon's good side by delivering the Malone character. He thought, "Serves the punk right, too."

Then he hurried upstairs to his bedroom bathroom to clean up and change his clothes before any of his men noticed the mess he had made of himself.

Thinking more like normal he realized that he could make a lot out of his association with the devil. "We'll see, he thought, we'll see."

After cleaning up, Joe went back downstairs. He saw Carlo being attended to by the doctor in his own room. As he went back to his study, one of the guys called out to him to see if it was all right if they went down and played some pool. A shaky feeling went through Joe's body. "You don't even want to think about going down there, ever, you understand? You pass the word to everyone that the pool room is off limits from now on. Anyone who goes down there will be the sorriest loser I've ever seen. Got it?"

Joe made it clear to his men that he was the most macho man they knew and if they questioned that then they didn't really need to exist, did they? He watched as they went to play cards in the party room next to the living room.

Charlie Wu found Linda and he reported what he had heard. He then added, "Since the head thug is making the pool room off limits that means that there is something there that he doesn't want anyone to see. Maybe after a while I'll check it out."

Back in his study after composing himself, Joe called a contact in the local Teamster's Union. "Ray? This is Joe, I need to know if you guys ship stuff for a little outfit in southeast Littleton called Technological Alternatives Inc. You check it out and let me know quick, hear me?"

Then he called his labor union contact but had no more luck there.

He sat and thought for a while. While he was thinking he noticed that the glass was back in the painting and that the wall was repaired like it had never been broken. "That little gook is all right." he thought. He got up and went over and inspected the wall. He couldn't tell where the new stuff started and the old stuff stopped. "Carlo was right about the gook." He shook his head, "Too bad Carlo and Hugo aren't here to see this."

Joe called in one of his house guards and inquired as to Carlo's condition. The guy didn't know because the doctor had taken Carlo to the hospital in Castle Rock. His injuries were too serious to treat without the proper medical equipment. But the guard said that Carlo was talking when he left so he would probably get well soon. "Rats." thought Joe "I'm losing guys right and left over a punk."

There was a knock on the door followed immediately by Wally Parnell, the mob accountant.

They talked for a while and discussed the legal entanglements that could result from Joe's single-minded revenge on this one guy. Joe was aware that Wally thought he was one really sick dude which is why the accountant didn't argue with him on anything.

Joe also noted that Wally carefully advised him while making sure he covered his own back side in the event things went sour. Joe sent Wally to see about getting additional men to help in the hunt.

Joe had thought about sending the stuck-up young snot downstairs to meet Mr. D. until he remembered that his marching orders were not to have anyone else bother the resident evil in the basement.

Joe sat and plotted at his desk until it was getting dark outside. He then called in the four men he had that were still functioning. He outlined what he wanted them to do and how. They left with their assignments and Joe called his attorney

"Hey, Seddler, it's Joe. What's with Johnny and his boys? When do I get them back? I need them right now." He listened as the attorney told him, "Joe, we got trouble this time. I can get the other three guys out by tomorrow morning, but Johnny... well; they're holding him without bail because of two outstanding murder warrants from Chicago. There is no way short of breaking him out of the Justice Center you can get him back in the next month." Joe shook his head. "The little rat didn't cover his tracks well enough. Seddler; just forget him and get me the other guys as quick as you can. Okay?" He got an affirmative and hung up the phone. Getting up he went looking for something to eat. He enjoyed watching the chink girl in her hot outfit make him a sandwich.

At seven o'clock p.m. a large truck ran Bob Wexler's Chrysler convertible off of the road near the TA plant. Bob escaped injury thanks to the air bag in the driver's steering wheel, but the car was a total write-off.

A bomb threat was called into TA and the main plant building was cleared and searched. Since there was only twenty people working on the second shift, not too much production time was lost and no bomb was found.

After the second shift was over, two of the women walking to their car in the TA parking lot were shot at by someone with a rifle. One woman took a round through the upper thigh and lost a great deal of blood before they got her to the Littleton Medical Center. The other woman wasn't hit but was thoroughly scared. She told the shift supervisor that she wasn't coming back to work at night until they could ensure her safety. The guard staring out into the darkness silently agreed with her.

When Jack heard of these crimes he was convinced that Joe was planning to seriously hurt him and his company in revenge for the drubbing he had received at TA that afternoon. He wanted to call Agent Rhodes but knew that he would have left for the day. In fact, he did call him anyway. There was no response from the number given to him for the agent's cell phone.

Understanding that he, and through himself, Laura, would be prime targets for the gangster's anger he decided to take himself and Laura out of the line of fire until things settled down. He explained his reasoning to her and she agreed that they should 'lay low' until the police or the FBI could deal with the madman.

Packing some clothes they put her little Dodge into the garage next to the Range Rover, locked up the house, and set the alarm system. Taking the Cadillac, they drove to the Marriott Hotel in the Denver Tech Center and checked into a suite for the night. They finally got to sleep around midnight, holding each other to keep the imagined terrors in the night, away.

CHAPTER EIGHTEEN

After all the working thugs left the mansion, Charlie Wu carefully checked to see that Joe Miland was thoroughly involved in his activities at his desk and that everyone else was gone. He wanted to be fairly sure that there would be no one to accidentally catch him while he was investigating the pool room. He quietly slid down the stair with every sense at full alert. He thought to himself as he neared the bottom, "Something's not right here. I've got a bad feeling about this." He stopped and analyzed his "bad feeling." It wasn't just nerves. He'd done this kind of thing for years for the Asian government before escaping to America with his wife.

Charlie knew that one of the major reasons they had abandoned their native land was that they had found Jesus in the most unlikely of places, a Manchurian prison. His mind suddenly flew back to that time as he stood in indecision on the steps to the basement of Don Miland's mansion.

------------------------ ****** ------------------------

Charlie had been one of the Asian government's agents and he had improperly fallen in love with another agent. This was frowned upon by the people in charge. But he had always been a wild card, toeing the line only to get to where he wanted to in the Communist Party and in the spy business. He knew when to act correctly and when to break wind at an official function. He recalled that he had pulled strings and gotten himself assigned to an investigation strictly so that he could be near the woman with whom he had fallen in love.

He was also aware that Linda had not known the young agent she was working with very well because they had only met twice before in the normal progress of their careers. She had told him later that she knew he was a great agent and very talented. She hadn't understood why he would want to work with a relatively new agent like her.

Charlie remembered the time flying by as they pursued the enemies of the state across the vast land that is China.

He found out later that she had eventually been attracted to him because of his good looks and professional mannerisms. Charlie hadn't known that she was aware of his interest until she told him that it had become clear to her that he was interested in her in ways that weren't official. She said it dawned on her when she had caught him staring at her like a moonstruck calf one day. Even though he denied it, he knew that she was right.

Charlie quickly realized that they were attracted to each other in many ways. Over the months of the investigation they had become deeply committed to each other. He was careful to not damage her reputation and left the sexual part out of their relationship until after they got married. He remembered thinking "After all, she is the daughter of a prince." If nothing else, Charlie always felt one maintained honor above all things.

As they grew more comfortable with each other's techniques and capabilities they begin to function as a team with almost instantaneous reactions to the other person's lead. Both were good agents with excellent field craft and had been in trained in several martial arts on how to take on more than one opponent at a time. Charlie continued to train with Linda so that together they were highly efficient in combat.

Charlie was a modern Asian man who had grown up as an atheist who had never considered religion or worship of God. This was as required by the ruling party. Linda had limited knowledge of the various religions that they ran into throughout China, but was not a believer in any deity. They kept their morals high because it was the right thing to do. Charlie remembered that all changed on the day they went to the prison in Manchuria to question a suspect involved in their investigation.

They identified themselves at the prison entrance and were admitted. Charlie had the prisoner brought to a small room to question him about a variety of leads they were following. As they were talking to him Charlie noted that he was a very humble and honorable man. There was a loud disturbance outside the door that suddenly burst open into their room in the form of three men brandishing homemade knives.

The agents jumped up from their seats and flowed into action like a well-oiled machine that had already rehearsed this exact event. They quickly disarmed and disabled the three men. To Charlie it was relatively easy. The problem came from the prisoner they had been interviewing. He yelled at the two agents to stop hurting the attackers even though he knew they had come to kill him.

Charlie watched the defeated trio as he and Linda drew back. To Charlie it had been very obvious that the three had meant to kill the man they were talking to and probably eliminate both Linda and him as well. He knew that the men they were investigating were powerful and had a long reach. Someone didn't want their prisoner to talk.

Hearing a moan they watched as the man at the table staggered to his feet and blood fell on the table. One of the attackers had managed to throw a knife and the handle of it was sticking out of the prisoner's chest. But, despite his injuries he drew himself up to his full height and faced the three men. His words startled everyone else in the room.

The man ignored the knife and the bleeding and in High Mandarin stated, "Do not injure them on my behalf." They don't know what they are doing." He looked upward and said, "I am the beloved of Jesus Christ and I know that I am on the upward path." The serenity of his expression made the deadly injury completely unimportant. He smiled wanly and walked past all five stunned people in the room and out the door. They watched as he reached the sunlight flooding through a high window in the hall. He just opened his arms and raised his hands in silent acceptance of his Lord's magnificence.

It looked to Charlie like the life flowed out of him in a rainbow ribbon and up into the sunlight. His body collapsed like it was boneless. Nobody said anything for several seconds. Then a half of dozen guards came rushing down the hall, stepped around the body, and charged into the room.

Awed and shaken by what they had seen, the two agents left the prison and began the long journey back to Beijing. On the train Charlie recalled that afternoon as the two of them went over the events in their minds and discussed what it would be like to have the security and peace that the man had shown. But how could they do that?

Like most couples the woman seems to be the instigator when it comes to the matters of the heart and Linda was no exception. She suggested that they contact one of the underground Christian groups they knew of and see what they could tell them about this.

Slightly over one week later, Charlie held his first Bible in his hands and began to read the sections outlined to him. God's Holy Spirit led his heart, and his mind followed quickly. Three days later both Charlie and Linda gave their lives to the Lord and were baptized into Christ's body in one of the underground groups they were commanded to destroy.

Charlie was acutely aware that this total change of mind and heart would be impossible to hide and within a week they had decided to leave China and seek their path as directed by the Lord. That path had led them to Denver, Colorado in the United States. After providing service to several undercover agencies, they met Sensei Grady and that relationship had led him to these steps.

---------------------- ****** ----------------------

Charlie reached out with his mind and spirit and prayed, "Lord Jesus, I am troubled by this action and the Holy Spirit has brought you to mind. Tell me what to do." A warm feeling of love flooded his spirit but an image of fearful darkness with two red eyes and white fangs sprang to his mind. Charlie immediately reversed his steps and flowed quickly back up the stairs and away from the basement.

CHAPTER NINETEEN

In the hotel room as Laura slept fitfully next to him, Jack searched for peace and rest. They were elusive. He had come to understand that he and his wife were pretty much alone against terrible odds. Regardless of his personal capabilities, his money, his anything, he was powerless to do anything about the danger threatening them. Wishing he had someone to turn to he stared into the darkness and hoped for reason to come up with a solution.

Contemplating a maze with no outlets and no signposts, he fell asleep worrying.

The automatic light controls had turned off the lights at Jack's house at eleven p.m.

Bill Wetzel and Karl Thock sat in a dark pickup truck parked down the street from Jack's house. They waited one full hour to make sure the occupants would be fast asleep. Karl started the powerful engine on the truck and drove slowly down the street showing no lights. He brought the truck to a halt directly in front of Jack's house. Bill got out of the cab carrying three packages. He looked around at the dark, sleeping neighborhood and seeing nobody he dashed up the driveway and threw the first package through a window in the garage door. The only sound was the breaking glass and a strident alarm bell. He ran across the front of the house and threw the second package through a front window. This time there was more noise and a lot more broken glass.

Bill sprinted around the left side of the house to the back and threw the last package through the kitchen window. His whole route had taken less than forty seconds. He ran back around the house and out to the waiting truck. As he climbed in, Karl drove off and then parked the truck down the street.

They watched as the alarm continued to sound for about one minute. Suddenly, three heavy explosions erupted inside the house and every piece of glass on the first floor exploded outward shredding the trees and shrubs. Huge flames leaped up and engulfed the first floor in minutes. Less than five minutes the entire house was a raging inferno. Bill punched

Karl in the shoulder and said, "Bingo!" Karl drove out of the neighborhood and back toward Castle Rock to tell Don Miland.

The first police officer responding to the alarms tripped by the breaking windows slid to a halt outside the house and radioed for fire trucks. He watched until the fire department arrived. They had to fight fires in the houses on either side of Jack's house because the ferocity of the blaze had caught them on fire as well. The officer conferred with the fire captain. Even though he had arrived in the first ten minutes he scanned the primary blaze and realized that there was absolutely nothing they could do to save the structure. The Captain told the fire fighters to concentrate on containing the fire as well as extinguishing it to prevent it from spreading. The Captain felt they were very fortunate that the night was cool with little or no breeze or the damage would have been much higher.

Jack and Laura tossed and turned in fitful sleep three miles away in the hotel.

Joe got the word from his police snitch at three thirty in the morning about the fire and that no bodies had been found in the ashes of the Malone home. Shaking with fear, he realized his men had exceeded their orders again. Dang! They didn't know it, but they were putting his head in the devil's chopping block.

He rolled his stocky body out of bed and looked back at Dixie, sleeping on the other side of the king-sized water bed.

Joe went into the kitchen and poured himself a cup of coffee from the steaming urn sitting on the counter. One of the night guards came in for a cup of coffee and nodded to him and then returned to his patrol of the exterior grounds of the mansion. Splashing water over his face to clear the sleep from his brain, he grabbed a phone. Getting the man he wanted, he said, "Get the word out. Two grand goes to the man that finds where that guy is staying. I want to know before anybody else when you find out."

Thirty minutes later the phone rang. Joe reached over and picked it up. "Yeah, what do you know?" The voice on the other end was a high falsetto belonging to a gay transvestite cross-dresser who trolled the Tech Center area for equally odd partners. "Don Miland? This is Bonnie D. I hear you are offering two thousand dollars for the first person who finds a certain Cadillac?"

Joe figured he could guess where this fag had found his target, but it didn't do to welsh on a reward. Next time nobody would rise to the bait. "Yeah, that's the offer. Although I distinctly said the first "man" that finds the guy, I'll still give you the money for the location. You know if you're lying, you're dying, right?"

It seemed that Bonnie D. had no intention of getting Don Miland mad at him. "Yes Sir, I do know that. Okay, the Caddy is parked in the parking lot of the Tech Center Marriott Hotel. I even went in and checked the register. The clerk was so sweet to help me. Anyway, the man you want is in room 1540. That's on the fifteenth floor."

Joe figured he had found a form of human life even less intelligent than Carlo. "Yeah, I figured that out all by myself. You can pick up the money from Willie the Pimp in the park at Colfax and Broadway tomorrow." He broke the connection and called his present number one hitter.

"Donny, I found the fink. He's holed up in the Marriott Hotel in the Tech Center. The Caddy is in the parking lot and he's in room 1540. I want you and a couple of the boys to go get him and anyone that's with him and bring them to me. Don't kill him! I mean it. There will be hell to pay, literally." Watch out for this guy, he knows all that Karate stuff. He beat Carlo to a pulp in just a couple blows. "Also, get word to Willie that he gives two grand to a fag named Bonnie D. tomorrow at the park." "Got all that? Okay, I want to see that guy here before breakfast. Move it! And don't come back without him."

CHAPTER TWENTY

Donny and his men approached the Cadillac cautiously. The time was four o'clock in the morning and the sky was still black. Donny stood watch as Manny slid under the car and carefully hooked the package to the floor of the driver's side and turned it on. He slid out and nodded to Donny. They headed for the side door to the Hotel.

Jack had jerked awake by an insistent beeping. He thought the alarm in the hotel room had gone off, but the luminous numbers on the clock said four a.m. and that was at least one hour too early for the alarm.

Suddenly, he sat up, got out of bed and stepped to the window. Realizing the beeping was his car alarm, he slightly opened the drapes. He had a good view of the parking lot where he left his car. He watched as someone slid out from below his car and joined a couple of other men. They all headed for the hotel. He considered his options. Obviously, Don Miland had found him and had rigged a bomb to his car. It was equally obviously they knew where he was and were coming up to their room.

He gently shook Laura and said, "Honey, get up. I think we are about to have uninvited company." He dressed quickly and shut off the pager which had responded to the alarm on his car. Laura was out of bed and getting into her clothes quickly and quietly. Jack thought to himself, "I love her and now I've really put her in the dumper." It occurred to him that he was quite willing to fight for what he considered right. But, did he have the right to offer her life up at the same time? How did she feel about facing the gang? No time to wonder now. There were no non-combatants for the minute. He would just have to do whatever he could to protect her.

Jack picked up the phone and dialed 911. The response was immediate. He explained that someone had probably just put a bomb on his car in the parking lot and they were on the way up to his suite, probably to assault him and his wife. He described his car, gave them the room number, and dropped the phone handset on the bed even though the woman on the line insisted that he stay on the line.

He grabbed Laura's hand and they ran to the door. He opened the door cautiously. Peering out into the corridor he could not see anyone. The hotel was still quiet at this hour. They left the room and shut the door which locked automatically. He led her to the right, away from the elevators and opened the door to the stairs. Listening carefully he ascertained that there was no one else in the twenty-story stairwell.

As they quickly sped down the stairs Jack kept listening for any other sounds that would indicate someone else was in the stairwell. To Jack the cold painted walls and the harsh florescent lighting was jarring to the point of being painful after being chased out of the cozy retreat of sleep. It also seemed like an endless spiral of walls and doors with the echo of their running feet bouncing back at them. But, finally they got to the lobby entrance of the stairwell. Breathing fast they rested and gulped in large amounts of air leaning against the wall for a few seconds. Jack then opened the door a crack and scanned the lobby.

It didn't take a trained observer to spot the cover man for this operation. He was standing by the elevators in a suede jacket and tennis shoes. Not your normal dress for a four a.m. jogger. The jacket sagged suspiciously under his left arm. No doubt he was armed.

Unfortunately, Jack could see that the man had a clear view of the stairwell exit. Jack carefully closed the door and they went down one more level to the first level underground parking garage. Stepping out into the garage they headed for the exit.

Rounding the corner they saw a steel gate shut over the exit to the garage. Since he didn't have a car to trip the treadle which opened the gate they looked around for another exit. The only other exit was the door they had just left. Returning to the door Jack found it locked. Searching his pockets he realized that they had left the room too quickly and he had forgotten his room key.

Feeling the panic starting to rise, he stood still and used a Zen technique to quiet his beating pulse and momentarily pictured himself next to a calm placid lake on a beautiful spring evening.

More in control of his autonomic nervous system again, he considered their predicament. Reviewing the options he led Laura back to the area behind the stairwell and out of sight of anyone exiting the door from the stairs.

Laura spoke for the first time since being awakened to a flight from danger. "What will we do if they come down here?"

Jack smiled. "I doubt that they will come down here, but, if they do, we hide. If that doesn't work, then you distract them while I sneak up behind them. How's that sound?"

She said, "It sounds like we'll both get hurt. But, I can't think of anything better. Wait a minute. Wasn't there a phone by the stairs?" Jack mentally reviewed his recollection of that area. "You're right. We can get hold of the police and they can get these guys."

They returned to the stairwell door and found the phone inside the box where Laura had seen it. Hearing noises on the other side of the stairwell door, Jack motioned for Laura to pick up the phone and move as far away from the door as possible. Jack jumped up and grabbed the metal supports jutting out of the concrete ceiling above the door and pulled himself up above the door. He then rotated his body so that he was facing downward and braced himself between the supports and the wall above the door. This was basic exercise for a rock climber.

Laura listened for the dial tone and dialed 911. As she started to speak the door began to open slowly. She stopped speaking and held her breath, her eyes wide with fear.

Manny opened the door to the first level of the parking garage and peered around making sure there was no one in sight. This guy has got to be around here somewhere,. he thought, he can't just disappear into thin air. Just then he caught sight of a movement behind the door. He stepped out quickly and leveled his pistol at the movement. He had time to glimpse a good-looking broad with her hair all mussed up before the lights went out.

Jack had waited until he was sure there wasn't a second man behind the first one before he acted. He lashed out with his left foot to strike the man's head and knock him out. The guy dropped to the floor like a boneless bag of flour.

Jack dropped from his perch to the floor of the garage and grabbed the door before it could close again. Looking back into the stairwell he couldn't see anybody else. One of the loafers had fallen from the man's foot when he was kicked. Jack used the shoe to prop open the door. He then went to the still form on the concrete. Finding a solid pulse he realized that while he was beating the tar out of people he hadn't killed anyone. Again his actions were because he had to, and again, because it was right. But, somehow it still bothered him.

Laura was still talking to the 911 operator as Jack used the man's belt to tie his hands behind him. There was sadness in his eyes when he looked at his wife. He saw the tears in her eyes and realized how frightened she must be right now. He picked up the man's gun and walked over to her and put his arms around her. Later on, he couldn't recall who was comforting who.

Laura was nodding her head. Jack looked at her face. She had an expectant but tentative smile trembling on her lips. It was amazing. She was terribly frightened and yet she still functioned at the necessary level. She covered the mouthpiece of the phone and told him, "The police are here in the hotel. She said that they haven't found either of the other two men yet, but they are coming down here to help us."

Jack nodded and went back to the body on the floor. Carefully wiping his fingerprints off of the metal he placed the gun near the unconscious man's body. He had a flash of remembrance and realized he had thought almost the same thing in the clothing store after shooting the man with a shotgun. "Gad," he thought, "I'm getting into a rut here."

Jack then went back to Laura's side. There was a sudden flash of headlights and then the red and blue flashes of the strobe lights coming from the emergency lights on top of a police car right outside the grill over the exit of the garage. Then the door of the stairwell opened and a policeman with a drawn gun and a portable radio looked into the area around the stairwell. He spoke into the radio and the gate at the exit started to roll up. Two more police stepped into the garage from the stairwell. They also had their guns drawn. When they saw Jack and Laura they lowered their weapons and began to search the rest of the garage.

The Sergeant with the radio stooped down and took a look at the face of the man tied up on the ground and checked the body for vital signs. He put the gangster's gun into an evidence sack. Two police cars drove over to the stairwell and their lights threw everything into sharp relief.

Laura handed the phone to the Sergeant and put her face against Jack's chest and clung onto him. The police checking the rest of the garage came back and held a quick conference. They then left the garage to search the parking lot outside.

The Sergeant introduced himself and asked them to accompany him back to the lobby. After they were seated in the office of the hotel manager, the Sergeant turned on a pocket tape player and had them relate everything that they could remember about the morning from the time they woke up until then. After the second telling he clicked off the recorder and stood up. "Okay folks, I guess that's all for now. I'll want you to come downtown tomorrow to sign the transcripts of this tape and, of course, there will be charges to file against the thug in the garage. He turned to leave the office and Laura asked him, "Sergeant, do they know who the man is?"

The Sergeant looked at the disheveled couple with understanding eyes. "I know the guy Mrs. Malone, "a real dirt bag." The world would be a better place without him in it. Mr. Malone, you did me a real favor taking him down without killing him. He killed a good friend of mine a couple of years ago and we knew it, but couldn't prove it, so he got to walk. This time he's going to go to the slammer for a long time. You see, he is a two-strike felon and having that gun just revoked his last parole." The officer was obviously displeased with the man.

There was a rap at the door. A police officer motioned to the Sergeant who joined him for a few minutes of whispered conversation. The Sergeant came back to Jack and Laura. "Is this your address?" he asked, holding a pad up for them to read the address.

"Yes, why?" asked Laura.

The Sergeant frowned, "I'm afraid I have some more bad news for you. Your house was destroyed by fire this morning. I'm sorry." He looked at them and they looked at each other in dismay. Laura's face clouded up, "All my things, my wedding dress, my car." She slumped in her chair and put her hand over her eyes. Jack turned to the Sergeant. "Did they say what caused the fire?"

The policeman nodded. "Yes sir, there was a report from a couple of kids who had been making out in a car on your street. They reported a pickup truck with two men in it caused an explosion and fire by throwing something into several windows of your house. It was definitely arson." He looked at Laura crying in the chair and Jack's concerned face. "Would you and your wife like to go into protective custody? We can keep you safe from the people that are trying to harm you."

Jack nodded as he held Laura close to him. "Yes, I think that we would like to do that."

The Sergeant also nodded and picked up a phone. While he was talking, one of the plain-clothes officers in the room stepped out for a smoke. Checking to see that no one was watching, he pulled a cell phone out of his pocket and speed-dialed a number. When the phone on the other end was answered he spoke quickly and quietly. "Miland, the guy you want is going into protective custody." He listened for a minute and said, "Yeah, I'll let you know."

"Thanks." Jack said as he shook the officer's hand and helped Laura to her feet. He left her in the lobby with two officers while he went upstairs with another officer and got their things out of the compromised suite. The door was broken inward off the hinges, but nothing else had been bothered. Apparently, they were the only items of interest for the Don's men.

CHAPTER TWENTY-ONE

Jack watched from a distance as the bomb squad placed the device they had removed from his car onto the wide bumper of the bomb disposal trailer. Upon examination the bomb turned out not to be a bomb but an electronic tracking unit.

The Sergeant told Jack that the Cadillac had a clean bill of health and said he would have it taken to a impound area later that day.

Jack helped Laura get into an unmarked car with their luggage and silently rode until they reached their new destination. Getting out of the police car at a small, three-bedroom ranch-style home in suburban Littleton, he held her hand as they walked in a daze to the front door and went inside.

Jack thought, "I do think that things are as bad as they can get." A few minutes after they had unpacked and settled down in the company of two young policemen, the phone rang. One of the officers answered it and talked for several minutes. Hanging up the phone he turned to the young couple. "That was the captain. There is the chance that this site has been compromised. You and your wife are to be moved to a different location."

Jack repacked their things and eventually he and Laura were shuffled into another car and went for another drive. He was glad that the police were involved and could protect them from the criminals. Instead of being driven to a new location they were taken back to their car in the parking lot of the Marriott hotel in the Tech Center. The officer told them that he had orders to let them drive to the next safe house. He gave Jack an address to where they would be taken care of. Jack wasn't sure that he liked the sound of that comment, but he didn't seem to have any choice.

As he drove north into town, Jack attempted to figure out why the gang had declared an all-out war on his family and his company. Probably to set that "example" that Jim had alluded to in their talks.

Jack was now sure that revenge was behind the attacks. He had been rough on Joe Miland when he got pushy. "Hah," thought Jack bitterly. "They probably don't know that it was me that messed up their stooges at the clothing store yet. Wait until they add up two and two."

He also realized that the normal, safe, quiet way of life was gone from his life for the time being. But, it didn't have to be that way for Laura. Jack determined to get her out of this mess and face it himself. She didn't have to go through all this. He looked over at Laura, who was staring out of the window at the downtown Denver area as they passed it traveling north on Interstate 25, lost in her thoughts or, most likely, replaying this morning's madness in her mind.

Jack switched lanes to pass a slow moving truck and said, "Honey? Are you all right?"

Laura seemed paler than normal but she turned to Jack and nodded her head. "I'm still trying to comprehend what has happened to our lives in the last twenty-four hours. We've lost our home and everything in it. We've been attacked by men with guns. A device, that was meant to track us, was put on our car." She stopped and slowly shook her head. "I know that what you did at the store and at the plant were the right things to do, but, is the price worth it? I mean, we have only avoided being killed a couple of times since midnight by the narrowest of margins. This Don Miland guy won't quit, will he? Can't the police or the FBI or somebody stop him from trying to destroy us?"

Jack put his arm around her and pulled her close to him. "Honey, I really don't know what can be done. But, I will do everything I can to find out."

Arriving at the address he had been given he found only an empty lot with other empty lots on either side. Checking to make sure he had read the address correctly, he found that he had. There just wasn't any house there.

Laura shook her head, "Why would the police give us a wrong address?" Jack thought for a minute. It seemed to him that things had gone terribly off track and they had been abandoned by the police. He smiled at Laura, "I don't know, but we're going to try to find out as soon as I make us harder for Don Miland to find."

She cocked her head to the right and raised an eyebrow. "And how are you going to do that, Houdini?"

He smiled, "Watch this." Traveling in the middle lane of I-25 southbound, he waited until the last second and suddenly switched lanes and exited the freeway without warning. Amid blaring horns he then took the Sixth Avenue East exit ramp as he watched for any other car that made the sudden lane changes. There didn't seem to be anybody following them. He steered the Cadillac east several blocks toward downtown.

Finding what he was looking for, Jack pulled into a large parking garage building that had a sign indicating long-term parking. Pulling the ticket from the automated ticket dispenser he drove into the down ramp entrance and descended four levels. At this level there were few cars, most of those had dust covering them indicating that their owners had left them there for many months. The place was dark and gloomy with only the occasional bare light bulb to light the deep darkness at this level. Jack found an inconspicuous corner and pulled the Cadillac into a stall between two SUVs.

They got out of the car and Jack took their two bags out of the trunk. He also took out the car tarp and covered the car. Securing the cover with a cable that ran underneath the car, he activated the cover alarm. Then he used his radio control button to set the Cadillac's alarm as a backup. He then picked up some of the accumulated dust from the corner of the garage and sprinkled it liberally over the tarp. Shaking it slightly he made it look like the Cadillac had been down there for an extended time, just like the other cars on that level. The fan-driven ventilation was stirring the dust on the floor which was quickly eliminating their tire tracks.

After walking across the cold garage level to the elevator he stopped and put on his sunglasses. Taking his cue Laura repeated the action with her own glasses.

When they reached the ground level, Jack spoke quietly to her and told her to stay out of the line of view of the man in the office. He then went to the office and made arrangements for the storage. She watched as he talked with the attendant and then paid the man in cash. The attendant used his phone and turned back to his book. Jack left the office and casually walked by the entrance where Laura stood waiting. She turned and walked to the other entrance away from the office hoping the man wasn't watching the camera view she saw high in the corner. She joined Jack as he turned the corner away from the office.

They waited outside in the early morning sun a block away from the garage for only about ten minutes when a taxi pulled up to the curb. They took the cab downtown getting out at a nondescript office building. After the cab had left them, they walked one block further to an auto rental agency which had a large sign announcing Hertz Rent-a-Cars. Again, Jack made the arrangements while she waited a distance away. Fifteen minutes later they left in a black, four door Cadillac. They had become far more anonymous and therefore safer in Jack's mind.

Jack was fairly sure that if they went to the TA offices, the wreckage of his home, or anywhere he normally went, this whole effort could be wasted because they could be spotted, and the attacks would begin again, even worse than before. So they went downtown to the Hyatt Regency and took a suite using the company name and credit card rather than his own.

Once they were in the suite and had ordered brunch from room service Jack placed a call to Agent Rhodes of the FBI. The man was not in his office and the cell phone number got no better results. Jack called Bob Wexler and found him at home recuperating from the auto accident of the night before. Jack brought him up to date and asked him to arrange for one of their staff to pick up some items from the plant and bring them to Bob's home. Bob would bring them to the hotel later that afternoon.

Jack thought about the look on Bill Martin's face again. Something about that look of peace and serenity called to Jack. "I think we should go talk to the people at the church where Bill Martin was an elder." He pulled his key ring out of his pocket and stared with regret at the key he had gotten from the dead man.

Laura didn't want to expose herself anymore than she had to. "I have a really bad headache and I don't want to go out where that horrible man might find us. Is it all right if I stay here?"

Jack was pretty sure that no one would find either one of them this time and he knew she needed some time to rest and pull things together. "I think you will be fine as long as you don't call anybody or go out, okay?" She agreed and went to take a shower and go to bed. Jack got the rental and headed out to southeast Denver.

CHAPTER TWENTY-TWO

Jack parked his car in the church parking lot. He felt somewhat nervous going into a setting where religion was the main topic. But, he kept his composure by remembering it was their choice how they wanted to spend their lives, praying to an invisible and un-provable deity. Then, he remembered the look on Bill Martin's face and his last words, which he said with a smile while he was dying, "Yes, Lord, here I am", as if he was responding to an unheard welcome. That a dying man would do that with his last breath most certainly didn't seem like nonsense at the time.

As Jack reached the front doors, he hadn't even given a second glance to the beautiful panorama spread out beyond the church buildings. The whole southern expanse of Denver and the foothills were framed by the Rocky Mountains. The evening sky was still light enough that the mountains looked black and the millions of lights of the city looked so peaceful. Jack though wryly, "For some people maybe."

Stepping inside he saw a sign pointing the way to the office. Opening the office door he found an elderly man talking to a middle-aged woman sitting at a computer terminal.

The man smiled and said, "May I help you with something?" Jack introduced himself and mentioned his participation at the time of Bill Martin's death.

The man introduced himself as Alan Throman, the minister of the church. He was a spry sixty-some year old man well dressed in a neat gray suit. There was intelligence in his eyes and he radiated a calm, peaceful nature that seemed perfectly suited to him. He shook his head and asked Jack. "It was very sad, the way Bill died. You say you were there when he was attacked?"

"Yes." replied Jack, "He only lasted a minute or two by the time I could attend to him."

Alan Throman tipped his head back and studied Jack's face. Jack recognized that the man wasn't staring at him but looking somewhere else for information. "You have some questions you need answers to, don't you?" Jack started, not realizing that he was that easy to read. "Yes, yes I do."

Minster Throman invited Jack into his office and had Jack sit in a comfortable overstuffed chair across the desk from him.

Feeling largely out of place Jack explained, "I am not actively involved in any religion so please forgive me if I don't understand everything. Actually, I normally don't have much interest in religion. But, I am interested in finding out what made Mr. Martin act like he did and say what he said." Jack still felt compelled not to mention the key or the burden placed on him by the dead man.

Jack recounted for the minister the events, words, and general impressions he remembered from that morning several weeks ago. When he finished, Alan Throman nodded his head several times. He thought for several minutes before he began.

The pastor looked directly at Jack. "Relax, Mister Malone. A large part of the world doesn't take an active part or have any belief in an organized religion. We see people who don't believe in God seeking truth everywhere. It is not uncommon for non-believers to be confused or misunderstand deeply religious events."

Sitting back, the Minister made an expansive gesture with his hands. Then continued to try and explain Bill's passing. "To a non-believer it might seem like a fairy-tale at best, or maybe like a fanatic activity at worst. To make you really understand Bill's attitude and last comments, it will be necessary, for the sake of this discussion, that you consider, hypothetically of course, that there is a living God who really exists. Who created everything, and is involved in the lives of everyone on the planet. Can you do that?"

Jack nodded his head. He could go along with this so far.

Seeing Jack's agreement the Minister continued, "If you are really interested in what happened, I need to give you a short version of history of the world according to God's Inspired Word, the Bible."

Seeing Jack's look of concern, the minister added with a laugh, "I'm not trying to convert you to Christianity. God seems to have that task already well in hand. I just need to explain our beliefs in our terms and they won't mean anything to you unless you have an open mind and accept that Bill believed these things also."

Jack saw the logic to that and agreed, for the sake of this discussion, to postulate a living God that created the entire universe, the Earth, and everything on it, including man. He was willing, momentarily, to see an all-knowing God that was present in each person's life all the time. The minister then proceeded to explain in short bits with big leaps in time, Genesis, the Old Testament, and the law according to Moses as described in the Bible.

Alan then described the New Testament, Christ's role as the Savior of all mankind, His tenure on Earth, His crucifixion, His death, and His resurrection. Ensuring that Jack understood so far, he explained how Christians believe in the unseen living God, the concept of the Trinity, the authenticity of the Bible and how God works in their lives because they have repented of their sins and truly believe in Jesus Christ as His Son. Central to this explanation was the fact that Christians know that Jesus, through God's Holy Spirit, is with them always. Alan then described the second coming of Christ and the end of the world. Needless to say these concepts were sketched in very brief descriptions for the sake of time. Jack was a quick study and had actually heard a previous version of this when he was a child.

When the Minister asked Jack if he was clear on the basis for Christianity, it caused Jack to ask a natural question. "How can Jesus be with each and every one of millions if not billions of people all the time?" The minister looked at Jack to see if he was really asking the question out of curiosity or actually seeking an answer. The look on Jack's face made him guess the latter. So, he answered by pointing out their original hypothesis, agreeing that God had created the Universe. The Creator of the Universe could not be considered bound by human constraints or even understood by human minds. The Bible states that Christ will be with each of us always. Not humanly possible, true, but for God, a small thing perhaps.

Continuing, he said, "There are only two things Christians have to do in this world to acquire the rights to heaven and fellowship for their immortal spirit with God after their death. First, they need to realize that God exists. This is normally done through learning or in many cases, when life overloads the person's ability to handle it. In their extremity and in desperation they reach out to Jesus for help. When He helps them, they begin to understand that He is real and that He loves them. They realize that the only true path to God is through Jesus Christ. They see how sinful their lives have been and they want to try and emulate the perfection Jesus displayed while He was on this earth."

"Then, secondly, when they are ready, which usually takes a period of time while the person prays and becomes familiar with their relationship with the Lord, they want to join Him and walk with Him. When they surrender their lives to the Lord, their sins are forgiven and God's Holy Spirit comes to dwell within them. The peace and contentment experienced at this time defies explanation to anyone other than the soul that was just eternally saved from death."

Minister Throman peered at Jack to see if he had glazed over. He found an active intelligence looking back at him. So he continued.

"At this point they normally seek a baptism in which they repent their sins and publicly admit they believe, in their hearts, that Jesus is the Son of God. The baptism symbolizes their death to this world and their birth into the body of Christ Jesus. The sins of their past are literally washed away and they begin life as a Christian. This is where you get the 'born-again' label." The only other thing a Christian has to do in this world is to glorify God in their lives and love others as themselves."

Jack asked the minister a question about the Bible that had bothered him for years. "I understand that many of the things in the Bible are contradictory and that you can support any view you want if you read the right passages. Is this true?"

Alan reached into a desk drawer and drew out a new Bible. He handed it to Jack who riffled the pages not sure what to look for. The minister smiled, "Go ahead and keep that for yourself. You study it and see if you can find anything that is contradictory. But, read it as a whole, don't pick a statement here and a word there and use it to support an argument that has no merit. Over the last two thousand years many great minds have searched the Bible to do just what you are suggesting. In fact some of the strongest Christians came from the ranks of those seekers of truth."

There was a knock on the door and the lady from the office opened the door and stuck her head in. "Alan, they are about to start."

The minister looked at his watch, "Okay, tell them I'll be out in four minutes."

She nodded and left, shutting the door. Alan Throman turned back to Jack and continued, "Bill Martin was a true believer in Jesus Christ. It wasn't a theory to him. It was true living facts, everything I've told you, he knew that they happened and were more real than this life to him. He wasn't hoping his faith was real, he knew, he absolutely knew that God is here and working hand in glove with mankind. He had a personal relationship with Jesus"

"Where or how he got his personal assurance, I don't know. But," and here the minister peered intently at Jack to emphasize his words, "When Bill Martin died, he was in the presence of the living God. He could also see the wonderful future he was entering into, right then."

The minister rose and when Jack stood, he shook Jack's hand. Smiling he said, "We all try to reach the place Bill was at in his faith. I liked to think I was well along in my walk with God, then Bill came to me one day and I could see Christ in his eyes. He was so full of joy, happiness, and peace it really humbled me. You see, God has ways of getting your attention when he wants it." Cocking his head to one side he finished up with, "Somehow I think you are going to need Christ in the near future."

As they left the office, Jack declined an offer to attend the service which was just starting. The minister said goodbye and went into the auditorium where sixty or seventy people had gathered. Jack lingered somewhat out of sight and listened to the first remarks and the opening song which was "Amazing Grace."

As he drove away from the church in the early evening twilight, he wondered about what he had heard and what it meant for him. He knew it had affected him somewhere deep inside because he had done something he normally didn't do. He had started crying as he listened to the words of the song. Something inside of him had agreed with the lyrics of the song written a century before. Jack shook his head and thought "I wish I knew for sure what to believe." He stared at the Bible on the seat next to him and wondered. What he was thinking would take some serious study. "Oh well," he thought, "I coincidently seem to have some time available."

CHAPTER TWENTY-THREE

The next day, Jack left the hotel room and went to a pay phone several blocks away. He called the police while Laura took a long hot shower. As soon as he identified himself and asked about the case, the officer that answered put him on hold. Jack took that for two minutes and then hung up and decided to get some more change from the store down the street. When he came out of the store he saw a police car driving fast, veer into the lane on his side of the street and another police car coming the opposite direction slide to a halt next to the phone booth he had been using. Both officers were out of their cars with their handguns drawn and were looking at the people around the phone booth. Jack shrank back into the doorway of the store and then exited on the other side of the store. He made his way back to the hotel and told Laura what had happened.

He called the FBI again from their room and this time the agent was in his office. Jack felt like a drowning man who saw a lifeline suddenly appear. "Agent Rhodes am I glad to talk to you." Jack recounted the events since Joe Miland had appeared at his office up till that moment, except that he left out his church meeting and the latest confusing melee at the phone booth.

The agent cleared his throat. "Well, Mr. Malone, it seems like you called it correctly as to who your visitors would be. It also appears that you certainly got Don Miland's attention. I have a summary here of the..."he paused for several seconds. "Will you excuse me for a minute?" He put Jack on hold.

Laura came out of the bathroom in her robe and noticed the look of concern on Jack's face. "What's wrong now?" She asked, her face mirroring the concern his showed.

"I don't know. I seem to be getting put off by everyone in authority no matter who I talk to."

The phone clicked and Agent Rhodes came back on the line. "Mr. Malone? Sorry I was interrupted there. I have another case, a major one, which I have been working on for the last four months. I'm afraid that I won't have a lot of time in the near future, so we'd better get together and work this out right away. Where are you staying?" Jack gave him the name of the hotel and the room number. Agent Rhodes promised to get there as soon as he could.

Jack sat there and thought for several minutes. Everything whirled around in his head. He had lost everything he owned, there was nowhere to turn and no one would help them. He knew nobody could save his wife from these animals if he got killed. Feeling very much alone he decided he had to do something, anything to stop worrying. So he turned on the television with the sound low while he waited for the FBI agent.

Laura came over and sat on the floor by his feet and rested her head on his knee. "When will we meet with the FBI?"

Jack said, "Soon, the agent is on his way here right now. You know, it seems like we are on our own, like two goldfish swimming in the sea with sharks hunting for us. The police are... "

Jack broke off as a picture of his face appeared on the television. He quickly ran the volume level up so that they could hear the newscaster.

The newscast continued ."... is wanted in connection with the deaths of two Denver policemen at a safe-house where the couple were being held in connection to another case. According to our sources at police headquarters, the Malone's apparently killed both of the officers while they were standing guard in the living room of the safe house. Jack Edward Malone, pictured here, is a martial arts instructor and is capable of doing a great deal of damage with his bare hands. It is suspected that he attacked Officers Van Carland and Morrison, shown here, while they were assigned as protection for the couple." Pictures of the two policemen that had been in the house for the few minutes Jack and Laura had been there flashed on the screen.

Jack felt like he had just had an ice bath. He thought, "This is totally unreal."

The newscast continued. "The police are searching the city and watching the airports, train station, and bus depots for the suspected couple. Roadblocks have been put up on all the major highways leading from Denver, especially the Interstate Highways, I-25 and I-70. If you are planning to use these highways today or tonight, leave plenty of extra time because there are already long lines at the roadblocks. The police expect to have the couple in custody soon. But if you see this man or woman..." Their faces returned to the screen. Publicity photos shot at a charity event earlier that year. ."..Notify the Denver Police, the FBI, or the CBI, immediately at the numbers shown on your screen. Do not attempt to apprehend these people yourself. They are considered armed and very dangerous." Jack's heart sank as he turned off the television.

Frowning, he thought for several seconds. A really nasty likelihood hit him between the eyes. He turned to his wife, "Laura, get..." he stopped talking as he saw her. She looked like she was in shock. Her color was very pale, her eyes were large, and she was breathing rapidly. Jack knew she needed time and tenderness, but he couldn't give her either one right now. He put his hands on her shoulders and looked her in the face. "We will have time to discuss this and try to figure it out later, honey. But, right now we either have to give ourselves up to the FBI for the murder of those two policemen or run and hide until we can prove our innocence."

Laura looked at him for a few seconds and then jumped up and grabbed her clothes. Dressing quickly, she grabbed what she could carry, including her handbag, and was ready when Jack met her at the door to the suite. Some of the color had returned to her face and she looked really determined, almost fanatical, and definitely teed off.

Not having time to psychoanalyze the situation Jack opened the door and peered out. After realizing he had just done exactly the same thing earlier that morning at the Tech Center hotel, he thought to himself, "I'm really getting into too many ruts."

Seeing no one, they repeated their flight down the stairwell and got to their rented car. Driving out of the hotel parking area Jack pulled to a stop at the light a half a block away. In his mirror he saw an unmarked police car pull across the exit to the hotel lot. The light changed and he carefully drove away and out into Aurora to another hotel.

Laura opened her bag while they drove. Jack was heartened to find that she was still thinking on all cylinders. She had grabbed a dark red wig full of ringlets. She combed her hair down tightly and put the wig on. It completely changed her looks. Changing clothes in the car she put on her gardening jeans and a loose shirt. Donning dark glasses and removing her lipstick made her almost plain. Jack waited in the car while she checked into the Sheraton Hotel under an assumed name and paid cash for their room. They sat down in the living room and discussed the trumped up charges and the murders of the two young cops.

Jack said, "It seems that Don Miland does have contacts on the police force, and now he has set us up beautifully. The police are probably searching for us with a shoot on sight directive. That way he could keep us from giving our side of the story."

Jack realized that any contact with anyone they were normally associated with would result in immediate arrest or assault by the police. Perhaps if they dropped out of sight for several days the intensive search and pent-up anger would dissipate. Jack remembered that this procedure had worked after the murder at the men's store. To Jack, that event seemed like a year ago, now.

Laura looked at her watch. "Your dad and his brother won't be arriving until Monday morning. That's five days from now. What will we do until they get here?" Jack thought about it and told her, "We stay here and don't make waves until we can get together with them, Jim, and Bob."

Jack used his Palm Pilot PDA and sent Bob Wexler an anonymous E-mail. He was sure that unless the National Security Agency was involved in their case the authorities would not be able to trace the E-mail since it was sent via the wireless connection. He told Bob to arrange to bring his dad and uncle to the Sheraton Hotel by a limousine service on Monday. He then told Bob to call the Dojo and arrange for Jim Grady to also meet them at noon.

Both Jack and Laura adapted subtle disguises. Laura stayed with her suburban housewife look and Jack took on the look of a computer nerd. The brown horn rimmed glasses and the baseball cap changed his looks sufficiently to throw off casual observers. Then they drove to a shopping center and split up. Meeting back at the car they had acquired sufficient supplies to last them a week if necessary. Laura wasn't actually looking forward to cooking in the tiny kitchen, but they had to limit their exposure in public. Jack used the time to exercise until he dropped, study the Bible and make notes. He wondered if the police or Don Miland could find them where they were hiding. He also wondered why nothing was going their way.

Four days later Jack was still wondering the same thing. The time of inactivity had been especially hard on him. He was used to being very active. He was also frustrated and had become somewhat overwhelmed by the feeling that the entire world had turned against him and Laura.

Jack watched as the television had carried a second story about the police seeking them for investigation into the deaths of the two police officers and possibly some civilians, too. It became even more obvious that Don Miland had incriminated them both in some kind of bizarre scheme to eliminate them. Jack had heard Jim Grady speak several times about how the police hunt cop-killers, no warning and no mercy. Miland had really known how to hurt them.

At that moment in his mansion, Joe Miland was sweating bullets because the police thing had gotten totally out of hand. He absolutely had to get Jack Malone alive and now every cop in town was looking for him to whack him. Joe knew that this would result in unimaginable horror for him and that was one thing he was determined to prevent.

Back at their hotel room, Jack Malone had eventually come to the end of his ability to handle the situation. He had gone over and over and then reconsidered every possible angle, and even every remote possibility, even the obviously unworkable, or dumb ideas. Never in his life had he been so ineffectual and stymied. His intellect, his abilities, his positive outlook, they were all worse than useless. No matter what he tried he was defeated before he started. This was the first time in his adult life he didn't have any control of his future or his immediate circumstances. It was an extremely uncomfortable and suddenly even fearful situation.

He had run out of options and knew that Laura didn't have anything to offer at this point. He didn't fault her for that because that wasn't his nature to blame others for his problems. He had caused the war with Don Miland. Jack knew their first support wouldn't be there for twenty-four more hours. He also knew they couldn't leave the country because they couldn't use their passports even if they had them. Plus, they didn't have the connections to have false ones fabricated by the underworld.

Jack was fairly sure that the full force of the FBI, the CBI, and the police were hunting them, the killers were hunting them and there was no where left to run. Their house and everything they owned had been blown up, every move they made seemed to be countered and bested. The sadistic killers seemed to be able to find them wherever they went and wouldn't let up until both he and his dear wife were dead. Jack felt the clutching of his gut which was fear and he couldn't deny it.

Laura had become more of a nervous wreck each day and for the first time in his life Jack didn't have a way to ease her concern. If he tried anything, they'd probably be killed. If he didn't do something soon, they would be killed anyway. It was a no win situation.

Jim Grady and all of their friends, and their businesses were being watched by the police, the killers, or both, and there was nothing he could do about any of it. They were quickly running out of funds and the police would jump on their credit card purchases if he used any of his or her personal cards. He figured they were probably onto the corporate cards by now as well.

For the first time in his life Jack found he really, really needed help. But who could he turn to? The police were probably living with his dad just waiting for Jack to call.

As he sat there mentally lost, he remembered some of the things he had read in the Bible and how Christ had said "I will never leave you, I will never forsake you." The Bible said that Christ is there for Christians when they need help.

Looking up at the ceiling Jack wondered how Bill Martin would have prayed to Jesus Christ and how he would have been comforted in his time of need. Jack thought, "A lot of good that did him when his killers jumped him." But then Alan Throman was clear about the fact that Christians should expect ridicule, hatred, even death because of their belief in Jesus. His mind visually replayed what he had read about the crucifixion of Christ. The concept of a truly innocent man being cruelly beat, whipped, spit on, and nailed to the cross so that he could remove the sins of mankind. The thought brought unbidden tears to Jack's eyes. Laura looked at him and her eyes were full of tears, too.

She came over and hugged him. "We'll get out of this somehow, won't we Jack?" She then buried her face on his shoulder and sobbed. Her total dependence on him was the last straw. It served to underscore how incapable he was to eliminate her hurt and fear. In his humiliation he could feel how much she was suffering and he thought, "Oh, God, if you are there . . . have pity on my wife. I love her so much and I can't do anything to help her. Please, please, save her." Finally humbled, Jack unselfishly turned to God to save the one he loved rather than himself.

As he sat there ashamed and numb with defeat, a brilliantly clear thought came to him. He sat up and untangled his wife's arms from around his neck. He felt galvanized and full of purpose all at once. He spoke softly to Laura, "Honey, go fix up your face, I've got an idea." She brightened up somewhat and obediently went into the bathroom to return several minutes later looking much better.

Jack drove the rental through the early Sunday evening traffic until he reached his destination. Although she was surprised, Laura didn't object when he led her into the church building. Jack remembered back in the hotel room how the sign in front of the church had been suddenly pictured in his mind. The service times were clear and there would be one at seven o'clock this evening. It was only six-fifty when they got there and the service hadn't started yet.

The lobby was full of people, happy people and bunches of kids, all of them completely oblivious to the fear and danger the two of them were in at the moment. Spying Alan Throman, Jack steered Laura over to him and introduced them. The minister greeted Laura warmly and asked Jack to take her back to his study until after the service. Jack declined and asked if they could come in and watch the service in the auditorium.

Alan thought for a few seconds and then agreed but asked Jack to wait in the lobby until the second song began. Noting Jack's confusion, he added, "We don't really want to have everybody trying to greet you as a guest right now, do we? You are a couple of pretty hot items on the news, right now and I don't think those disguises will stand a close look." He smiled at Laura, patted her on the hand and added, "Although I must admit your picture doesn't do you justice."

Jack and Laura slid into the back row of the auditorium after the second song. The service was short, maybe 45 minutes including the first part which was praise and worship. Classical and modern music accompanied the singing and it all had a refreshing quality. They read the words to the songs as they were scrolled up a wall and sang along with the others. Laura had a really good singing voice. Jack wasn't too sure if he added or took away from the songs, but he stuck it out and gave it his best.

The sermon was short and to the point, about forgiving others so that God would forgive you. Jack wondered if he would ever be able to forgive Don Miland and the men who were attempting to kill them. During the prayers Jack had concentrated on trying to visualize the words and their meanings.

After the service, most of the people filed out of the auditorium while some stood around and talked to each other. Laura reached over and gave Jack's hand a squeeze. Smiling she said, "Thanks for bringing me here, I feel better than I have for a long time."

Alan Throman came up to them and escorted them to his study. Closing the door, he sat down behind his desk. Smiling at them both he said, "You took quite a chance coming here tonight. Were you aware that you made the national news on television at five o'clock?"

"No, I wasn't" said Jack, "but it wouldn't have mattered, we are out of options at this point. I'm not sure why I came here tonight and brought Laura. It was kind of a spur of the moment thing."

The minister peered over his glasses at Jack, "Your idea?"

Jack thought for a second, "I'm not sure it was. But then, you are also taking a risk you know, something about aiding and abetting known fugitives."

The minister smiled, "Aiding and abetting are sometimes necessary talents for Christians. You remember that Jesus was branded a criminal also? When I heard the news, I was with the elders of this church. I told them about how you tried to save Bill Martin when he was attacked and killed."

The elderly minister looked from Jack to Laura and back again. "We prayed for you both and prayed that God would grant us the ability to help you. The consensus here was that you two are not guilty of the charges and that Satan has placed an assignment on you both. Satan seems to want you very badly."

The minister got up and walked around the desk and sat down between the two of them. "Satan is a liar and a cheat, but, he will win against you if you don't have the Lord's help. Christ wants to help, but you need to believe in Him and ask Him for that help. The Lord has put it on my heart to help you as much as possible. I'm fairly sure that you are just beginning to see the answers to your problems. What you need to do is decide to resolve your faith."

Jack was only sure that he was no longer sure of anything.

The minister asked them both, "Are things so rough that you feel that you've hung on as long as you can and now you're running out of rope? Do you feel that you have nowhere to turn for help? Is everyone in the world against you? Do circumstances conspire to trap you and prevent you from winning through?"

Laura nodded. The minister looked at Jack and said, "All right, here is a chance for you to see if what I'm telling you about God's concern for you is real. At the same time you can ask him to handle your burdens. He will, you know." The minister's straight forward, honest statements gave credence to his faith and wasn't a 'hard sell'. This meant a lot to them. "Jack, remember when we hypothetically proposed a living God so you could understand Christian Belief?" Jack nodded. "Good, now I would like the three of us to pray and I want you both to give your cares and worries to the Lord."

The minister smiled an understanding smile. "You can't handle them, but He can. You need to admit, both to yourselves and to God that you can't handle what life is doing to you. Jesus stands knocking at the door, open the door and let him come into your life. His yoke is easy and his burden is light. He created the universe and each of you as well. I know He wants to help you. Give your worries and cares to God. He'll gladly take them from you because he loves you. He really wants to help."

The minister continued, "Jack, you said that you have been searching the Bible. Then you know that all of us are born into a life of sin. All you have to do, in your heart, is to admit that you have sinned and ask him for forgiveness for your sins. He will forgive you and gladly welcome you. Tell Him you are in over your head and you need Him to handle it."

The tears came unbidden to Jack's eyes. There was an ache in his heart and when he glanced at Laura he could see that she was feeling the same things.

Not at all sure that God would forgive him or shoulder his burdens, Jack still agreed and so did Laura. Feeling a thrill and scared at the same time Jack fidgeted while Laura blew her nose and they prepared to start the prayer. The minister asked them to repeat the prayer of salvation after him. Jack reached into his pants pocket and withdrew the key ring with the key Bill Martin had given him on it. He thought of it as a security blanket from Bill Martin. He clutched the key ring in his left hand.

As they bowed their heads Jack realized the minister was right on about one thing. There was nothing he could do to solve the problems. At the rate the attacks on them were increasing it was a good chance that he and his wife wouldn't make it through the next day. The ache in his heart drew him on with a spark of hope.

The minister began the prayer, "Oh most wonderful and magnificent Father, we praise Your name and stand in awe of the power and majesty of Your kingdom. Jesus, we come before You with two lost souls who are seeking You and your eternal love."

Alan Throman squeezed their hands. "Jesus, I am a sinner and live in a fallen world." Jack and Laura repeated the words after him. "I believe that you came to Earth to save me Lord. I believe that you were crucified, died and on the third day you were raised up, back to life. Jesus, I want you to come into my life and be my Lord, my King, and my very best friend. I give everything I have including my life to you Lord. Cover me in your powerful blood Jesus and guide my life from now on. I pray this in your name Lord Jesus."

The minister squeezed their hands again and continued. "Lord God, we are asking your help for Jack and Laura Malone. Father, this world has burdened them beyond their ability to deal with the injustice and viciousness the evil one has directed towards them. They come seeking a life with you desperately needing your protection. Father, without you they are powerless to stop the powers and principalities of darkness arrayed against them. Help them Father, and let them see Your Hand in their rescue."

Focusing his mind on a picture of Jesus' face he remembered from grade school, Jack earnestly prayed for help. He felt something deep inside of him swelling up and he felt choked up. Tears again flowed from his eyes and he found himself yearning so hard it was like the worst heartache he could ever have.

Listening to the words of the minister Jack found himself crying out in his mind, "Forgive me God, I'm such a prideful idiot for thinking I was in charge." Jack remembered reading in the Bible "*Pride goes before destruction, a haughty spirit before a fall*." And he realized that his pride was an affront to Almighty God,

All at once a wave of peace and warmth flowed throughout his body. He felt a sudden breaking and a release and it really felt as if all his burdens and cares had been lifted off of him. Things suddenly became crystal clear in his mind. He knew he hadn't generated the peace and joy he was feeling. It definitely came from outside of himself and it made him feel so good. He wanted to jump up and shout Jesus' name.

A sudden, sharp pain in his left hand made him open his hand and drop the key ring. He stared at the key ring. Both the minister and Laura were sitting with their heads bowed and their eyes shut, so they didn't see that the key ring did not fall when he let go. It hung there for just a second and then Jack grabbed it again. But he knew what he saw.

Now this was something tangible his scientific mind could understand. Jack was very familiar with the Law of Gravity. It didn't play favorites. Well, he thought, at least it didn't play favorites with people. No human was able to contravene that law.

Jack had asked for help and maybe a sign that his faith was founded on something other than blind belief. He had gotten an answer that only he had seen and could understand. He silently thanked God and felt the joy swell within. Jack Malone had just become a believer.

The minister finished his prayer, "In Jesus' most Holy Name, Amen." He looked up at Jack and he knew, without words, he knew. He got up and hugged Jack and then Laura.

Stepping back he smiled, "You both got your answer, didn't you?"

Laura's tears ran down her face. "I never knew how loving He could be."

Jack nodded, "He is here and He cares." It didn't sound or feel foolish at all for him to say those words, because he knew they were true. "I have been so blind..."

Even though it had been a quiet night, Jack realized that a wind had blown up while they were praying. He identified sounds of dust and a stray tin can blowing across the parking lot. There was a sudden blast of wind against the church building which rattled all the windows. The minister sagged against his desk and looked shaken, even a bit ashen. He straightened up and took Jack and Laura's arms and led them out of his study. Jack said, "What's the matter, are the police outside?"

Alan Throman sought the direction of the Holy Spirit and got a definite answer as to what to do next.

"No" replied the older man, "Something much worse than the police." He hurried the two of them into the empty auditorium. Everyone else had left the building and gone home.

As they hurried down to the front of the auditorium the Minister said, "Remember, I told you that Satan is a liar, a cheat, and completely evil? He can cause trouble of serious proportions. I don't think he is too pleased that you have come to know the Lord." Another heavy gust of wind hit the building and something broke somewhere and began slapping against the roof of the lobby.

The storm seemed to grab the large building and shake it. Somewhere the wind found a crack and a scream-like whistle sounded loudly throughout the building. Suddenly the lights went out and Laura let out a short scream. The emergency lights came on and gave a pale illumination to the large room.

The storm's fury intensified by the second and many things started banging and pounding on the outside of the church building. Jack imagined it sounded like all the demons in hell were beating on the church. The three of them reached the pulpit area and the minister fished out some keys and unlocked two large doors that opened up the baptistery. Jack shouted over the noise of the storm, "What are you going to do?"

The minister looked somewhat shaken and yet very determined. "By realizing and accepting your relationship with Jesus, you have been granted salvation. But always remember, whenever you have a victory the enemy comes to try and steal your gain back from you.

"Satan is seeking the opportunity to frighten you as new Christians, to try to make you walk away from God. But if you two truly believe that Jesus Christ is Lord, and you publicly admit it, in the enemy's face so to speak, he is defeated. At this crucial moment he is using the physical force of the storm to try and scare you both into thinking God is powerless. The Holy Spirit showed me that if you two are baptized right now your public admission that Christ is Lord is a symbol Satan can't overcome. You go down in the water, symbolizing your death to your 'old body' that was operating in Satan's world, and are born again into the body of Christ as a 'new man and new woman' and thereby out of Satan's world. This public admission weakens Satan and his attempts to dissuade you will be defeated." They had reached the side of the open pool of water at the side of the altar. Just then, the minister suddenly grabbed at his chest and his face turned bloodlessly white.

He coughed and sputtered, sagged against the side of the baptistery. Jack was afraid that the man could die right then and there. Then, with a determination that amazed the young couple, he drew himself up and shouted, "You foul existence! In the name and the blood of the Lord Jesus Christ of Nazareth I demand that you get thee away from me. In God's words, 'The Lord rebukes you', Satan. The Lord, who has chosen Jerusalem, rebukes you! Is not this man a burning stick snatched from the fire?"

It was like a macabre scene from a Steven King horror show, Jack thought, yet he knew in his heart it was terribly real and was happening to both him and Laura. He could sense the immense powers waging a tug of war over that bottomless, unseen, gulf he had felt before.

The minister seemed to gain some strength and some color back. Reaching down, he untied his shoes and told Jack and Laura to do the same. "We are going to stand up to this mischief and he will flee from all of us."

With a tremendous crash, something collapsed near the front of the church building, shaking the auditorium even more than the battering it already had taken from the wind blasts.

Acting very spry for a man of his age and apparent heart condition, the minister did a reasonable side vault over the low wall and landed in the waist-deep water of the baptistery. He urged Jack and Laura to join him. A noise which quickly rose out of the range of hearing, but could still be felt, assaulted them with a teeth-clenching screech like finger nails down a blackboard. This high-frequency shudder felt like it was jellying their insides and they lost no time in getting into the water next to the minister.

Suddenly, Jack heard the roof of the auditorium groan loudly like it was being squeezed and crushed at the same time by a giant hand. He could see the whole structure begin to shake and disassemble around them. Between the groaning of the roof, the screaming of the wind and the banging and slamming at all points of the outside of the building, it was becoming almost impossible to hear anything.

Alan Throman leaned close to both of them and shouted, "I'm going to ask you a question. Do you believe that Jesus Christ is Lord and that God raised him from the dead?"

They both replied earnestly, and quickly, "Yes."

The minister then said, "Do you receive Jesus Christ as your Lord and Savior?"

Jack and Laura both replied, "Yes, I do receive Jesus as my Lord and Savior..."

A large section of the front lobby glass blew in just then and both main doors of the auditorium were hurled open. Through the blowing dust and debris Jack could see a violent, whirling dark mass being propelled by the storm into the church sanctuary. To Jack it looked like it was moving with purpose, toward them.

The minister was now shouting at the top of his lungs, "I therefore baptize you both in the name of Jesus Christ." With that he placed his hands on their heads and strongly shoved them both completely under the water.

Under the water it was suddenly quiet. Jack again felt that endless calmness and peace. Time seemed to be suspended and he sensed the presence of God.

He was suddenly pulled up from the water and the minister was giving them both a group hug.

Whether it was coincidental or not, the wind which had been screaming, suddenly died down as if a wall had suddenly been put in place between the church and the storm. The whirling mass was gone and with a last gust, which sounded suspiciously like a cry of frustration, it quit altogether. Papers and debris settled to the floor and the doors of the auditorium sighed and slowly closed as the pressure of the wind fell off.

After climbing out of the baptistery, the minister found some towels for them to dry off with. While they were getting somewhat back into shape, the minister came over with a smile and said, "Mr. Malone, I want to thank you for blessing me tonight."

Jack looked around at the demolished church and shook his head. "I'm sorry about the damage. Are all your baptisms this strenuous?"

"No... No, this was a first for me. That was why I feel so blessed to have been involved in it. The Father obviously has an important place in His plans for you two, or else Satan would not have dared to attack a house of worship to try to get to you like that."

Jack realized that this mighty man of God might prove important to their survival. "Excuse me minister, but if you have some time tomorrow I would like you to join us in a discussion of our problem at our hotel around noon."

Smiling faintly, he agreed to be there. The look on his face told Jack that he probably was secretly wondering how much of the hotel would be left.

As he escorted them around the collapsed roof of the front porch, he gave them some advice. "God will handle your problems, but He will expect you to do your part. Your walk with God already seems to be in high gear, so learn all you can as quickly as you can." "Read the Bible, it is God's Word. God Bless you both, Brother and Sister in Christ." He waved good-bye and started looking over the damage to the church.

Jack noticed that the minister hadn't taken the opportunity to ask them to become members of the church, or what was left of it. He had a hunch he knew why too.

CHAPTER TWENTY-FOUR

The next morning Jack woke with new determination. He was not going to lose to the devil or the world against him, not with God on his side. He talked things over with Laura and made plans while they waited for reinforcements.

The front desk called up and asked for them under their assumed names. The desk clerk informed Jack that his dad and uncle were there with a Mr. Wexler. Jack asked him to send all three men to their room. Laura hugged Jack's dad and uncle when they came into the room. Looking like the proverbial "Mutt and Jeff" they were similar in appearance but his dad, at six foot, was about two inches taller than his three-year older brother. Both had thinning hair but looked fit and tan for two men in their mid fifties.

Jack and Laura explained some of the things that had happened, but wanted to wait until the others were there before recounting everything that had happened to them since they had talked a week before.

Jack answered another knock on the door and admitted Jim Grady and another man. Jim bowed to his student and then to everyone else in the room. "I would like to introduce Mark Connelly." He indicated the new member of the group who shook hands all around and sat down.

Jack appraised the young man. He was in his late twenties or early thirties, about six foot one or two, with dark black-brown hair and an intense, no-nonsense look on his face. He handled himself with confidence and that, coupled with his close haircut indicated a military or ex-military type. He was built a lot like Jack but was probably somewhat heavier. One thing Jack noted immediately was his constant scanning of everything in the room. He was doing it unobtrusively but on all levels of sight, hearing, and touch. The action, which would have seemed nervous in a less confident person, came across as one of heightened alertness from Mark. The overall impression one got from Mark Connelly was one of subdued power just held in check. When he spoke his voice was a pleasantly deep baritone.

Jim took in the tenseness in the group at the intrusion of an unknown party and explained his presence. "Mark is a friend of mine who flew in from the Middle East last night at my request. He is a specialist in counter-terrorism who was trained in the U.S.Navy and was the leader of a SEAL team. He did a stint with the Marines as a counter-terrorism instructor. He left the military five years ago and has continued to provide his skills to those who need them around the world. I am as proud of Mark as I am of you, Jack, because he also graduated as a second Dan in Jujitsu from our school. He left just before you started Jujitsu. You were in your second year of Karate when he went into the military."

Jack's opinion of the man increased considerably. Jim Grady did not give his approval to just anyone. Jack nodded his head to Mark and asked, "I assume that Jim feels that you can help us with our gangster problem. It has gotten a lot worse since yesterday."

There was one more knock at the door. Jack went to the door and let Alan Throman into the room. Jack introduced the minister to each of the other men and invited him to sit down. "Alan" Jack started, "I was not totally honest with you the last two times we met and I wanted you to be here so that you could understand the reason that I didn't come clean with you."

The elderly minister nodded his head and waved his right hand in a gesture of 'go on'.

Jack explained about Bill Martin and the run-in with Don Miland's man at the Dojo. He then went on to detail all that had happened to them since the guard's announcement of the two cars at the front gate of the TA plant up until that moment. Laura added considerable play-by-play color and gave Jack's rendition some of the terror and unrelenting violence that had been their companion for most of the last week.

Jack's dad was shocked that the criminals could get away with such activities and that the police would buy such a put-up case in the murder of the two policemen.

Jim Grady held up his hand to stop everyone from talking at that moment and calmly updated the situation. "I have an old friend from the force who has gone on to be an assistant director at CBI. He called me this morning and gave me some interesting news. They immediately identified your assailant in the garage as Manny Dimette, a shooter and bomb man for Don Miland. But, as the young people will say, some is good news and some, bad news."

He had everyone's rapt attention. "The bad news is that the CBI has an on-going operation against Don Miland. They were on the verge of completing their investigation and securing the evidence they need to put him away forever, but, they have run into a serious snag. Don Miland has just discovered their operation and is now has their operative as a hostage."

Jack threw his hands up and declared. "Wonderful. So, my wife and I have to wait until this animal kills us so that they don't ruin their investigation?"

The Sensei was shaking his head. "No, I don't think so, Jack. I don't think that neither Don Miland nor the CBI want you two hurt, or especially dead. When you disappeared you gave the CBI the slip, too. They are aware of the frame up that Don Miland did on you two about the deaths of those two policemen. Their problem is that they can't tell the police because they are sure that Miland has an inside man in the police department. They just don't know how high the person that is on Don Miland's payroll is, in the department. So, until they know who the mole is they can't call off the manhunt for you without tipping their hand."

"They were going to spirit you two off to their own protective custody until they could put Joe in jail. That is, they were until Don Miland discovered their agent."

Mark Connelly spoke up for the first time. "I assume that they can't get their man out without endangering his life. What's the good news, Sensei?"

Jim smiled at Mark. "Something right up your alley, their agent had informed them that Joe Miland is after the Technological Alternatives Company simply as a ruse to get at Jack. From what she was able to figure out, Don Miland's big-time partner, who has his fingers on everything, wants something that Jack has. Joe and his partner think that Jack knows or has something that is of great value to Joe's partner. She couldn't find out what it was they wanted, but only that they want it badly enough to kill anybody that gets in the way." He turned to Jack and Laura. "She was caught trying to find out what they wanted from you. Essentially, she blew her cover trying to prevent them from getting to you."

Jack, his dad, his uncle, and Bob Wexler all tried to speak at once. Again, Jim held up his hand to silence them.

The Sensei continued. "I believe, knowing this pinpoints why they are after Jack, and most importantly, why Joe is trying to get his hands on Jack and Laura."

Jack shook his head. "I'm not so sure he wants to get his hands on me. The set-up with the two dead policemen has every cop in the state out gunning for us, probably with a reward for our dead bodies."

The Sensei shook his head. "We think that the operation got more animated than Joe wanted and it got out of his control. The word my friend has is that Joe is desperately trying to find you before the police do so that he can solve whatever problem it is he has with his partner."

Mark sat back. "That is good up to a point. But, until we know what it is that Don Miland wants to get for his partner, we can't determine what, or who, we need to protect, or how."

Jack looked at Laura and searched her eyes. She nodded her agreement to his unspoken question. Jack turned back to the group. He smiled at the minister. "I think I can tell you exactly what Don Miland and his partner are after. But, you are going to have to have some pretty open minds to understand what I am about to tell you." He looked at each person for a few seconds. "Two days ago I would have passed off what I am about to tell you as fairy tales or overheated imagination. Nothing could be farther from the truth." He was so very serious that everyone decided to listen carefully.

"Simply put, Laura and I seem to be the focus in a battle between good and evil. I mean good and evil as in Jesus Christ and Satan." Jack eyed the group and plunged on. "Last night Alan Throman baptized Laura and me into the body of Christ. The church was almost destroyed in an effort to prevent us from being baptized. If you have any doubts about these facts, look at the front page article in the Denver Post today." His dad, uncle, and Jim all nodded, they each said that they had seen the article but hadn't known the cause or that Jack and Laura were involved.

Jack continued his story, "I have always thought of myself as reasonably humble, but the events of the last two weeks have proved to me that I need to be a lot more humble than I was." He fished his key ring out of his pants pocket and held the key up. "This key has the secret to whatever Don Miland is trying to get for his partner." He went on to relate how he had come by the key and the events that led up to last night. The minister was quietly nodding his head as he listened to Jack's tale.

Jack shook his head, "I don't know what this 'Holy Treasure' that I have been given the key to could be. But, I intend to find out and keep it out of the hands of the Don Miland's of the world. I need all of you to help Laura and I resolve this problem. I think that when we have the solution to the secret of the key, then we may be able to stop the attacks and get the CBI to prove to the police that Laura and I haven't committed any crimes."

Mark cocked his head to one side. "You think that Beelzebub is so hot to acquire that key that he would kill for it?" It was a statement of concern by Mark about things on a spiritual plane that he had no control over or even knew how to operate on.

Jack looked him frankly in the eye. "Absolutely, I already saw them kill one man for this key and they have tried to kill us twice."

Steve Malone got up and walked over to his son and sat down on the couch next to him. "I'm so glad that God opened your eyes to the realities of this world and the next. What is it you think that we ought to do?"

Jack sat back and took a deep breath. "I've given this a great deal of thought in the last twelve hours and I think that we need to retrieve whatever it is that is in the locker at the bus depot and then make further plans. There is no reason to keep playing hide and seek with Don Miland's men and the police until we know what we have."

Laura was listening to the group talk about going to get whatever the key was the secret to and shook her head. She stood up to get everyone's attention. "I think that we, as a group, need to pray for God's help and protection before we charge off and try to resolve this by ourselves. As Jack and I learned last night, we can do nothing without God's help or we will be trying to solve this thing in our might rather than in God's might."

Everyone agreed and the group bowed their heads in prayer. Jack led the prayer with a heartfelt supplication to the God of the Universe for guidance and protection for everyone there.

Jack felt a definite sense of satisfaction and reward for turning to God before they acted.

It was decided that Larry Malone and Mark would be the best ones to retrieve the package because they were the least implicated and therefore would probably be the least watched for. The rest of the group would wait at the hotel until the object was brought back for examination. Then they could brainstorm their next actions.

CHAPTER TWENTY-FIVE

Larry Malone considered their vulnerability fairly low as he rode with Mark Connelly who drove to the downtown area of Denver. They parked the car and entered the bus depot. Finding some convenient seats with a good view of the locker area they sat down and acted like they were friends having a good conversation between bus rides. Actually, they watched everyone in the area, especially anyone looking like they were watchers camped out.

Looking at his watch Larry saw that an hour had passed. They were satisfied that no one was watching them or the locker in question. Larry sauntered over and using Bill Martin's key, unlocked the door and opened it. He held his breath as he reached into the locker and withdrew a small cardboard box. Roughly, eighteen inches long, four inches wide, and only three inches high, the box was very heavy for its size.

Larry carried the box back to Mark and they casually left the bus depot watching for anybody trailing them. Eventually, they returned to the hotel and the room.

Jack asked if they had encountered any trouble. They shook their heads. Larry laid the box on the table and looked at Jack. "Here you go. I sort think that you should be the one to open it since you've been in the hot box because of it."

Jack looked at Alan Throman. Alan indicated with a nod of his head that Jack should do the honors. After all, he was the one entrusted with the key.

Jack slowly opened the cardboard to find a wooden box about the same dimensions. The box looked like very old wood with a crude hook and eye fastener on one side and two small brass hinges on the other. Testing his new found spiritual relationship with Jesus, Jack said a little prayer for guidance and undid the hook. Opening the box he saw a metal spike, about twelve inches long, with a crude head on one end and an equally crude point on the other. The spike was lying on a soft pad of purple material. The metal was iron and was grossly discolored over most of its length.

Everyone had crowded around to see what was in the box. Jack looked at the minister and asked the obvious question. "Could this be one of the nails that the Romans used to crucify Christ?"

Alan Throman shook his head, "I don't know. The very fact that Satan wants it bad enough to kill people and even attack a house of the Lord lends credence to that concept." Looking at the velvet-like cloth supporting the metal spike Alan noticed a loose section in the lid and a corner of a piece of paper sticking out of the wood. Reaching in carefully, the minister was able to withdraw a thin book from under the cloth. He looked at the writing in the book and went back to sit down under the light. Jack studied the rest of the people in the room as they all waited patiently for Alan to tell them what was written on the small pages.

Taking his reading glasses out of his coat pocket, the minister leafed through the pages and then returned to the first page. Looking up he said, "Yes, it is one of the three nails that were used to pin our Lord to the cross. This little book gives us various notations by the different people that have protected the spike, and a little of the history from Christ's time. Since it is on paper rather than parchment I can only assume that it has been copied from the original.

The minister continued. "Apparently the original author is unknown but it seems to indicate that an unnamed Christian who lived in the period of Christ's crucifixion and resurrection was given this spike by Nicodemus. Here, let me read some of this to you."

The minister began reading from the pages, slowly at first, because the text was in Aramaic.

"On the evening of our Lord's crucifixion, Joseph of Arimathea, secretly one of us, and Nicodemus were given permission from Pilate to remove the body of our Lord from the cross and entomb Him because of the Holy Day. Struggling mightily, the two men and a soldier were able to get the cross laid down on the ground and got the crossbar loose from the main pole. Not wanting to damage Jesus' body anymore than already had been done, they worked to remove the nail from His feet, removing the other two nails in the crossbar afterward. Nicodemus helped Joseph to wrap the Lord's body and entomb it in the garden near Golgotha. Nicodemus, at some later date, gave this nail to me to keep for the church." The minister nodded, "That agrees with the Gospels. There's more here by other authors, sort of a hodgepodge." He continued to read.

"Many heathen temples have been built in the neighborhood of the Holy Sepulcher. But the Empress, Saint Helena, after a long and difficult search, found the remains of three buried crosses. She had a piece of wood from each of these applied to a sick woman and the one that affected her cure was declared the True Cross. She had this cross enclosed in a silver shrine and placed in a church built on the spot. The Empress gave one of the nails to her son, Constantine. It is said that he had the nail beaten into the inner fillet of the Iron Crown of Lombardy. There's something here about the crown being bestowed by Pope Gregory the Great to Charlemagne in the year 774 a.d. It's pretty faded and hard to see." Then there is a list of names of people and dates."

The minister raised his eyebrows. "This page tells of the time that the agents of Satan killed the keeper of the nail in 1355 a.d. and stole it. Apparently the thief wanted to look at it before turning it over to his master. The tale says this. I was following the two men with the box holding the nail. They stopped and argued. Then one of them opened the box and took the nail out. He screamed and fell to the earth. The other man ran away. I went to retrieve the Holy Treasure and saw that the dead man had a fearful look on his face. I prayed to the Lord and was able to pick the nail up and replace it in the box. I now keep the Holy Treasure for the Lord. He spoke to me." The minister looked up, "That's all it says. There are a list of twelve names here, with the last one being Bill Martin with the date of 2004." "That was the time that he became so sincere."

Jack asked, "What are we going to do with it?"

Alan Throman said, "I think that, again, we should pray to God for an answer to that question." All of the people in the room bowed their heads to pray in their own fashion. Afterwards, the minister got up and said to Jack. "I believe that this is yours to protect for the time being." Taking a small pen from his pocket, he carefully inscribed the name 'Jack Malone' and the year '2011' at the end of the list. Having done that, he carefully slid the book back into its place under the cover.

Jack looked at the cruel piece of metal in the box. Its texture deeply stained brown from dried blood. Jack thought, "That is the blood of my redeemer." He took a deep breath and carefully reached into the box and touched the nail with his right index finger. There was no inherent power in the nail itself that he could detect. As Jack held the nail he thought about the terrible day of the crucifixion. He was only faintly able to imagine the physical pain and agony the Son of God allowed himself to suffer. But he had come to understand that the real pain the Savior suffered was the separation from God the Father as he accepted all of the world's sins on himself, a sinless man. Trying to imagine what the crucifixion must of felt like to Jesus he suddenly felt sharp agony and terrible pain throughout his body, but, before he could react to the pain, it was washed away with an overwhelming feeling of peace and love. He felt the presence of the Lord in a way he could never describe later. He knew without any doubt the Kingdom of Heaven was real, spiritually close by, and that the master of that domain smiled on him.

Jack came to with Laura holding his head in her lap and her tears falling on his face. She kept saying his name over and over again until he said "What?" She looked into his now open eyes and smiled and kissed him.

Everyone else was crowded around and a dozen hands helped him to rise to his feet. He swayed slightly and shook his head. He looked around and asked "What happened?"

His dad said, "You reached in and touched the nail before any of us could stop you. You froze with a horrible look on your face for a long time."

Mark Connelly added, "Yeah, that was a long ten seconds."

Steve Malone continued, "Then you got this peaceful look on your face, smiled and collapsed to the floor. We didn't know what had happened to you. You scared us half to death, especially Laura."

Jack thought for a minute. "He is right here with us now, you know. Jesus I mean. He is very much alive and involved in everything we do. I can't give you any specifics but I can definitely tell you that He loves everyone in this room and is confident that we can succeed."

Jim Grady said, "We can succeed at what, Jack?"

Jack shook his head, "I don't know what, just that we can be victorious."

The minister got up and went to the box on the table. He carefully closed the lid and fastened it. Turning to the group he said, "I don't think that any of the rest of us should try to take the journey Jack just took." He smiled ruefully, "As much as I dearly want to, I don't think it would be prudent." He set the box down and stared at it.

Jack sat there and pondered for a few seconds. The thoughts came together in his mind and he spoke to the others in the room. "The nail doesn't have any power of its own. It's more like it allows you to take that next step in belief and the Lord is there with you. At least that seems to be what happened to me."

"What do we do now?" asked Mark.

Jack looked at Mark, "We can't wait until the wheels of justice roll on at the CBI. Laura and I won't last that long. We need to get our own proof that we didn't kill the police officers. How we do it I'm not sure. We need more information on the charges. Jim, can you get what we need?"

Jim Grady shook his head. "I'm locked out of this whole matter by my association with you. But, I can come up with the computer codes to access the information if we can find a terminal that will not be suspect by the police."

Laura said, "I know one that is available and I have the passwords to use it. It's mine at work. I'm on vacation and nobody is going to suspect me to show up at my job and waltz into my office. Give me the codes and tell me what I need to look for."

CHAPTER TWENTY-SIX

Jack had mixed feelings about Laura going off alone. He went over to Bob Wexler and took one of the little packages Bob had brought in his briefcase. He opened it and gave it to Laura. She recognized it immediately. It was the fourth of Steve Malone's inventions that Jack was producing. It was a 'HEAR ME!'

Jack told the others about the 'HEAR ME'. It was a personal locator device similar to the ones used in aircraft to assist rescuers in locating it if it crashes. This one was about the size of a package of 100mm cigarettes, it was coated in waterproof rubber and had a small lanyard attached for carrying purposes. Once activated, it started transmitting an emergency beacon on the 900MHz emergency band. The small Lithium battery would allow it to continue transmitting bursts every minute for over 96 hours. It had been well received by skiers, hikers, hunters, and recently by the military. It had saved over a dozen lives in the first three months after it went on sale.

Jack noted that, interestingly, nine of the fourteen rescues had been children under the age of ten. He was spurred on by interested parents and designed a second generation device that had an 'electronic leash' capability. If a child too young to activate the device was to use it, the electronic leash automatically started the transmitter if it moved over a preset distance from the base unit. That alerted the parents and they could track the child immediately. He showed them how it was designed for use in remote areas but testimonials had also been coming in about it's effectiveness in places like amusement parks and zoos.

Jack put the small unit in her purse and told her to activate it if she even thought she was going to be in danger. She nodded and grabbed him again and kept her arms around him before letting go and stepping back. He smiled at her and gave her a quick kiss. He remembered again how much she really loved him.

He had a serious look on his face. "How are you going to get to your office?"

She smiled and put on her sunglasses and a hat over her red wig. "I'm going to take a taxi, that's how." She squeezed his arm and left the suite.

Jack wasn't sure he liked her going alone. "Is she going to be safe out there by herself?"

Mark answered. "Probably a lot safer than she would be if she was with you." To Jack's frown he continued, counting off points on his fingers. "First, this gang of Don Miland's is looking for you. I doubt that they even know what she looks like. Second, since they don't apparently know where you are right now they won't pick her out of the crowd as she leaves. Third, since the police are looking for a couple, Laura will be safer on her own."

Jack was nodding his head in agreement. Mark continued, "We need you here now anyway to help us determine what we need to do. And we need to do something soon because Don Miland isn't going to sit still while we wait. Since he can't find you and the package you've just inherited, he'll be taking whatever steps he can to either secure control of that box, or destroy you."

Jack realized Laura was better off away from the action. He was happier that she would be safe than he was sad that she wouldn't be near. So, he said a prayer to God to protect her, left his heart with his love and concentrated on the planning.

Jack knew that contrary to the movies there is a great deal of hashing and rehashing of details to determine the right sequence to do things in a life and death situation. Unfortunately, there was no script to go by in this case.

CHAPTER TWENTY-SEVEN

As the small group in the hotel room discussed their options and possible avenues of action, Mark Connelly felt right at home. He totally trusted Sensei Grady and had a good feeling as to the capabilities of the other men in the room. Mostly they were amateurs, sure, but they weren't paralyzed with fear. They wanted to face this threat and if they lost then they would go down fighting. He realized with a start that he understood the religious angle and agreed with it. He knew that he had been a Christian for a long time. He also knew he had done a lot of things that church members would frown on, but if his occasional reading of the Bible, and asking Jesus for forgiveness when he strayed, was on target then he should still be in God's good graces. He noticed that this meeting reminded him a lot of the team meetings when he was running a Navy Seal Team. He sat back in his chair as the ten-year old recall enveloped him.

------------------------ ****** ------------------------

To Mark, the jungle had been pitch black but vibrantly alive with sudden and violent noises. He noticed that the brightness of the pre-dawn sky outlined the tops of the trees and made the darkness below even more complete.

Mark felt the heat and humidity generated during the day which had not dissipated and was amplified by the heavy closeness of the air within the trees. He could feel the sweat running down his back and chest. In his nose, the cloying stench of rotting vegetation was mixed with the sweet smell of fruit and flowers. The aroma overwhelmed his sense of smell.

He listened to the continual cough, roar, snap, hiss, and occasional death scream of animals which stood out over the constant background roar of insects and covered any small noises of his passage through the jungle. His ability to filter through this sheer volume of noise and detect 'strange', and definitely, dangerous sounds did not seem like much of an advantage. He had survived long enough in this type of environment to have developed the distinct impression that the jungle at night went about conducting its life and death business in a centuries-old manner which didn't care one iota about his presence.

The light was blinding, coming as it did out of the complete darkness of the trees at the edge of the field. Mark watched the scene being played out in front of him from the safety of a small depression with a covering screen of dark brown tree roots and leafy ground cover. The acrid tang of the decaying vegetation his face was buried in almost brought tears to his eyes. Seeing the overpowering odds against the people on the trail reminded him of the daily battle his dad had to fight to keep their farm in Nebraska. It represented the same type of courage somehow.

As Mark watched, the little family was starkly outlined in brilliant white in a world whose complete dimensions were defined by the light. Every thread in the coarse material worn by the man, woman, and child stood out in vivid detail. The whole family stood pinned in place, much like deer caught in the headlights of an onrushing car.

The man raised a hand to shield his eyes from the light and attempted to see what was causing it. The woman only hugged her baby closer to her breast.

Hector Ruiz stood in the dark behind the searchlight and studied the little tableau in disgust. "It is just another wretched peasant family wandering around in the dark." Now he had given away the element of surprise and notified the entire world as to his position. "For what?" he thought.

He ordered the man and woman to come over to him immediately. Turning to the sergeant manning the searchlight he ordered it turned off. The sudden darkness in the jungle was as dense for Ruiz and his squad of soldiers as it must have been for the man and woman struggling to cross the twenty yards of coarse grass from the trail.

They were having a hard time keeping their balance in the uneven terrain. The man gave the woman a hand as she struggled with the baby. Ruiz was angrier than when the oaf of a captain had posted him in this hellhole. This peasant family was going to feel his anger. He had no problem inflicting great pain on the defenseless people of his country. In his view they weren't worth the cost of a bullet to put them out of their misery, and he felt great shame that his country was populated by such happy, ignorant people.

Captain Ruiz was pleased he was known for his ruthlessness with anyone he considered unworthy. Having been educated at the University he looked down on the great mass of the population of his little South American country. He was very unhappy that people like this peasant family were the ones that the world judged him by, their lack of education, lack of grace, and their very poorness.

Hector knew in his heart he was much better than that image, and, he would rid his country of as many of these peasants as he could manage. His twenty-man squad had already executed over three hundred of the worthless trash since he took charge three years ago. His 'death squad' was one of the most feared in the country. He glared at the faint blur made by the little family. These two idiots and their worthless offspring would shortly disappear into the jungle. First the man would die, next the woman and finally the baby. Of course his men would want to look the woman over first to see if she could buy a few more minutes of life by pleasing them. He would have to take an interest in their motivation soon. They had started out as good soldiers, obedient and dedicated to the military way of life. Over the last two years they had lost all pretense of military conduct and had become a little too insistent on the rape and pillage aspects of their assignments rather than the missions themselves.

Like children who want dessert without eating their meal first, sloppy attitudes which would need attention. Perhaps he would attend to that matter with some selective discipline as soon as the threat of American incursion into their country had been dealt with properly.

True, a controlling faction in his government had condoned the kidnapping of the American Assistant Secretary of State and his family. Equally true, his superiors had looked the other way even though the Americans had poured much money into his country's economy. But, orders are orders and he had been directed to stop the anticipated raid into his country to recover the family. He felt pride that his superiors had given him such an important task.

The fact that the entire military command was on alert and his little group had been stuck watching a jungle path did nothing to diminish the honor in his mind. It was several days too early for the huge machine that made up the government and military of the United States to get up the anger and chest beating needed to authorize an incursion into a foreign country. By the time they got the first ransom demand from the radical militants the entire military of his country would be on full alert. The world press would condemn the Americans for any actions against the small country. Eventually he would become a leader and be able to spit on the great countries of the world. He ruefully put aside his contemplation of future glories to attend to the approaching peons.

The man and woman must have hit an unusually bad hole because, without warning, both of them fell down and disappeared into the complete blackness of the ground. Ruiz slapped his forehead in exasperation. Suddenly, several of his men fell to the ground. He spun around to discipline them when two more of his squad were knocked off their feet. He couldn't see much in the dark but he heard the thwack-splat made by a silenced rifle round. Yelling to the sergeant to turn on the light he pulled his sidearm out of his holster and turned towards the dark trail. As the light flared on he saw a sight that stopped him in mid-stride. The woman had risen up to her knees and snapping her arm forward she threw the baby directly at the searchlight.

The small child flew in an arc and had almost reached the spotlight when it exploded with a blinding flash and a huge roar. The Captain's dying thought was that he had been killed by a stupid peasant and a woman at that.

Mark waved his arm forward and thirty men and women dressed in full battle gear quickly flowed out of the trees and approached the decimated squad. Dressed in jungle fatigues with their faces and hands covered in battlefield cosmetics they seemed almost like dark ghosts to Mark. They would be barely visible and then fade into the background when they stopped moving. That they were professional was evident in the economy and silence of their actions. Everyone knew their job and there were no wasted moves. Silently, they spread out and quickly checked the remains of the twenty-eight men who had made up the death squad for signs of life. The six who hadn't died immediately were going to die and were beyond being saved by any known medical help and were quietly and efficiently put out of their misery to end their suffering.

Mark and his men could find no sign of either the Sergeant or Captain Ruiz, both of who were closest to the two pound C4 blast and were probably totally disintegrated.

Mark talked into his battle microphone and the 'peasant' man and woman ran up the squad and quickly took off their disguises. They redressed in their field battle outfits quietly and quickly. Under Mark's watchful eye the soldiers cleaned up the area to eliminate any sign of their presence and called in their perimeter scouts. Mark took the lead as the entire battle group slipped into the jungle and disappeared into the night. Mark listened to the jungle which was already back at full roar and knew it wouldn't be long before any trace of the death squad was removed by nature's janitors.

Ninety minutes later Mark saw Lieutenant William Caroll of Roanoak, Virginia stop walking and go to one knee. At the same time he held up his left hand with his fist closed. The entire group went to ground silently. They had been moving at a double-quick pace through the jungle. The pitch blackness of the jungle night was no barrier to Mark's night-vision goggles. These were the same light amplification goggles the entire squad was wearing.

Through his light-enhanced and magnified view Mark made out the two sentries almost three hundred yards away that Bill Caroll had spotted, long before they could see him.

As a Captain and the officer in charge of the mission, Mark knew that Bill Caroll was more than capable of deciding what to do. He had been training the young man for the last year to replace him. His last assistant squad leader had gone like the three before him. Mark smiled. Every time he got a new officer trained up to his own level of competency the staff pried them away to run a group of their own. He really was flattered that they were so confident of his training, and he knew that was one of the rules of the game, but still... He glanced at Bill Carroll, confident that he knew what to do. But, they always maintained tight control. His people had come through some really horrendous fire fights because they trusted their officers implicitly. The reason they trusted them was because they acted professionally and competently.

Huddling close together he and Bill whispered back and forth. Mark checked the sentries with his night vision glasses and turned back to his second-in-command. "Double tier?"

The question was battlefield shorthand inquiring as to the number of lines of sentries, one row, or one row with a second row several dozen yards behind the first one.

Bill Carroll referred to the tattle-tale IR detector he held in his left hand. The tattle-tale device was much more discriminating about human body heat than the wider vision glasses. Two dots floated alone on the tell-tale's miniature screen. Looking up carefully so as not to click their night-vision glasses together he whispered back, "Single, eliminate?" At Mark's thumbs up sign he pumped his left hand up and down twice in the air. Two darker blurs moved forward and stopped at the Lieutenant's position. He pointed out the two guards and made a slicing motion across his throat. The two soldiers, one a man, the other a woman, quickly slipped out of their battle harnesses and slipped off their helmets. Quickly the two assassins closed on their targets. Mark had made sure everyone knew that the clock was running and the time for the successful completion of the mission was only measured in the hours of darkness left in this night.

As the two assassins slid silently forward through the night Mark watched as they circled the stationary guards and approached them from the back and to the outside of each guard.

The guards had sat in the exact same places for several nights at least with nothing happening and nothing to do to stay sharp.

Sergeant Mary Vorland crouched two feet behind a sentry chewing on a root. Her face was concealed by battlefield cosmetics and she gave off no detectable odor whatsoever. The eight inches of Cold Steel Tanto fighting knife in her left hand was black anodized and reflected no light. As she waited for the 'go-signal' she tensed herself and focused on the guard that was her assignment. An errant thought reminded her that she could be doing homework in a Loyola University dorm right now rather than laying face down in God knows what about to take the life of another human being. She had been accepted and could have gone like her mother wanted her to do. But, sensing her need to establish herself she had volunteered for the service and here she was. She mentally shrugged and pushed the odd thought out of her mind. She knew if she wasn't one hundred and twenty percent sharp she could be the one dying in the next few seconds. Breathing deeply through her mouth she mildly hyperventilated to provide her muscles with sufficient oxygen for the coming struggle.

When she saw the single red dot from Sergeant Bob Gorkee's attack pack, she rose up and closed with the sentry in one smooth movement. Her right hand went over the guard's mouth and her right knee smashed into his back. Using the full-power stroke she had drilled in for months, she pulled the blade from where she held it extended behind her and drove the full length of the Tanto into the man's left kidney.

She had been trained and understood that in the sudden confusion of the unexpected attack, the crushing enormity of the pain felt like a carbon-arc welding flame applied directly across his brain inside his head. The pain was so overwhelming he couldn't utter a sound. It didn't matter if he had been able to at any rate. He died of renal shock before he could identify what was killing him. Mary pulled the Tanto out of the guard's back. It came out with an ugly sucking sound. She then quickly executed one swipe from left to right slitting the exposed throat of the dead man. Training was thorough in her unit. Too many 'dead' men had come back to life from a theoretically fatal wound not to make sure.

She gently laid the man's body on the ground and blinked her attack light two times aimed at the rest of the squad. Sergeant Gorkee's light also blinked twice.

Mark led the rest of the unit as they moved up and spread out around the dead guards like a silent black river. The two sergeants retrieved their battle gear and joined their teams.

Mark saw Mary make the sign of the cross as she moved back to her position. He knew she was asking God to take the soul of the man she had just killed. Each of them had their own way of coping with their emotional reactions to causing violent death.

He stopped and took a deep breath. He was getting too wound up. His concern with all the details of the assault had crept up on him until he was strung wire tight. It distracted his focus and could make him miss the very detail he needed to recognize. He wiped the sweat off of his forehead and moved toward the point.

The dank, fetid, hot air of the jungle was broken slightly by the breeze that blew inland from the ocean and made its way to the American troops. They were positioned on the landward side of a group of buildings situated in the edge of the trees. There was approximately two kilometers or 'klicks' of more or less open ground from the buildings to the beach. Mark checked his watch, holding the cover back from the luminous dial. 0330 hours. They had reached their objective twenty minutes ahead of schedule. He reached over and pressed the staff recall button on his commander's battle pack.

In response to the summons the four team leaders moved up close to Mark and waited. The Intel they had from NSA, Navy SatCom, and Air Force over flights indicated that the buildings were surrounded by a six-foot fence topped by razor wire. The sensitive Air Force detectors had picked up a frequency hum from the fence that indicated a probable sensor grid or fence wiring. Either one would give early warning of their presence and bring all available guns to bear on them very quickly.

Since this contingency had already been discussed and the means to surmount the problem determined before they set off, Mark simply confirmed that the plan was a go and that they would begin in exactly two minutes from then. The team leaders melted back into the darkness and Mark was alone again. The two minutes seemed more like two hours as the time dragged by with possibility of discovery always looming over them.

The recon that the COMM/ECM team members did after the guards were removed indicated that there were electrified wires woven into the fence wiring rather than a separate grid. Trying to electronically bypass the sensor wiring was risky since there were many different coding schemes to prevent just that occurrence. With all the high-tech electronic cat-and-mouse games being played these days, Mark had opted for a back-to-the-basics approach to surmount obstacles such as these.

As the time ran out, Mark watched as teams of four ran up to the outside of the fence. One member went to one knee and prepared to provide covering fire into the compound if necessary. Two of the others laid down their rifles and turned with their backs to the fence one full pace away from the wire and poles. The fourth member timed it out and ran at the fence full speed. As the fourth member jumped for the top of the fence, the two standing team members grabbed hold of a leg and helped propel the human cannonball over the top of the fence and into the compound.

The two people helping get the soldier over the wire were referred to as the Jet Assisted Take Off team or, JATO team. This was a technique that they practiced constantly and it went off quietly and rapidly. As the fourth member cleared the top of the fence and came down inside the compound, the falling soldier executed a forward roll to absorb the shock and to reduce the sound of the landing. This team member then moved ten yards into the compound and took up a defensive role in a prone position.

Team members then ran forward and were boosted over the fence one by one. Then the original JATO team was replaced and they were, in turn, boosted over the fence. The whole procedure took less than three minutes and when it was over there were twenty-six of the unit inside the compound and four outside serving as a rear guard or reserve force if necessary.

After the fence was crossed, the teams split apart and moved in on the buildings to carry out their assigned roles. Mark and Bill Carroll headed up the team that moved to the main building and approached it from the side. No one challenged them at this quiet hour of the morning. As Bill set the det-cord to the side of the house Mark thought about their objective. The United States Assistant Secretary of State, his wife, and their two teenage daughters had been kidnapped during a bloody raid on a downtown assembly hall. Twenty-seven people, including seven American Secret Service Agents had been gunned down and the Secretary and his family forced into a van. The demands wouldn't be made known to the world until nine a.m. tomorrow, local time. Everyone expected the demands to include the immediate return of a notorious drug-lord who had made himself president-for-life before he was captured and brought to the USA.

The new American president ordered the rescue attempt by Mark's unit within two hours of the kidnapping. CIA and NSA had been on top of the event almost from the inception. One of the directors of the CIA had actually warned State about rumors before the Secretary's trip. Unfortunately, the tense relations required the affair to go ahead regardless. Mark felt it had been unwise of the Secretary to endanger his family, but that was the way things happened in government circles.

Mark knew it had taken less than two hours to determine where the family was being held captive, thanks in large measure to the long-time local recruitment by the CIA of agents-in-place. By the time Mark's unit was ready to leave from an Air Force Base in Texas, detailed floor plans of the target had been provided with detail fine enough that the team knew what the captives were tied up with and where they were normally positioned in the building. To Mark, that meant that the CIA had an agent inside, hopefully the local agent had the sense not to be there when the rescue went down.

Bill moved back to Mark and held up the detonator. Synchronizing their efforts with that of the other teams, they waited roughly twenty seconds and then set off the det-cord. The magnesium-cored line burned fiercely and quickly. At the same time there were numerous small sounds coming from the various other building and areas around the main building. The other teams were eliminating the bulk of the enemy soldiers.

At this point the det-cord was finished burning and three team members gave a hard pull on cords they had fixed onto the section of wall inside the det-cord burn. A six foot section of the wall, including the supporting vertical studs was suddenly ripped loose from the side of the building and fell with a crash to the ground. Mark, Bill and three other team members rolled in through the hole in the wall and spread to either side inside the building. Three guards were inside and got off several shots before they were gunned down.

As they had entered, Mark had seen the captives on the floor and had dived over the Secretary's wife. He rolled and came to a crouch between the captives and the guards. Bill hosed a figure-eight of 5.56 mm rounds at the guards. Three rounds punched through the head of one man before the force of the rounds threw the dead man against the wall. Six rounds slammed through the second guard and he died from hydraulic shock before he could get off a single round.

The third man had been shielded from Bill's attack by Mark and had blasted away at the intruders. His first two rounds struck Mark in the chest as he protected the hostages. The breath knocked out of him, Mark waited for the sound of the bullet that would kill him. It didn't come. The man's gun had jammed and he was working furiously to clear the chamber. Mark overrode the pain of the bullets, he rose and executed a front round-house kick and knocked the rifle out of the man's hands. Mark then fell to his left and landed on his hands with his fingers open. Pulling up his right leg he made a quick sweep from left to right and knocked the man's legs out from under him. The guard had pulled his pistol out of his waistband after he lost his rifle. As he fell backwards he fired one shot. This last round went ballistically upward through the ceiling, unintentionally killing the officer upstairs who had just jumped out of his bed. Drilling up through his groin and chest the bullet exited the top of his head.

As he fired his pistol he was shot four times by the third member of the penetration team. Dropping the pistol he had shuddered twice and died.

Mark rubbed his chest under his protective vest and felt the inward dents in the trauma plates made by the incoming rounds. He knew he would have some major bruises in the morning but no cracked ribs. He turned to the family on the floor and set to work helping the other team members release their ropes and help them out of the building as quickly as possible.

With the crash of the wall section and the rounds fired by the guards, all pretenses at stealth were abandoned by the entire unit. Several explosions marked the end of the generator building, the radio tower, and the parked vehicles. The second team reaching the main building brought extra protective vests for the freed hostages and as a unit they all begin moving away from the base toward the sea.

A sharp explosion ahead of them destroyed twenty feet of the fence and the entire inside unit ran through the hole and back into the jungle. The four man reserve team had hauled tail around the compound and met the group there. The entire operation had taken less than five minutes from ignition of the det-cord to the disappearance of the entire squad with the former hostages.

They continued running and helping the Secretary and his family keep up until they reached a large open section of the beach. The COMM/ECM operator had been talking to an AWACs controller since they left the compound. By the time they reached the rendezvous point the familiar sound of incoming helicopters was building to a roar. Three Sea King choppers settled into the sand while two heavily armed Apache helicopters hovered over the edge of the beach facing the compound. Mark and Bill helped the family into the first chopper and it immediately rose into the air. Accompanied by one of the Apaches it quickly circled around to the south and headed back out to sea and the nuclear powered aircraft carrier waiting ten miles off-shore.

The rest of the team climbed on the other two Sea Kings and were quickly evacuated to the carrier. During the run from the shore the copilot gave Mark a set of headphones and a microphone so that he could communicate with the carrier. His tactician, Sergeant Walter Konig, brought him up to date. Over the roar of the Sea King's jet engines Walter's voice came through clearly. "Great job, sir" The Commander sends his highest regards for you and your team."

Mark pressed his microphone button. "Thanks Walter, is there any response from the garrison, yet?"

"Yeah, they weren't expecting us for at least two more days and we caught them with their pants down, big time. They realized what was happening and are about to rush a platoon of soldiers over to the compound any minute now. The only smart thing they did was call in a flight of their jet fighters to intercept your helicopters."

Mark frowned at the darkness. "When will they get here?"

"Don't know, sir" was Walter's answer. "The Captain of this floating air field wanted to get into the act and had pre-launched two flights of F-18 Hornets. They were airborne just as you evac'ed the enemy camp. I think when the local jet jocks saw the flights with over fifteen U.S. aircraft coming their way they became distinctly disinterested in this part of the coast. As far as I can tell they didn't even land at their own airfield. Heck, they're still headed west running full afterburners."

The Sea Kings were settling to the deck of the carrier at that point and Mark noticed that the Secretary and his family were already off their helicopter and into the waiting hands of the Navy. As he was preparing to get his gear, the Secretary walked over to him and held out his hand. Mark shook it and smiled at the man. Over the roar of the engines the politician leaned close and asked Mark a question. Mark just smiled and shook his head. The Secretary was then hurried away with his family and the rest of the team jumped to the deck. The flight crew was trying to get the helicopters out of the way so that they could recover the fighter aircraft that were returning.

In their assigned quarters a few minutes later, Bill tapped him on the shoulder. "What did the Secretary want?"

Mark smiled, "He wanted to know my name so he could thank me properly."

Bill laughed, "Did you tell him that your name is privileged information and if you told him what it was you'd have to kill him?"

"No, I just told him he didn't have the necessary need-to-know." They both laughed at that.

The rest of the unit was unwinding and preparing for the debriefing sessions before they could get some rest. Mark took a quick shower and put on his Navy Seal uniform. As he was combing his hair a yeoman stopped at his side. "Captain Connelly, the Exec asks if you would join him in his quarters as soon as possible."

Mark nodded and followed the rating to the Exec's quarters. Rapping on the door frame he heard the bass rumble of the gruff Executive Officer rattle the curtain in front of him. "Come in, dang it!"

Mark entered to see the Exec sucking his thumb and turning a light shade of red up his neck. At Mark's look of puzzlement the officer took his thumb out of his mouth and stared at it for a few seconds. Shaking his hand up and down, he pointed to the chair in front of his desk. Mark sat down and waited to find out why he was there.

The Exec glared at a cabinet inset in his wall with the door of a safe poking out from behind the door of the cabinet. "Danged thing swung shut and very nearly made me a nine-fingered second officer."

Shaking his head again he stared at his rapidly purpling thumb. With his other hand he picked up a set of papers and handed them over to Mark.

Reading the papers Mark raised his eyebrows in amazement. When he had read them all the way through he looked up at the officer. "Why?"

The Exec opened a refrigerator door next to his desk and got out two soft drinks for them and an icepack for his thumb. This was obviously not the first time he had needed one. He then pulled the papers back to his side of the desk. As he read the orders he took a couple of sips of his drink and grinned slightly looking at Mark. "Son, you and your people just pulled off one of the slicker raids I've had the privilege to be a part of. It seems the President had absolute faith in your ability to do just that. These orders were cut two hours ago. You hadn't even reached your objective at that time."

Mark remembered that he had nodded absently because he was already figuring flight times, approaches, and pitfalls of the next challenge facing his team.

----------------------- ****** -----------------------

The hotel room snapped back into view and Mark shook his head as if to clear away the memories. A lot had happened since that little walk in the park. Now he was in business for himself and an especially important part of his earlier life had asked for his help. Getting up he stretched his six-foot, two-inch frame. It warmed his soul to help his teacher. He owed the man more than he could ever repay him. He looked out the hotel window and smiled when he realized he might be making a sizable dent in that debt really soon.

CHAPTER TWENTY-EIGHT

Laura walked through the lobby of the hotel amid dozens of other people who were going about their business completely unaware of her and the events of her life. It gave her a sense of unreality about the suite upstairs. It was like it was a television show that she really wasn't a part of, only an observer.

Straightening her posture and striding purposefully towards the front door she glanced at her reflection in one of the mirrors in the lobby. She looked calm, cool, poised, even though she was still wearing her wig and glasses. Even in the harried packing of the night before, she had picked out a nice spring dress that would even look good at work. Thinking about her clandestine trip to her office reminded her or her duties at her job. I'll let them know that we're innocent and that I'll be back as soon as we clear this up. Her positive thought drove the dark events of the preceding evening and this morning further back in her consciousness. She set off for her office by having the doorman hail her a cab.

After paying the cabbie, Laura walked across the concrete courtyard in front of her building. After reaching her company's floor, Laura explained some of the situation to Mr. Brighton. She then contacted everyone concerned with the Dilby contract to insure its success. While she straightened things up in her office, she glanced around. Everyone was in on her secret and acting like she was not even there. She powered up her computer and input the network address Jim Grady had given her. A few minutes later, using the codes he provided she had access to the files concerning their case. The access codes that Jim had given her allowed her unlimited access to things that even most police could not have gotten into. She quickly downloaded all the copies onto a thumb drive and powered down her computer. She knew that they had the ability to tag files to sound an alarm when they were accessed and to provide the location of the computer accessing those files. Jim Grady had been very precise in his directions that she should leave immediately after she got the information. Otherwise she would be arrested as soon as the police got there.

She thought about calling Jack at the hotel but thought that he would not want her to leave a call on her phone to the hotel since the police could possibly trace it. She called a cab and arranged to have it meet her at the front door of the building, realizing belatedly that the police might be able to trace the cab company from this phone call. Well, she would just get off somewhere else and ride a bus or walk to the hotel.

Len Craxis stopped her to ask a question and, like normal, managed to monopolize her time enough to make her late getting downstairs. She saw the cab waiting and ran across the front walk and hopped into the taxi. She gave the driver directions to a restaurant several blocks from the hotel and sat back to wait out the trip.

As they headed along Broadway toward the downtown area, a dark blue Buick Century pulled alongside the taxi and suddenly swerved to the right. The cabby swore and stabbed the brakes. Being a veteran cab driver he avoided the other car and swung around the back of the Buick with an observation on the legitimacy of the marriage that produced the driver of the Buick.

Laura had been bounced around by the swerving of the cab but had gotten a good look at the men in the Buick and was terrified by the look the driver gave her. Not the cabby, her! She suddenly wished she had never left the hotel suite and Jack's embrace. Remembering the little locator in her purse she dug it out and put her fingers on either side on the red circles.

Jack had explained the operation of the locator to her when they were skiing last winter. The only way to activate the device was to press on both of the small red circles on either side of the rubberized package. That activated the Lithium battery and started the transmissions. High frequency pulses went out once every minute and were accompanied by the wink of a sub-miniaturized red light-emitting diode at the top. This was to ensure the user that it was working.

She was sure that the man in the Buick meant her harm, but she delayed in starting the HEAR ME! because she couldn't live with a false alarm that could bring Jack out in the open for no reason.

She had a reason less than twenty seconds later when the Buick again pulled up on the driver's side of the cab and the passenger in the Buick stuck a gun out the window and motioned the cabby to pull over. She pressed the buttons on the locator and put it back into her purse. The cab driver looked at the gun pointed at him and slowed down. Reaching under his seat he pulled out an even larger gun and waved it at the man in the Buick as if to say, "Mine is bigger than yours and you had better leave me alone."

The response was swift and brutal. Three shots crashed through the driver's window of the cab and two of them hit cabby's head. Laura screamed as the, now driverless, cab swung to the right and smashed into a wooden fence surrounding an abandoned house on the north side of South Broadway. The crash threw Laura into the back of the front seat and onto the floor of the cab. The force of the crash was such that she hit the floor hard enough to knock her out.

Back in the suite in the Hyatt, Jack was in an animated conversation with Mark and Jim about what the mansion the gang lived in was like. His father, uncle, and Bob Wexler had set up the handheld receiver for the 'HEAR ME!' beacons and had supplied one to each of the others in the room.

Suddenly the receiver gave an alert tone and beeped once. For several seconds nobody moved. Then Jack said, "That has to be Laura. She's in trouble." Striding over to the receiver he pressed a switch and looked at the readout. Quickly walking to the other side of the suite he stopped and waited. When it beeped again, he pressed the button again. The electronics in the unit did a quick extrapolation and triangulation and gave readout of approximate distance and bearing to the signal. He repeated the sequence.

Jack said, "She's headed south." Jim pointed at Jack's dad and uncle, Minister Throman, and Bob Wexler and said, "Stay here." Jack, Mark, and Jim rushed from the room with the receiver.

Providence provided them with an elevator and a non-stop ride to the garage where Mark led them to his car. Jack took in the black Chevy SS with black tires and blacked out chrome. He noticed that the car had gone through some definite changes in performance and outfitting. The engine sounded like it might have four hundred horsepower as they paid the attendant and roared out of town bearing south on Broadway. They had to detour the site of an accident involving a cab since Broadway was blocked off by police and other emergency vehicles. Jack was relieved to see that the locator beacon did not indicate that Laura was in that mess.

Each beep of the receiver gave an update on the location of the beacon. Three beeps later Jack announced, "It seems to be stopped about a mile ahead of us and maybe a couple of blocks to the right."

Zeroing in on the location of the beacon they isolated it to a cinder block building three blocks south of Broadway and about eight blocks east of Hampton.

Jack was all for charging in and getting at whoever had kidnapped Laura. Mark shook his head. "We don't know how many are in there and we don't know that they won't kill her as soon as we break in. This whole thing may just be a trap with her as the bait to get to you. Did you think of that?"

Jack stood there with his teeth clenched. "I don't care. If it's me they want then I'll face them, but I'm not leaving her in there alone."

CHAPTER TWENTY-NINE

Laura's first thought as she came to was, "If only her dad would get the smelly, fat man off of her and let her breathe she'd be okay."

Laura fully regained consciousness with a raging headache and a terrible taste in her mouth. She gagged and tried to reach up and clear the vile thing stuffed into her mouth. She realized that her hands were tied behind and below her and she couldn't reach her face. Panic flared and she felt that she had to vomit from the smell and taste of the thing filling her mouth. She realized that if she threw up while laying on her back, unable to roll over, and unable to remove the object in her mouth she would choke to death.

Forcing her stomach to relax and fighting desperately to gain control she silently prayed to Jesus for control and rescue. The taste and smell receded and her body relaxed in gradual stages as her autonomic nervous system slowly gave control back to her conscious mind.

After several minutes she deliberately took stock of her situation. She was definitely tied, hand and foot, to a metal cot. A smelly rag of some kind filled her mouth and was held in by a big piece of duct tape. She couldn't find any real damage other than a pounding headache and stiff neck.

She tried turning her head and was rewarded with a little success. She could see that she was in a small, windowless room which contained nothing else but the bed to which she was tied. The room was dingy and the air she could smell was musty with the distinctive odor of a room long closed off and unused. She tried to move her arms and legs but found she was secured tightly to the bed and could only just raise her head an inch or so. She thanked God that she was still fully clothed and apparently alive. She shuddered involuntarily as she remembered the cabbie's head coming apart at the impact of the bullets.

Her stomach threatened to revolt again and she calmed herself by thinking of the surface of a calm lake as Jack had told her. Unable to do anything but wait, she thought of her mighty woman's attitude when she left the hotel. It didn't take a truck to run over her to make her aware of the vile seriousness of the men that had taken her and what they probably meant to do with her, after they've killed Jack. Her thoughts raced trying to find a way to warn him. She craned her neck to see if her purse was anywhere in sight. She couldn't find it. It was probably still in the cab with that poor dead man.

Laura had never made a conscious effort to despise and hate people until this time. Now the consuming hatred of what they were doing to her and her husband threatened to overwhelm her. Then she remembered the Scripture. "Judge not, lest you be judged by the same measure." If they came to get her and took her bonds off, she'd try to hurt them as badly as she could. She didn't harbor much hope that anyone would find her or help her. She realized that she probably wouldn't get out of this alive.

She started to cry big hot tears which rolled down the sides her face as she thought of all the things she hadn't done and how much she and Jack would miss each other. Then she realized that she had been saved already. Suddenly, as if a bright light shown on her she realized that her death wasn't as important as it had seemed before. She thought of Jesus and his love. She felt much more at peace than she could of even imagined two days ago. "Thank you, Jesus" she murmured through her gag. She almost giggled thinking how unintelligible that sound would be to anyone but the Lord.

CHAPTER THIRTY

Mark had walked around to the trunk of his car. Opening it he pulled out three of a half dozen Kevlar vests and gave one each to both Jack and Jim. "Put these on." When Jack hesitated Mark said, with a smile, "This is just in case you can't stop the bullet with a Ninja technique." As they put the vests on, he opened a case and pulled out three new Ruger P90 double-action .45 caliber automatics. He smoothly racked the slide on his and slid it into his holster which was part of the vest. Jim Grady noticed the drapes on the ramshackle home they were parked in front of being tightly pulled across the window. No doubt the residents did not like what they were seeing.

The other two men followed suit with their pistols. Mark handed each man a black cap with an insignia on it. The insignia looked very much like a police badge until you got a close look at it. Then the logo 'Born to Kick Butt' was evident. Obviously most people mistook it for a genuine police badge until it was too late.

Picking up a utility bag, a small box and a Remington Defender 1200, 12-gauge shotgun, Mark closed the trunk of the Chevy. There were no windows on the side of the building where they approached. A two-story cinder block structure which had six-foot chain link fences to the right and left faced them.

Giving Jack the shotgun, Mark unzipped the utility bag and pulled out a rope with a four-point hook on it. He stepped back and whirled the hook in a vertical circle until it reached a high speed. He then launched the hook upward towards the roof of the building. The hook sailed over the parapet and snagged on it when Mark pulled on the rope. The hook was padded with rubber and had not made a noticeable impact when it reached the roof.

While Mark was scaling the rope to the roof, three young black men came around the street corner on the far end of the block. Seeing them, Jack jacked the slide on the 12-gauge to chamber a round. The men stopped, looked at the action and turned around and went back the way they had come. Jack was gratified that in short order all three men and the equipment were on the roof of the building.

Mark walked carefully against the far edge of the roof to the right hand side and then with hand-signals, had Jack and Jim hold his feet and lower him, headfirst, down to the top of the window below him. After several seconds he motioned to be pulled up. Moving to the front of the roof, he then took a careful peek over the front of the building which faced into a parking lot and away from the street. No one was around although there was a blue Buick parked in the lot near the building. A small balcony with a French style door in it was directly below him. He conferred with them in whispers. "There is no one in the room below. We are going to go in there and work our way through the building."

"Okay? Now remember, no noise. This is an old building and the floors will creak if you put weight on the wrong board. If we are discovered we need to move very quickly." He looked at Jack.

"If you have any doubts about shooting anyone in this building you had better stay up here." He wasn't unsure of Jack's commitment, just reminding Jack that most likely several people would not walk out of this building after the three of them went into the room below. Jack didn't hesitate. "They've got my wife. I'll do whatever I have to do to get her back."

After Jack said a short prayer asking God's help in rescuing Laura, Jim took Jack's arm and looked him in the eye. "Focus your thoughts. Regardless of your concern for Laura, you must become a professional soldier if you want to save her. That means careful, deliberate actions." Jack took a deep breath and centered himself emotionally. He nodded that he was ready.

Mark lowered himself down to the balcony and used a Marine KBAR fighting knife to pry open the lock. He carefully opened the door and slid into the room. Jim and Jack followed. Jack handed the shotgun to Mark and carefully closed the door in case someone would look up from the parking lot. Jack and Jim drew their pistols. Weapons training for Ninjitsu meant old and modern weapons including automatic pistols. Both men were quite accurate with pistols and knew how to shoot under stress.

The three men worked their way to the door of the shabby room and Mark eased the door open a crack. Opening it all the way he moved into the hall. The other two men followed and surveyed the area. The room they had come out of was one of two spanning the second floor of the building. There was one more closed door on the hall and then wooden steps that led downward. The rest of the building to the rear of these two rooms was a single two-story open bay and was a warehouse storing old cable reels. Jack saw that there was no other way down other than the steps.

Jim moved noiselessly to the other door and listened at it. He didn't attempt to open it because it was locked with a new padlock and hasp. Mark indicated with hand gestures that the other two men were to stay put. He handed Jack the shotgun and carefully walked to the stairs. Dropping lightly to his stomach he took a quick peek over the edge of the landing and pulled his head back. Moving back he whispered, "There are three guys down there but I can't see your wife. If your locator is right, then she has to be in that other room." He pointed at the door Jim was standing near.

Mark eased over to the door and taking a small bore out of his utility bag he silently bored a small hole through the wood of the door. Peering through the hole he nodded. Using his knife as a wedge, he slid the blade under the padlock hasp where it screwed to the door. He carefully and slowly rotated the blade. The thick shank of the KBAR forced the small screws out of the wood with barely a noise. Pushing the door open with his left hand he entered the room with his pistol at the ready. Jack reasoned that Mark hadn't been able to see the entire room from the small hole he had made and didn't want to be surprised by a guard that he hadn't seen. But the only person in the room was one very awake and very frightened Laura.

She was tied hand and foot to a cot. Her mouth was gagged and her clothes were torn and mussed. Jack held his finger over his lips to indicate silence to her and her big eyes above the gag glistened with tears as she nodded in understanding.

Taking Mark's knife he cut the ropes holding her to the cot and undid her gag. They had stuffed another rag inside her mouth to insure her quietness. It was obvious that she almost lost the contents of her stomach when she pulled it out and threw it onto the floor with a liquid splat. She grabbed Jack in a silent hug and looked to the men with a question on her face as to what to do.

That was decided for her as pounding footsteps on the stairs indicated several people coming up from the first floor, fast. Mark hunkered down and shut the door most of the way. Jack looked around, there were no windows in this room and they were effectively trapped. Jack had Laura lie on the floor and stood in front of her. They may be trapped, but they were not toothless." he thought, as the first man reached the landing.

The man leading the rush was firing a pistol he held in his left hand. Aiming the shotgun, Jack returned the fire. The impact of the double-ought Magnum shotgun blast launched the man's body backward into space over the heads of the next two men on the stairs.

Jack threw the shotgun to Mark who opened the door and shoulder rolled to the right. Jack stepped to the door with his pistol held in a Weaver grip and aimed it at the stairs. The two men behind the leader had paused to duck while the first man's body finished describing a bloody arc and crashed into the floor at the bottom of the stairs.

The two men exchanged looks and reached over the top of the landing with their pistols and fired off as many rounds as the clip held. This was not good planning on their part. Both men ran out of ammo at the same time and before they could reload Mark was standing over them with the shotgun pointed at their faces.

Both men realized the hopelessness of their position and dropped their guns and raised their hands. After the roar of pistol shots and the explosion of the shotgun the silence was electric. Mark looked down the stairs and again checked the floor below.

Mark motioned for the two captives to precede them down the stairs. He said, "Come on, quickly, we have to be gone before the police arrive."

After securing the two men with riot cuffs and gags, Jack, Jim, Mark and Laura went to the door closest to where Mark's car was parked. Mark motioned to the rest and they clustered near the door. Suddenly Laura turned and ran back towards the front of the building.

Jack raced after her. She ran to the area where the men had been sitting and looked around. Locating her purse on the floor she grabbed it and together they ran back to the side door.

The group walked quickly to Mark's car and loaded the guns and gear into the trunk. The trip back to the hotel was uneventful with quiet conversation between Mark and Jim in the front seat and Jack and Laura in the back. After a few minutes she wiped her eyes and spoke to Mark. "Mark, I owe you an apology. I thought that most everyone, deep down, was basically decent, even the people that were after us. But, after seeing them viciously killing that poor, innocent cabby I came to realize that they are horrible people and you need to deal with them in their own fashion. Secretly, she knew that every one of the gang members would get to stand in front of Jesus and be judged for their crimes. Eternity was a much longer sentence than life. But, she had no interest in allowing them to do as they wanted without resisting them. Not any more.

Mark looked at her in the mirror and nodded. "I'm sorry that you had to have this type of introduction into the realities of the criminal world. I have seen too much of man's inhumanity to man to be very judicious about my solutions. There really is only one way to handle trash like those men in the warehouse and I'm glad to have some help for a change."

Jack spoke up. "If those two guys you left there tell Don Miland about this he'll probably re-double his efforts to find us, right?" Mark shook his head. "No, I don't think so. Those two guys will clam up when the police get to them. They both probably have records and will be grilled thoroughly. Don Miland will probably be upset that he lost your wife but he won't care about the men. This is business as normal for him. But what will worry him is who took her?"

Jack shook his head, "If Don Miland's' partner' is in the know as everyone thinks, they'll know who took her. I'm fairly new at this but I think we need to pray for guidance." The rest of the trip was spent in silence.

CHAPTER THIRTY-ONE

Jack stood at the open window and breathed deeply. He stared out into the nighttime that had fallen over Aurora. The air was cool and the lights of the city spread out around the Sheraton Hotel. Jack felt energized by the team of people that reconvened in the tenth floor suite.

Recent events had bonded the team in their purpose and determination to see their little war through to the end. Jim Grady had explained that the possible penalties were great but the kidnapping had been a rallying cry and her rescue gave hope of success. The data that Laura had gotten from the police files showed that the police had definite doubts that the Malone's were the ones that had killed the two policemen at the safe house.

After having a dinner via room service, Jack insisted that everyone pray together to God for direction and help. Jack was in the middle of his thanking the Lord for his wife's rescue when he felt the presence he had felt when he touched the crucifixion nail.

While he still felt terribly unworthy, Jack was so grateful for the love and peace and the power he felt. He fell deeper into whatever place he was at and a point of light appeared and began to grow, or come closer. Jack thought that it was interesting because he knew his eyes were shut.

The light grew until it was close enough that Jack could make out a figure in front of the light. The figure was dressed in a long white gown or robe that glowed like light itself. The face was shining and the eyes were bright gold and hard to look at. The powerful figure spoke to him. "Jack Malone, Your Lord has a task for you. I have heard your prayers and will intercede to teach Satan a lesson." His voice was like that of a bass drum but still easily understood. "Take the treasure you have and allow your enemy to steal it from you. Don't worry, it will be safe. Then go to the house of Joe Miland and take it back from him. I will be with you." Suddenly the figure disappeared and Jack opened his eyes to see the rest of the group still bowed in prayer.

It turned out that while Jack was the only one to get the message, everyone had been touched by the presence of the

Lord. There were more tears than men normally admit to but they went unnoticed by anyone else.

Jack slowly repeated what the figure, which he felt was Jesus, had told him. Mark at first thought that Satan could be tricking Jack in order to get possession of the nail. But the minister shook his head. "I tested the spirit and it was our Lord." Everyone agreed that Satan wasn't the presence that had been with them in the room and doubted that Satan could have talked to Jack while the Lord was there. Therefore it probably was Jesus and they needed to have faith in the Lord.

Mark then said. "We are all agreed that the Lord wants us to get the nail to Don Miland and then go in and take it back, probably at his mansion, right?"

Everyone in the room either nodded or spoke their concurrence. Mark sat back and continued. "To do this right we need recon and some Intel of the buildings. First, that means we have to drive by and get some photographs. Secondly, we need to get whatever building plans are available from the local building department. Third, we need to plan our assault, because that is what it will be, in all major areas."

We need to know where we are likely to find Don Miland and the rest of his thugs. We also need to determine where we might find any records of his setup operation, if there are any, to definitely convince the police that Jack and Laura did not kill two of their own. Then we need to determine how to get to those places. You plan the objectives, not every detail. You also make contingency plans, and backup plans." He stopped and smiled to the rest of the people, "Because as soon as you make contact with the enemy, all the planning in the world goes right out the window."

"All right," said Jack, "I can get us an aircraft and some fairly good shots of the place."

Jim interrupted him. "No need, I can get us all the photographs of his place we need and I can probably get us a roster of who is in there along with their mug sheets. I can also supply profiles of their daily activities. All of these records are on file from the normal police surveillance done on a suspected organized crime location or from my contact at the CBI."

Mark was pleased. "That's great. I'll go to the Castle Rock Building Department tomorrow morning and secure the floor plans and ground layouts."

Jack looked at Bob Wexler. "Bob, I think you need to rally the troops at TA and lock the place down tight. We know the gang will attempt to do something there if they can't find me."

Mark added, "Bob, you need to make sure you don't let in any inspectors or survey teams or gas maintenance personnel until after we hit Don Miland's tomorrow night. That is one of their favorite schemes to gain entry. Turn away everyone and post guards on the roof of the building with rifles. If anyone tries to come over the fence, stop them."

Bob looked somewhat sickly at the thought of a TA guard shooting an innocent trespasser and said so. Mark relented somewhat. "Okay, just fire warning shots into the ground and see if they stop. If they won't, then you have to shoot to kill. Remember, no normal person is going to scale an eight-foot chain link fence topped by razor wire by accident or as a prank."

Bob agreed that it was unlikely, but still had a problem. "Where am I going to get rifles by tonight?"

Mark looked at Jim, who nodded. "Don't worry, we'll see that you get enough rifles and," he added raising an eyebrow at Jim, "they'll have night scopes on them because that's when they are most likely going to come at you. Do you have any guards that have experience with light-amplification scoped rifles?"

Jack answered that. "Yes, the two Sergeants were both in Desert Storm and both had sniper training or experience. I don't think they have forgotten how to use them." Privately, Jack thought that both Sergeants would dearly love to shoot back at the people that had been sniping at them lately.

Alan Throman spoke up. "I am quite sure that the 'vision' that Jack had was real. And I think Jack is obviously a focal point in this collision between God and Satan. There have been too many events to doubt that. I am told I have prophetic gifts, but I'm still not sure of my role in the ongoing operations. I think my place is back at church with a group I know. We will be interceding for all of you in the spirit realm. I think you will need all the spiritual coverage you can get." After some more discussion, he left for Littleton.

Jack's dad had a thought. "Mark, do you suppose that they could identify this hotel and room soon?" At Mark's agreement he continued, "Then I suggest a relocation of our 'headquarters' to the house in Littleton that we have ready for the NovaStar demonstration. We know that it has probably the best security this side of the Federal Center and it has room for everybody. And, we would be a lot closer to our objective from that location."

After everyone agreed, Jack kicked the ball into action. He watched with pride as everyone agreed on their appointed tasks. Bob and Jim left to procure the weapons for the plant defense.

Jack and Laura packed up what little belongings they had and carefully checked out of the hotel.

Leaving the hotel they took care to see that they were not followed. They then took a circuitous route to the posh house on the hill in an exclusive neighborhood in Littleton, southeast of Denver. There were expensive cars in front of many of the houses in the area. One house even had a matching pair of 2013 Rolls Royce convertibles parked in front of their ornate front entryway.

A half-block away, a black SUV sat in the driveway of an expensive home. A man with binoculars watched the five people as they walked from the garage to the front of the house. He picked up his cell phone and punched a preset number. After two rings it was answered. The man continued to watch the house as he talked. "Hello, Miland. What was the reward for finding that Malone guy? Yeah, I found him. He's with his wife and three other guys. One looks like a cop and the other two are old guys. Actually, I was just following up on a lead on the house. It's owned by Malone's dad and uncle and it's got a new type of alarm system in it. It was nice they showed up while I was checking the place out. Here's the address."

As Jack and the others approached the front of the house Mark saw that it was a medium sized, classic two-story manor in red brick. It was normal except that there were no windows to be seen anywhere. A nicely landscaped yard surrounded the building. The garage was detached and would hold up to four cars. The Chevy SS of Mark's and the rented Cadillac were easily contained on one side of the structure and invisible after the doors were closed.

As the five people approached the house a floodlight came on and illuminated the entire area around them. At the same time a sign lit up in a niche in the stone wall on the right hand side of the path. The lettering on the sign read, "Please identify yourself before moving forward, you are approaching a building defended by a NovaStar Defense System. This will be your only warning."

Jack's dad spoke into the small microphone set into the panel. "Steve Malone, unlimited access."

There was no appreciable delay. As he finished speaking, the floodlight went out and the path to the door was softly illuminated. The panel lit up with the words, "Steve Malone identified. Unlimited access granted."

As they walked to the door and opened it, Mark kept his hand on his pistol, just in case. Mark was familiar with pricey homes because his parents had been affluent during his childhood. But this was really top drawer. He noticed that the front entry hall was elegantly styled and softly lit by indirect lighting. The soft blue-green carpeting was plush and the room smelled of furniture polish and flowers. It gave one a sense of security, which it was apparently designed to do.

As the group walked into the main living area soft, indirect lighting automatically came on and a small waterfall next to the ornate stone fireplace began to splash and gurgle. Mark ran his hand over some of the wood on the couch in the room. The whole room was done in fine woods and textures. Mark noticed sensors mounted in two corners but could not detect any other defensive equipment. He didn't give much credit to automated alarm systems because they were normally not effective and easily bypassed. He noticed that something in the house was out of place or strange. It was tugging at his memory but he couldn't place it right then.

Laura asked Steve Malone to show her the kitchen. Mark watched her. The lighting that came on in the kitchen was still indirect and gentle, but when she went to put a pot of coffee on the stove more direct overhead lighting came on and allowed her to see exactly what she was doing in the stove area.

As he went through the house it was obvious to Mark that the interior decoration was done by someone with class and taste. These two qualities were seldom applied at the same time.

Everything from the furniture and fixtures to the tile and toilet paper was excellent quality and pleasing to the senses. Mark noted that a great deal of attention had been paid to the scent of each area. There was a fruity/grainy smell in the kitchen and a floral fragrance to the bathrooms.

He detected a pleasant fresh air smell created by an ion generator in the main rooms. He was a little envious. He would like to be able to live like this someday. That is, if he lived through tomorrow. His profession didn't come with a future, just a roaring, life-on-the-edge present.

Mark's subconscious had been working in the background on that nagging question he had and it made the connection. Mark slowly walked over to the middle of the living room and stared intently out the large picture windows in the side and front walls. Then he turned to Steve Malone and asked, "Okay, how do you do it?"

Steve just smiled and said, "It's all just smoke and mirrors."

Mark moved closer and examined the view. It was pretty close to perfect. If he hadn't noticed that there were no windows on the outside he wouldn't have given the view a second thought. It looked like glass and he could see everything outside including the flowers and dimly, the lawn and the street. Cocking an eyebrow he turned around again, "Sweet. That's better than the special effects in the movies. How big are these screens?"

Steve laughed, "Those are screens alright, but they're not video screens. We designed a way to eliminate peeping toms, drive-by shootings and the loss of all that heat or air conditioning as well as strengthening the walls of the house." He walked over to a small display unit sitting on a cabinet and brought it over to Mark.

Pointing at the model he explained the operation of the invention they decided to call 'The Viewport'. The walls were actually four feet thick and the 'window' screen, which was real glass, was mounted on the inside wall. The outside view was from a large lens in the outer wall which was reflected and amplified by optics rather than with video so that it worked off natural light just like a real window. This allowed a nine inch lens to fill a four foot tall, six foot wide window with a view that was highly effective. Steve said that was thanks to the vacuum filled transmission box which darkened the window. Or the fact that it was lots easier to reduce the amount of light at any given time or, if desired, to shut it off completely by internally shielding the lens which also darkened the windows.

Mark was amazed. "I would bet there are other uses for this technology, right?"

Steve nodded, "Yeah, what if I told you that we can give you a four by six view from the second story level while you are in the basement? We developed that for underground houses with people that are claustrophobic and for city, state, and federal buildings." He tilted his head to the doorway. "Come with me and see the ultimate nature bedroom that we've set up as a side sale for the NovaStar system."

Jack, Laura, and Larry were familiar with the display and let Steve take Mark and Jim upstairs to show them the bedroom. As they walked into the special room it didn't look too special. Just a ten by ten bedroom with a bed centrally located in the middle of the room instead of against a wall like normal. Mark noticed that there weren't any other pieces of furniture in the room either. Steve closed the door and motioned for Mark and Jim to sit on the bed. After they were there he turned a control knob on a remote control unit.

Suddenly it was like being transported into a garden at night. The walls and ceiling disappeared and they were surrounded by trees and plants and over it all was the starry night with the glow of Denver to one side. Even more amazing was the sounds and the breezes which blew from one way and then switched to another. Mark could have sworn that they were actually in the garden. He tracked a buzzing insect as it flew from one side of the room to the other and he had a lot of history with insects. This sounded real and he could feel the coolness of the night air starting to chill him somewhat.

Mark turned to Steve and asked to see the remote control. Steve handed it to him. Mark turned the major control to the left and the lights came up and they were back in the bedroom again. He had to do it two more times to believe it.

As they came back downstairs Mark said, "I want one of those." Jim chuckled and added, "If we all make it through tomorrow you'll have to stand in line behind me." Steve had sobered up and shook his head. "It just doesn't seem real that we have to go after these people. But you will both get one of the first production units when Jack's company starts making them next year. We should have all the bugs, no pun intended, out of it by then." As they rejoined the others Mark said, "What bugs? That was great."

Everyone was given a bedroom and plans were laid for the morning. Mark prepared for bed reasonably sure that Don Miland's people wouldn't find them in this place tonight. He was equally sure that there was a good chance they would find Don Miland tomorrow night.

He took a shower and was tickled by the operation of the BathBot as it cleaned the shower stall and tub while he finished drying off. Checking his .45 for a chambered round, he slid the pistol under the pillow next to his and laid down. It had been a full day and while he was concentrating on the arrangements for the morrow, sleep overtook him.

CHAPTER THIRTY-TWO

Outside the demo home and a half block away a delivery van pulled to the curb and the lights went out. No one exited the vehicle which sat there dark and silent.

Whitey knew that the delivery van would not normally be in this area after business hours. He smiled, the reason it was sitting at the curb would have become obvious to anyone looking inside. He, and four of his men, sat silently waiting. Each man was dressed in black and armed with a variety of silenced pistols, garrotes, and knives.

As the leader of the group, Whitey ran a tight ship. He was a lean, thin man who always seemed angry. While two of his team were black, his name had no racial overtones. He hated the fact that he was called Whitey simply because his hair was pure white. His hair had been pure white since birth. He realized that this may have accounted for some of his anger. He'd had to fight his tormentors since kindergarten. After an abortive tour in the U.S. Army he had been booted out for being too vicious. He had beaten a fellow soldier in a fair fight. That hadn't been the problem. He had continued to beat the man to a pulp even after he was unconscious. The Army had found him guilty of sadism and dishonorably discharged him.

After that, Whitey had built a covert paramilitary group of his own. Men like himself who were military castoffs for a variety of reasons. They had all left the service under less than honorable ratings. But, they were well trained by the service and were professional enough to earn top dollar for specific tasks that most mercenaries wouldn't touch. Whitey knew their loyalty was as flexible as their morals. He kept a close watch on them so that they didn't enjoy the cruel aspects of their jobs too much.

Don Miland had hired Whitey and his crew to break into this particular house and rip off a box. Miland had described the guy who had the box for Whitey. Joe was sure that if the guy was there then the box would also be there.

Whitey thought that Don Miland must really want this box. So much so he had added big bucks as an incentive.

Whitey had been staying at a motel on Santa Fe Boulevard around nine o'clock that night when he got the call from Miland. He went over the call in his mind while they were waiting for everyone in the house to go to sleep.

------------------------- ****** -------------------------

"Hello Whitey. This is Joe; I got some good news for you. There are four guys and a woman that just arrived at a house in Littleton. I've got a score to settle with all of them. I don't care what you do with them, just bring me a box they have."

Whitey smelled a rat. Don Miland's reputation was well known. He usually made a guy work without all the details and then tried to screw him out of any profits. In Whitey's line that could get you dead, quick.

Whitey had decided to push the minor league gang leader a little, even though it was rumored that he now had some major connections. "Well, now, Joe, I don't think we can do it for the normal price. In fact," he continued before Joe could butt in, "I think it might cost you triple."

Don Miland had told him, "I'll pay you double if you kill all five people in the house and get the box. But, if you can't find the box then I want the Malone character alive. That's the best deal you're going to get." This last was almost shouted into the phone.

Whitey knew he had pushed it far enough. He wanted to kill a few people anyway. This way he also got an extra hundred grand for doing what he liked most. "Okay, we'll do it for double. But, you'd better be straight with me Joe. Is there anything you're not telling us about this hit?"

The Don chuckled. "Nope, it's just that I had Billy and two other guys snatch the broad this afternoon and stash her at a little hideaway I got in South Denver. These guys broke into the place and took her. In the process they wasted Billy. Does that make you reconsider?"

Whitey remembered shaking his head, before he realized that Joe couldn't see it. "No, but if these guys are players then we will be a little more careful than we would for a normal hit. Okay, Joe, I want half the money in my bank by eleven. Then we'll make the hit tonight. Deal?" Silently Whitey was glad somebody had finally wasted that little whacko of Don Miland's. Funny that Joe lost both Hugo and Billy in the same month. "Maybe Don Miland is not so well connected any more." he thought to himself.

Whitey had called his twenty-four hour computer banker and made sure that Don Miland had deposited one hundred thousand dollars into his account. He knew if Joe didn't come through he could call off the hit.

Whitey knew his guys were professional hit men and they had worked as a carefully orchestrated team for over a year now. He knew they made Joe's normal crew look like the amateurs that they really were.

------------------------ ****** ------------------------

By one o'clock in the morning Whitey was sure everyone was asleep and the neighborhood was silent. A cop had cruised by twice in the last three hours. He probably would make another round in another hour. By then they would be long gone.

The team pulled on ski masks to hide their faces more from reflecting light than to hide their identities. Exiting the van they noiselessly moved up the circular driveway to the front of the house. Then they fanned out and approached the house from several, well-rehearsed directions. It bothered Whitey that there weren't any windows in the whole house. The place was built like a bank. The NovaStar sign flashed on and the floodlight lit up as Whitey and one man approached the front door to the house. In one fluid motion Whitey raised his silenced .22 caliber pistol and the floodlight went back out with a tinkle of glass.

Chuck Billings slid like an extension of the black shadows in the back of the house into the lane created by the side of the garage and the house. At the end of the walk was an inviting door, probably to the kitchen. Scanning the area he noticed the signs indicating some kind of alarm system but he had his wires and meter to bypass any known system a household would have.

Sensing no one, he quickly slid down the path making no noise. He began to have a bad feeling about something as he entered the lane. By the time he was halfway to the door his heart was beating rapidly and sweat was breaking out on his face even though the night was cool. He shook his head to clear it and moved closer to the door. All at once he knew, beyond any doubt, that something horrible was just on the other side of the door. The feeling of dread increased with every step he took. His steps faltered to a halt eight feet from the door. The icy dread he was experiencing continued to mount until he knew he had to flee or he was dead. He turned and ran into the night behind the house.

Whitey had already gained entry to the house through the front door. He watched the two men on the far side of the house as they managed to open a side door and also gain entry into the living room area. There had been no wires or glass sensors so Whitey suspected ultrasonic or infra-red detectors. This was a common ploy by wealthy home owners which could be circumvented through slow and careful movements and the special clothing they wore which reduced their thermal signature below the trigger level of most systems.

Whitey and the man with him had slid slowly into the room. They had opened the front door with a jimmy and not tripped any alarms. This was too easy.

Suddenly, as they began to move towards the stairs in total silence, pandemonium broke loose. Whitey sensed a movement to his right and spun quickly and fired three silenced rounds from his .22. While he was shooting a huge form rushed at him and slammed into him. The next thing he knew he was tightly wrapped up and falling to the floor. He could see that the other men were in similar situations except that the man behind him was caught to the wall by a big net. One of the men on the other side of the room, also wrapped in a tightly clinging net said in a low voice, "Where the crap did Spiderman come from?" He continued to struggle when suddenly there was a hiss and a sound like a stick had been whipped in a quick circle. Amidst a tinkling of glass a mist rose up around the struggling man and he went limp. The man behind him also quit struggling.

Whitey got a whiff of the knockout gas and held his breath until he couldn't hold it any longer. The gas was dissipating quickly thank goodness. He couldn't turn his head too far due to the tightness of the net around him. But he could see the other man caught to the wall. Whitey said, "Can you get to your knife?" The man grunted "Yeah" and struggled to get his knife out of the sheath on his leg. He got the knife out and there was another one of those hisses. Whitey held his breath but there was no gas this time. His man against the wall suddenly stiffened and started to shake. The big Rambo-style knife flew out of his hand and slammed into the floor one inch from the side of Whitey's head. "Watch it, you fool, you dang near killed me!" But the man in the net on the wall wasn't listening. He had passed out. Whitey could see the pair of filament-like wires dangling from the stun-gun darts sticking through the man's pants into the thigh of his right leg. Whitey suddenly went limp and stopped moving. He knew now why Don Miland wanted him to tackle this place.

A human voice startled Whitey as he lay motionless on the floor. "Throw your gun to the side, now!"

The voice was brooking no nonsense and Whitey wasn't about to argue. Hoping that the movement would not bring some nasty reaction, he threw the .22 as far as his constraints would allow. The lights came on in the room. A second later he felt a large caliber handgun pressed against the back of his head. For a second he thought that the end had caught up with him while he was trussed up like a fish in a net. But, instead of a bullet, several other men moved into view. One of them used an aerosol can and sprayed the net holding Whitey. It fell away like it was alive. He was completely free but the cannon against his head suggested he lay still.

They searched him and his unconscious team and stripped them down to their underwear. They tied up the others and then had Whitey kneel with his hands on top of his head with his fingers intertwined and his ankles crossed. He couldn't make any sudden moves without taking an inordinate amount of time. The hard guy with them asked the questions. It was obvious that he would get the answers regardless of Whitey's silence. The other men would talk even if he could resist the hypodermic full of something the man had. Whitey had been led down the garden path by Joe and he didn't feel like playing prisoner of war to protect the little slime ball. He told them the truth about who hired him and what for. It was obvious that they hadn't been there to sell Girl Scout cookies.

After a conference, the tall, younger man with the green eyes asked Whitey what his code to Joe would be if he succeeded. Whitey tried to stall and think of something cute but they didn't give him time. The tough guy advanced on him with the needle and he blurted out that they didn't have any code. He was just supposed to deliver the small box to Joe to get the rest of his money.

He noticed the good-looking chick staying in the background. As he watched her he was surprised by one of the older guys who walked up to him and broke a glass vial in front of his face. He jerked back and involuntarily took a deep breath. Things got dim in a hurry after that. In fact, they went totally black.

CHAPTER THIRTY-THREE

Jack looked at Mark as his dad tied up the unconscious leader of the hit team that had invaded the house. "Do you think he was telling us the truth?"

Mark nodded, "Yeah, I think this old boy was ready to play ball when he got a look at that needle. I think he's seen or possibly used one before."

Laura asked Mark, "Was that really truth serum and would you really have used it on him?"

Mark smiled. "Sodium Amaytol and you bet I would. This guy was here to kill us and I would have gladly stuck this needle through his brain if it would get us the answers we needed." Mark smiled a devious smile. "Fortunately for him, the thought was enough."

"What do you want to do with these five guys?" Larry asked.

"Five?" asked Mark, "I only count four."

Steve laughed, "I forgot to tell you that one of their troops ran into the SCARE System at the back door and took off through the back yard." Seeing the odd look of confusion on Mark's face he added, "SCARE is short for 'Simulated Cortical Activity Radiated Energy' system. Don't worry about him getting away, he ran right into the pool defense and then was slammed into a brick wall by the pulse water cannon for his trouble. He's still sleeping it off in the back yard. Larry and I will go get him." He started to move to the back door when Mark stopped him. "How do you know there isn't a sixth man out there with a rifle?"

Steve thought about that and agreed that there was no way to be sure. Mark got two of his bulletproof vests and he and Jack slipped out without lights and got the fifth man and brought him back into the house. They repeated the search and strip procedure for him. They had an impressive stack of weapons on the living room floor by this time.

While they had been bringing in the thoroughly soaked man from the back yard, Mark had been thinking. "Let's call Jim and have these guys put on ice until after tomorrow night."

Jack shook his head. "Okay for the four hired thugs, but the leader is going to be our Judas Goat." "I think that he will be our method of getting the nail to Don Miland as Jesus told us to do." "But," he turned and looked at Mark, "If you have a really good miniature tracer we could bury in the box then we would have a place to go when we go to get it back."

Mark said, "Yeah, but how are you going to get him to cooperate?"

Jack smiled, "Appeal to his sense of decency and honesty." When every one there looked at him like he had lost all of his marbles, he continued. "I mean, we have Jim make him a plea bargain he can't refuse. For example, he could give the thing that Don Miland wants the most to him, pick up his money, and get to go free if he does what we ask him. Of course, we will be monitoring him visually and audibly. If he screws up, then he loses everything and goes to jail."

Mark frowned. "I don't like letting the likes of him go free. Next time he'll be more prepared for the NovaStar system and could come back to get revenge on you."

Jack thought for a minute. "No, I think he hates Don Miland more now than us. Anyway, if Jim puts a tracer on him, then he can go free, but probably not for too long, how's that? Anyway, the NovaStar system has many other surprises for a repeat offender."

Mark grinned. "I like the way you think."

Steve Malone agreed with that idea. "That way Don Miland will think we are history and have his prize. Of course, he could kill this guy and find the bug."

Jack shook his head. "No, I think that would be against his better judgment because he might need Whitey later and Whitey apparently has the smarts to cover himself in a way that Don Miland would lose a lot by killing him rather than paying as agreed."

Mark nodded his head. "I think Joe was using our boys here as trained dogs to find the nail. What he didn't plan on was the NovaStar System." Mark was very impressed with the way the system neutralized the hit team. He had never seen anything like it in an automated system. He thought back to the sequence of events.

194

He had been awakened by Jack on an intercom he didn't even know was in his room. Jack told him to come to the master bedroom because they had company. He arrived with his pistol only to watch on the 52" TV the elimination of the attackers. He had missed the split screen action of the man in back because he was fascinated by the clear, bright coverage of the four men working in what they thought was pitch black surroundings. He had seen light-amplification devices before. In fact he had several scopes and sets of night glasses in his car. But this was clear, black and white, not greenish and blurry. The actual capture and subduing of the team had taken less than fifteen seconds.

They called Jim Grady and in short time a panel truck backed up to the side entrance to the house and the four unconscious henchmen were placed in the back and secured with handcuffs. The SWAT team that picked them up looked very competent to handle the bad guys. Mark gave them a sack containing the accumulated weapons and talked to the leader of the team for several minutes before they left and he came back into the house.

When he returned he had a package which he opened and spread the contents onto the dining room table. There were many photos of Don Miland's mansion and grounds and each and every one of the inhabitants of the house. Jack pointed at a picture of Carlo and said, "He's the one that tried to beat on me at my company."

Mark pointed out another picture. "This is the CBI operative, Carol Nolan, alias Dixie Tuccine. They went through the mug shots and rap sheets of the other members. Several would not be there to bother them that evening. One of them was the one they killed at the warehouse. Jack pointed out the ones he had taken out of action both in the underground parking garage at the Marriott Hotel and at the men's clothing store where this whole series of events had started. Jack pointed out the thin faced Billy Ortiz. Jack mentioned that Ortiz was the only one he had run into twice.

Mark commented that for Billy Ortiz things had just gone from bad to worse to fatal.

Jack watched the sun came up while they ate breakfast. Mark and Steve had left to find the building plans for the mansion. Jack and Laura exercised and then went back to bed. It had been a short night and the next one promised to be a long one.

By two p.m. they all gathered in the dining room again. Mark had found a fairly recent set of plans of the buildings on the grounds and was laying out the basic attack sequence. There were obvious alarm systems and then there were the dogs. The police photographs clearly showed six different Doberman Pinschers. The dogs were lean, hungry looking dogs. They were alert and in each picture at least one of the dogs was watching the hidden photographer. They could be a problem.

At three o'clock Jack opened the door for Jim Grady. Jim showed up with two surprises, Charley and Linda Wu. The two 'servants' were able to provide a great deal of detail and flesh out the skeleton that they had built of the inside of the mansion. They recounted the routines for the personnel and what times the sentries made their rounds and when they changed the guard inside and out.

Then Charley Wu described what they had witnessed at the mansion in the last few days. "It seems as if all reason and sanity is leaving the men at that place. They openly act like brutes and animals. I've had to keep Linda away from the place and even then one of the men wanted to have sex with me. I wanted to kill him but just told him that I had tested positive for HIV and he changed his mind. But the carnal lust and appetites that are being expressed there are just horrible."

After imparting their information, the Oriental couple left. They were warned not to be anywhere near the mansion tonight.

Jack had a thought and made a phone call. After he was done he looked at the other men and his wife. "That was Minister Throman. What Charley was talking about is the effect of Satan or one of his demons being so close to them. They are encouraged to revert to their bestial natures and because they are amoral to begin with, it is an easy step. I doubt that they even realize what is causing their behavior. To them it is a lot like being drunk at a college party. Everything goes no limits. That is scary." Everybody agreed and they were a great deal more somber than before.

Mark had explained the alternatives to Whitey after he had regained consciousness and he had eagerly agreed to dupe Don Miland, indicating that the bozo had it coming to him for all the crap he had done. He listened to the good things that could happen to him if he performed properly, and to the bad things that could happen to him if he screwed up.

Jack watched Whitey's face and estimated his attitude from the changes. Jack figured that Whitey realized that they probably had a snitch in Don Miland's employ and he would not step out of character. Anyway, Jack saw on Whitey's face the greed when he found out he could still get the rest of his money and not have to split it with anybody.

Mark turned Whitey over to a special 'minder' team that Jim had assembled from friends on the force and sent him on his way with the box and the nail inside.

Jack blew out a big breath. It was five o'clock and they had worked out a feasible plan of attack. Mark, Jack, and Jim would go over the wall at eleven p.m. and eliminate the dogs. They would then penetrate the mansion and reduce the opposition until they could get their hands on Don Miland. They would take him prisoner if they could and get the nail back and find his records. If possible they would turn enough incriminating information over to the CBI that their case would keep Don Miland out of circulation for a long time and prove the Malones innocent. They would try not to kill him. Jack thought that they would probably end up killing him because he would force them to do it in self-defense.

The biggest question mark of all was what would his evil partner do and what could they do if he did anything? Would God protect them from the evil one? Since there was no way to answer any of these questions they decided to trust God and leave it to Him.

Steve and Larry Malone would stay outside the walls and the gates of the mansion with the longer rifles and provide long-range backup for the attacking troops, and to keep anybody from leaving. Laura would handle base communications and be on hand to drive the escape vehicle if they needed it.

Mark went to his car and brought back several items of interest. First he showed each man the use of the 'Blinder'. The Blinder was a small flashbulb with a power source that fit in the palm of your hand. If you needed to temporarily disorient an enemy you put your hands up and pressed the switch on the reflector. The resulting light, especially in a dark environment, would blind him and give you a chance to disarm or eliminate him.

They were interrupted by the 'minder' team captain. He explained that Whitey had done his part excellently. He had left the nail with one of Don Miland's men and had watched the remainder of his money being transferred into his special account. He then left and when last seen he was headed south at the maximum speed limit. One bad note was that his tracker unit quit working about forty-five minutes after he left. He really was free, for the moment.

The second item was a set of night goggles for all five men. These worked like the Starlight scopes on the long rifles. They amplified the available light so that a person could see in the dark much better than his enemy.

The last device was a 'flash-bang' grenade. Used by many anti- terrorist and police forces around the world, this grenade gave out a blinding light and a stupefying noise that disoriented everyone within range of the explosion. It wasn't meant to kill, only to stun.

Jack watched as they brought in the guns they would use. Mark brought in three special pistols for the men going into the mansion. Modified, silenced 9mm automatics. The operation of the gun was minimized to keep the entire firing sequence very quiet. Mark detailed the reduced performance of these guns due to the modifications.

They checked their main auto pistols, the .45 caliber Ruger and cleaned the actions again.

Larry took a regular M-16A2 with a silencer and a Starlight scope on it. Steve needed more power and precision because of the ranges involved in providing backup for the men inside the mansion. Mark went out to the Suburban that Jim had brought with him. He returned with the biggest rifle anyone else in the room had ever seen. Mark set it on the table and explained the weapon to the awe-struck audience. It fired a .50 caliber round that was almost as long as the magazines in the 9mm pistols. It was bi-pod mounted and had a huge recoil pad on the butt stock. The scope had three settings; Telescopic (20 power), Light-amplification for night shooting, and a thermal imaging setting that allowed for targeting warm bodies behind walls or other surfaces.

Larry wanted to know if it would shoot through 'walls or other surfaces'. Mark assured them that it would indeed go through almost anything. Steve experimented with the various scope setting and decided he liked the gun. He had been an avid member of the NRA for years and spent many hours on the pistol, rifle, and shotgun ranges. He was impressed with this weapon for its intrinsic value more than just because it threw huge slugs at high velocities.

They checked their protective outfits and then took a break. After a light supper everyone relaxed in the best way they could. Jack and Laura sought a quiet corner and held each other and talked. Laura shook her head and said, "I still can't believe that it is us, doing this."

Jack agreed with her. "It doesn't seem possible that three days ago the worst thing I was worried about was the poor job the gardener did on our lawn." That thought brought back the fact that they didn't have a lawn anymore, or a house.

Almost too soon, Mark got up and after a very heartfelt group prayer for protection and success, picked up his duffel bag and said, "Okay troops, let's go hunting." They all got up and picked up their gear and trooped out to the garage. The Chevrolet Suburban that Jim had brought was an especially equipped police command and control center. No one asked him how he got it.

Jim explained that the vehicle came with an extremely powerful tight band transmitter and receiver and a dozen portable hands-free radio units. These units could transmit to each other through the mobile base station in the truck and therefore didn't need the extra power or weight required to be a major transmitter themselves. The portable units utilized a microphone like that of a telephone Star Set. A small plastic boom extended from the earpiece to a point directly next to the mouth. Changes in air pressure caused by talking were transmitted up the boom to a microphone element in the ear piece. Normally a small momentary switch activated the transmit function when it was pressed. The units could be switched to an automatic transmit mode also. When the modulation of a voice triggered the microphone it also caused a VOX or voice-operated-transmit switch to turn on. This keyed the transmit button of the headset for hands-free operation.

Laura could talk to any one of the portables, any sub-set of the total, or all of them at once.

It was a determined but grimly silent group that drove towards the mansion that night. Each person was lost in their own thoughts about the coming battles, the physical one and the spiritual one.

Jack knew that the battle was only partially in the physical plane. The powers involved in this struggle included principalities, powers of darkness, and evil in all forms.

CHAPTER THIRTY-FOUR

Jack took a deep breath. The high-altitude night air had a crisp chill to it this early in the spring. He checked the nighttime conditions. A cloud cover had moved out from the mountains and the quarter moon was hidden completely. The gray clouds which scudded by were driven by a brisk wind from the west out of the mountains. Jack knew that Mark had planned on the darkness and the wind to cover the sounds of their entry onto the property. At ground level the wind translated itself into a breeze with occasional gusts that pushed and pulled at you, tugging at your clothes and your hair.

Laura had kissed Jack passionately before she let him go. The five men tried on the headsets and cautiously talked to each other and to Laura. They were using a frequency that the police normally didn't use just in case someone caught one of their low-power local transmissions. They had pulled off the road just after leaving the Interstate. Using the photos and maps they had used two rutted trails to approach the outer wall of the mansion from an unexpected angle. This also kept them from being seen by casual on-lookers. Using the night goggles they had come in without lights.

The five men shook hands and parted company. Jack and Mark watched as Steve Malone turned south and climbed a small rise. He then strapped the .50 caliber rifle to his back and slowly climbed a tall rock which provided a clear field of fire all the way to the mansion itself. Once on top he set up the rifle. Jack thought his dad was making himself as comfortable as one could while laying face down on a rock.

Mark touched Jack on the arm and pointed. Larry Malone had worked his way further south until he was just slightly in the trees near the front gate to the property. They both heard Larry as he triggered his radio switch. "This is four. I've got two watchers at the gate."

A second later Laura's voice came back to all of them. "Roger that four. All are aware of the watchers." Apparently Larry had dropped below line of sight and lost direct contact with the three man crew going into the property.

Through the earpiece Jack heard Larry say, "Five, this is four, how do you copy me?" Steve's answer was crystal clear. "I read you Five by Five, four." Jack wasn't sure if that was a joke or not but at least Larry wouldn't feel so all alone anymore.

As they approached the wall surrounding the estate, Mark took a small electronic field meter out of his pocket and studied it intently. As they reached the wall it stayed dark. He put his rifle against the wall and Jim and Jack each made a sling out of their hands and Mark used them to stand in as they lifted him to the top of the eight foot high wall. The red LED on the meter came on bright as he neared the top. He said, "Wait, don't lift me any closer to the wall yet."

Slowly moving the meter around he got a fix on the energy beam running along the top of the wall. Then he had them let him down. "It's no good. We can't scale the wall." he whispered. They've got a laser beam fence pulsating all along the top of the wall. We've got to find another way to get into the place." This could really throw a monkey wrench into the works.

The wall was at least three to four feet thick and probably five to six feet deep into the ground. Jack looked south and north along the wall and spotted what he wanted. "Come on", he said, and picked up his rifle and gear and ran quietly north from their present position. The other two men followed him quickly. It was almost eleven and they hadn't even gotten onto the property yet.

Jack slowed when he reached a tall pine tree that almost reached the wall. Mark was perplexed. "What can this do for us? It doesn't reach far enough to let us jump the wall. Look, they're not stupid. They've cut off all the branches that come near the top of the wall." Jack saw Jim smile. He knew what Jack was planning.

Jack strapped his rifle to his back and started climbing the tall thin pine tree. He worked his way to the wall side of the tree when he had passed the place where the branches had been trimmed away from the top of the wall. As he started to climb the last third of the tree's height it began to bend towards the wall. When he was high enough the tree bent all the way over the wall and Jack let go and dropped onto the estate. The tree hadn't triggered the laser fence because the limbs that would have broken the laser path had been cut off.

Jim followed Jack's example and soon he and Jack watched Mark duplicate the feat. They were all three squatting in the tall grass when Mark heard the first dog. They had planned for this. Donning their night vision goggles each man drew a special weapon. These were dart guns with a knock-out mixture that would have Bowser sleeping for the next hour. The three men moved about three feet apart and waited. Soon two of the Dobermans came rushing through the grass at them. Two carefully aimed darts brought the dogs down without a sound.

As they worked their way towards the house they eliminated three more of the dogs. That left one unaccounted for. About fifty yards from the house Mark held his hand up in a fist and the other two men froze. Going to his knees he signaled to get down. A few seconds later two of the guards came walking towards them through the grass. There was a little reflected light from Denver bouncing off of the bottom of the clouds. That was all the light the guards needed to see where they were going.

To the three waiting men the guards were clearly visible and vulnerable. The guards were griping about the missing dogs. One was saying "Dang dogs, always running after rabbits and never paying any attention. I think Joe ought a get Rotweilers. Those dogs are so mean they don't even like themselves."

The guards were dispatched with no more trouble than the dogs before them. Jim and Mark made sure their shots were neck shots for a sure knockout without any noise.

Approaching the north wall of the house Jim and Mark were peeking around the front of the house where two more of the guards were standing by the front door. Suddenly a guard who had been relieving himself in the bushes came around the back of the house and spotted the two men by the corner. He hesitated unsure whether to grab his gun or his portable radio. That hesitation cost him dearly. Jack came up behind him and reached around the front of his head and grabbed his left arm with his right hand while he placed his left hand on the back of the man's head. He applied pressure with his right arm to the man's neck before he could yell out. He held the pressure until the man had passed out. He grabbed the unconscious body before it could fall and placed it in the same bushes the man had so generously watered seconds before. Using plastic riot cuffs and a gag, he secured the man in the event he would happen to wake up in the near future.

Mark talked to Steve. "Five, One, two, and three are going to go in high. Watch the linebackers at the front door for us, Okay?" He heard a distinct 'Roger' from Steve. He then moved back to the rear of the house and checked the wall with his meter. Getting a clear reading he used the trellis and the vines growing on it as a ladder and in seconds was on the second floor balcony which faced the mountains. Jack and Jim quickly joined him.

His meter told him that the window was wired and he could see the glass breakage sensors on it. He moved to the door. It only had a magnetic switch at the top. He took off his backpack and took out a small device with a thin plate on it. He pushed the plate part way into the crack at the top of the door where the magnetic switch was. A pin-sized red micro LED lit up. Mark pulled the plate out and reversed it. Carefully reinserting it he slid it all the way into the crack and between the magnet and the switch. The little package was a battery operated magnet itself. Once the proper orientation for the magnetic flux was determined, the plate replaced the door magnet as the force holding the switch closed.

Mark took out a lock pick and in less than ten seconds had the door unlocked. He whispered to the other two men. "There may be additional security devices such as motion detectors and infra-red heat sensors inside. If any type of alarm goes off, we try to eliminate the obstacles on our way to Don Miland, right?" Everyone agreed and Mark swung the door open. They were inside the lion's den.

CHAPTER THIRTY-FIVE

Don Miland hauled back his fist and drove it into the girl's stomach. The smack of flesh on flesh was accompanied by a visceral grunt from the woman. Carol Tuccine's legs gave out on her again and she spit blood and parts of a tooth onto the rug at her feet from an earlier blow to the face. The room spun in circles around her in a haze of red pain from the beating she was taking. Suddenly something cracked into her head and she fell into a great silent darkness.

Joe looked at the unconscious woman and told his two men to take her to the basement and strap her into a chair. He'd continue questioning her when she came back to life. As they dragged her out of the room Joe turned away and grabbed his right hand in his left. "Ouch!" he thought, "that idiot girl's head probably broke every bone in my hand." Shaking his hand to quell the pain he regretted again trying to hit her in the face that last time. She'd swooned and he'd hit the top of her head instead.

Rubbing his hand he looked down on the floor at the busted open hair dryer with the tape recorder in it. "Dang, I really liked her too."

Joe's thoughts, as normal, turned to his 'partner' and recalled the demon's casual comment about the hair dryer and the faithfulness of his 'woman'. Don Miland had little time to waste on speculation as to who wanted to hurt him and, again as usual, found his favorite target. "I'll bet it was that turkey Fredo again. I'll bet he stuck her in here to spy on me."

Joe thought about the package that he had sent to Fredo that afternoon. "I'll bet he wets' himself when he sees that box." Joe grinned when he thought about his neat solution when he found out that one of his new boys was really a plant from Jose Fredo's organization. He'd shot the fink himself and then had him decapitated. Then he set the fink's head in a box and had it delivered to Don Fredo's by Federal Express. "That'll show that SOB who he's playing with." His thoughts of the satisfaction offset the pain in his hand. He went to get a drink. Looking at the clock over the mantle he saw it was almost eleven p.m. He realized that he had acquired the package his partner wanted almost eight hours ago. But he had been busy and wanted to savor the favorable reaction when he presented it to the demon himself.

CHAPTER THIRTY-SIX

Mark and Jack moved down the stairs from the second floor cautiously. According to the Wu's information this was just about shift change time for the guards. The new guards would be waiting for the other guards to come in before they left to relieve them. Normally they waited in the kitchen and drank coffee. Jim covered their descent from the landing balcony on the stairs.

Hearing voices in the kitchen the two men moved to the door leading into the kitchen from the dining room. The door was slightly ajar. Mark indicated to Jack to go to the other kitchen door in the hallway. He spoke into his microphone which he had switched to hands-free. "We go in on three and knock everyone out. Ready? One, Two, Three!"

On the count of three both doors swung into the kitchen and the four men inside turned to see who was coming in. They were expecting the earlier shift of guards and were startled to see the two strange armed men. Their surprise didn't last long. Mark shot the standing man in the neck and the quick-acting formula of knock-out juice turned his switch off immediately. Jack took out the one on the far side of the table. The other two men grabbed for their guns but never reached them. Mark shot the man across the table from him in the chest. Jack's second shot hit the last man in the back as he reached for his pistol. This caused him to slump into his uncaring partner who was in the process of toppling backwards to the floor.

Mark had just stepped into the kitchen to make sure the four men were really out, when two bullets struck him in the back and threw him into the kitchen and on top of the unconscious bodies there. Jack had just put the dart gun away and drawn the silenced 9mm. As he swung to his left he saw one of the front door guards charging towards the kitchen and shooting as he came. Jack yelled into his microphone, "All numbers . . . shoot, shoot!"

Jack fired three shots at the on-rushing man. The first shot hit him in the right arm and hit the bone in his arm. The fierce pain made him grab for his right arm with his left hand. The second round went through his left hand and into his right arm again. The last round hit him in the forehead. But, by that time the man was in shock from the pain and died without knowing it. The man fell face first onto the rug and performed an awkward bloody slide that stopped at an armchair.

A deep rolling boom reached Jack's ears just as the other front door guard flew through the front window next to the door. Jack snap-aimed at him but dropped his gun down when the man caromed off of the entryway wall and fell on his face like a limp rag. The man was quite dead, although the bullet had struck the rifle he had been carrying. It appeared that the power of the .50 caliber slug, instead of simply tearing the rifle out of the hands of the man, it had also broken the rifle in half and punched through the man. The distance he had traveled testified to the power of the .50 caliber bullet that had been fired from two hundred yards away.

When a popping noise was heard from the house and Mark's call came over the headset Larry pulled the trigger on his silenced M-16. The blast from the .50 caliber rifle on the rock above him roared as Larry's first round caught the first gate guard squarely in the chest. This guard lost all interest in his surroundings and dropped like a sack of potatoes to the pavement. The second man jumped behind the stone pillar holding up the gate and fired back in the direction he thought the shot that dropped his partner had come from. Unfortunately, he was shooting the wrong direction and exposed his back to Larry who immediately dispatched him with two well-placed shots.

Back in the mansion, Jack stepped into the kitchen to help Mark. Mark was standing up by then. He shook his head and asked Jack to rub his back. As he did, the two slugs from the 9mm pistol that had hit him fell to the floor from the dents they put in the Kevlar vest.

Suddenly, Jack saw movement in the living room near the front door and shoved Mark away from him and fell backwards. That quick reaction was the only thing that saved both their lives. Carlo crouched behind the couch in the living room and fired a shotgun at the two men in the kitchen.

As Mark fell forward and Jack fell back the load of buckshot passed between them and cleanly decapitated the sleeping man on the far side of the kitchen table. Jack scrambled behind the column that made up the corner of the kitchen between the doors. Mark dropped to the floor next to the refrigerator. The next shotgun blast tore the back window out of the kitchen. The smell of gun powder and blood was thick. Jack tried to get a shot at Carlo but was driven back by another blast of the shotgun. Obviously Carlo had an automatic shotgun and plenty of ammunition.

All at once Carlo cried out and jerked up from behind the couch. Two stun darts appeared in his chest and he touched them with a surprised look on his face. Then his eyes rolled up into his head and he fell over the back of the couch. Jim walked downstairs and reclaimed the throwing star that was stuck in Carlo's left leg. When Jack and Mark joined him he shrugged. "Sorry it took that long to stop him. I had to do something to distract him or he would have seen me on the stairs and that shotgun reloaded too fast.

Jack looked at Carlo's unconscious body and saw the full length cast on his right leg. The damage Jack had done to his knee would have some companion pains now. He looked around at the gun smoke filling the room like a low-hanging cloud layer. "Okay. Where's Don Miland?"

Jim Grady said, "Well, according to this tracking device that Mark gave me, the box is directly below us right now.

CHAPTER THIRTY-SEVEN

Don Miland looked at the package that Whitey had finally secured for him after killing that Malone punk and his friends. He knew the power in the next room was thirsting to have it presented to him. After, of course, all the proper rituals were performed. This was a thing of power from Mr. Goody-Two-Shoes himself, the big JC. Joe had never really believed in either God or the devil. Now he wasn't too sure. He looked over at the barely conscious woman tied to the chair. "Idiot woman," he thought. "After I'm done with her I'll give her to my 'partner' for dessert."

The flunky that had brought the box in from Whitey was standing there grinning from ear to ear like he was proud and he wanted Joe to reward him. "Okay, I'll give him his reward." Joe remembered what the power in the next room told him about trying to handle the metal in the box. How all sorts of horrible things would happen to him if he wasn't protected or one of those sissy Christians. He looked up at the punk and smiled. That really got the kid pumped up.

Joe pointed at the box. "Take that metal thing out of the box and put it on my desk." "We got to make sure that it is the real thing."

The kid was eager to please. He worked the catch and opened the box. Reaching into the box he grabbed hold of the spike. He lifted it out and started to turn around. Suddenly he stopped in mid-turn. His eyes rolled up into his head and he fell to the floor. Joe stood up for a better look. While Joe stood there looking at the spike and the kid lying on the floor, he heard the kid scream the most horrible scream he had ever heard. And Joe had heard some really bad ones. The scream which seemed to come from the pool room, died away into a really dreadful whimper.

Joe jumped and covered his head with his arms as a deep voice came out of the other room. The timbre of the voice made Joe's bones hurt like they were grating together. "You FOOL! Didn't I tell you NOT to OPEN the box? You will pay for this forever!" Joe wasn't sure if the entity in the other room was talking to the kid or to him. He didn't have long to wait to find out. The voice came again, this time twice as loud and painful. "Get that box in here now, you miserable little human being. You don't want me to have to come out into the light and get it do you?" Somehow, Joe couldn't think of anything that could be worse at the moment.

But he had a problem. How, to get the spike, on the floor back into the box. He didn't dare touch it and he didn't want to tell whatever was in the next room that he had a problem. Something he had heard in his youth reminded him about powerful people that tended to kill the bearer of bad news. Suddenly he had a bright idea. He ran over to his fireplace and grabbed the fireplace tongs. Picking up the spike with the tongs, he carefully maneuvered it back into the box and shut the lid. Congratulating himself on his cleverness he picked up the box and turned to go into the next room.

CHAPTER THIRTY-EIGHT

Approaching the door to the basement carefully, Jack, Jim, and Mark slowly filed down the stairs. At the end of a short hall there was a closed, sound-proofed door. Jack was ready to kick the door in when Mark stopped him. Mark reached forward and turned the knob and the door opened quietly inward. Inside wasn't quiet. In a flash the picture was clear to the men at the door. Carol Tuccine sat in a straight backed chair. Ten or twelve ugly red welts dotted her body especially her arms. Her face looked like she had tried to break through a door with it and there was blood all over her legs.

Don Miland stood there with the box holding the Holy Treasure in his hands as he turned to see who was stupid enough to interrupt him. His eyes grew wide at the sight of three heavily armed men standing in the doorway. All three pistols were aimed directly at him. He dropped the box and put his hands into the air above his head.

Jack motioned him to back away from the moaning woman. He did as he was instructed. Mark kept his pistol aimed directly at the man's chest. Jack could see that Mark's knuckles were white with the effort he was exerting not to fire the entire magazine into the man.

Jack and Jim Grady cut the woman's bonds loose and moved her to a couch. Jim saw a sink and got a wet rag and wiped the blood off of her to determine the extent of her injuries. Surprisingly, she was still alive and even functioning. She had lost two teeth and had a terrific shiner around her right eye. Several other bruises were starting to form on her face and abdomen and she had those nasty welts over her arms. For some unexplained reason, Don Miland had not resorted to stripping her and attacking her that way. But, at least she didn't seem to have any broken bones and the blood was mostly from her mouth and some superficial surface wounds.

She coughed and Jim helped her to a sitting position. Jack was mad enough to seriously hurt the crime boss. "What caused those welts?" he asked her.

She started to answer and had to try for the second time. She pointed at Joe, "Mr. Macho there wanted me to tell him who I worked for and I didn't want to. So he used an ice cube to deaden the skin and then put a hot cigarette against the skin. That way you get a really deep burn before you feel anything."

Jack turned and walked over towards Joe like the angel of death. But Mark stopped him with the comment, "We need some information from him first." Jack gritted his teeth and backed off. Looking around he spotted the box that held the crucifixion nail and went over to it. Picking it up, he opened it and made sure it was intact, which it seemed to be.

Jack was turning to tell Mark to take Don Miland upstairs when there was a malevolent scream of rage from the next room.

The fact that the scream was inherently evil and that it shook the entire room wasn't lost on any of the men. Mark and Jim grabbed Carol and made a run for the door. Joe, realizing that he was in more trouble than he could imagine, made a run at Jack in an attempt to retrieve the box.

Sensing Joe's move, Jack turned, drew his pistol and shot Joe in the leg. The Hydro-shock hollow point bullet imparted so much power that it spun Joe around in a circle and dumped him on the floor. His whole right leg was numb and he couldn't move it.

Time seemed to stand still suddenly. The wall between the room they were in and the one behind it seemed to melt and collapse at the same time. Jack's soul felt a fear that he had never known, much worse than when he was being baptized. A Stygian blackness existed behind the wall and began to flood into the room. As the three men and the woman turned to run, the door slammed shut before them and they were trapped. The darkness pulsed with evil and a sick hunger.

Jack realized he was facing a power far beyond his capabilities to understand, let alone handle. In a few seconds both he and his friends would be consumed and damned forever. Jack tried to hide the box behind him, but a shadow swept forward and knocked the box out of his hands and to the floor. Jack felt like his skin was slimy and imagined that he could feel every hair on his body writhing around like worms. He was filled with a feeling of total failure. The though raced through his mind that this is what he deserved and he wasn't worth anything. A horrible malaise came over him and he wanted to hide. He was ugly, miserable, and God had walked off and didn't want him at all.

Then the memory of the peace he had felt when he had touched the spike in the hotel room strengthened him. "That wasn't right!" Jack was still a brand new Christian but one thing he was absolutely sure of was that the love of God never wavers. Once you accepted Jesus and were saved by putting on Christ in baptism, God never left you, ever! He fought through all the pity and guilt he was feeling and concentrated on Jesus. The ultimate peace he had felt when he had touched the spike came back. Not completely, but enough that he was sure that it was man that walked away from God, not the other way around.

Jack turned to the only hope he had. Instead of continuing to quake in absolute terror like his body and soul demanded that he do, he prayed. He prayed out loud to the Son of God to save them. As he remembered it later, this was an extremely earnest prayer. He had been in the presence of the Lord God almighty and he was eyeball to eyeball with a principality of darkness and this was as real as it could get.

With a sensation of a building being slammed to the earth, all movement and all sound stopped. There was complete silence in the room. Not just quiet with little background noises but an absolute total lack of sound. A light whiter than white flooded the room with a visible power. The flood of white light enveloped Jack, Mark, Jim, Carol, and the box and pushed the malignant blackness away from them. Jack smelled a beautiful fragrance of flowers and the peace of the Holy Spirit filled them all. The terror he had felt melted away as if they had never been there.

Jack felt a calm, beautiful, and even more powerful voice say, "Be gone evil one, these people are mine. You can have the one who served you. You were going to get him anyway." Jack saw the mouth of Don Miland making a word that looked like NO! Over, and over, and over again.

Don Miland was closer to the wall of darkness and it surged over him. Jack watched as the big man was shaken like a rat in a terrier's fangs. His being seemed to shimmer and distort The man let out a deep bass, gut-wrenching scream of horror which was cut short and a desiccated husk of what had been a human being was discarded to drop lifeless and apparently empty onto the floor.

The blackness receded and faded before the light. Gathering itself with a silent scream of rage that Jack couldn't hear, but somehow understood, the darkness seemed to very quickly recede into a point and disappear. The bright white light faded away and with a crash, noise returned to the room. Jack thought that he had never seen such an astonished look on the face of his mentor. Sensei Grady had just had a serious attitude adjustment and was attempting to assimilate a great deal of new concepts that were not just theory anymore.

Jack recognized a thought forming in his mind, "I will be with you, forever."

Jack could tell that the other people in the room had heard the same message. He was more aware of the fact that God had always been with him and would always be with him, even through an eternity after the end of this life.

He turned and looked at the mask of horror etched deeply onto what had been Don Miland's face. Compared to Bill Martin, it was obvious that Don Miland had a rougher ride ahead of him. Jack looked over at Carol and started to ask a question. His mouth was still so dry no sound came out. He swallowed twice and licked his lips and tried it again. "Do you know where the late Don Miland has his files? My wife and I would like to be vindicated in a couple of murders."

Carol took a deep breath, nodded and holding her stomach she limped over to the stairs. Walking underneath them she pulled on a coat hook and a section of the wall came out. Inside were two file cabinets. The men helped pull the files out of the cabinets. Mark and Jim started quickly going through them and pulling out the ones that the police and CBI could use.

Jack looked around the basement while this was going on. Seeing another coat hook like the one that worked the secret file room door, he pulled on it. Sure enough, another door opened in the other wall. He walked over and flipped on a light switch next to the door. Looking up he whistled. At that, Mark came over to join him. Carol did too. She looked inside and said in an awed voice, "I never even knew this was down here."

The room was full of guns, boxes and boxes of grenades, mortar shells, dynamite, C4 Plastic Explosive, and thousands of rounds of ammunition. The room probably ran the full length of the house above it.

Mark walked over to an armored panel and studied it. Then he shook his head, "Jack, I think that there may have been some other rules or switches you should have used before you opened this door. He pointed to the countdown timer that showed that the time left was twenty minutes. He looked over at Jim and asked, "How much Plastique do you think we have here?"

The Sensei had the files they needed and had joined the others in the basement armory. He estimated the number of packages and boxes and declared, "About a good half-mile's worth." Jack knew that this meant that they had better be more than a half mile away when the balloon went up. Mark agreed.

They left the room and Mark started to shut the door when Jim stopped him. 'What are you going to do with the men upstairs? If you leave them here, you might as well of just shot them."

Mark looked at his watch, estimated the time and said, "They actually deserve it," as he looked at Jim. But, we'll load them onto the back of the Suburban and leave them outside the property. They can fend for themselves when they wake up."

Grabbing the files they wanted they started up the stairs. Suddenly Carol said, "Wait a minute." She hobbled back down to the basement with Mark right behind her. They came right back up with two big briefcases that looked heavy from the way Mark was carrying them. She looked at the crew and said, "Let's go." They quickly ran to the first floor and, dragging the sleeping men out through the front door and out onto the front porch, they cleared the house in record time. Laura was there with Steve and Larry who were standing guard. Everyone helped pile the sleeping guards into the back of the Chevy Suburban. Jack quickly ran around back and got the guard they left in the bushes. It took three people to get Carlo onto the top of the stack of unconscious thugs. Everyone then piled into the Suburban and Laura took them carefully back to the gate so as not to spill bodies along the way.

Larry had located the key on one of the guards and that opened the gates. He had hidden the dead guards in the bushes. Carol looked back at the mansion and commented, "You guys do neat work. I can't even tell that anything happened here." She pointed at the two men lying in the bushes, "Let's dump the rest of the scum here with their buddies." They quickly laid the rest of the men in a neat pile out of sight of the road.

Looking back Jack had to agree with Carol. At the distance of the gate which was about two hundred yards, the mansion looked perfectly normal. The only outside damage that would be visible from this side was the window next to the door that Steve's shot had catapulted the last guard through and that had a curtain hanging over it.

Mark laughed, "It won't look like nothing has happened in a few minutes."

Laura drove away towards the interstate when she suddenly said, "I see car lights coming towards us."

Mark said, "Turn off the road to the right here and go into the woods." Laura quickly did as she was told. The Suburban was in four-wheel drive anyway and she had been driving without lights using her night vision goggles so as to not attract attention.

Three hundred feet into the woods she stopped the truck with the emergency brake so that there wouldn't be a flare of brake lights to give them away. They all watched as two limos and a van roared by on the road to the house. Jack asked Mark, "Reinforcements?"

Mark shrugged, "Could be, I really don't know but they're not policemen." Then he turned to Laura. "Drive on a little farther up the trail. I think we can see the house from the top of this rise."

Laura stopped the truck near the top of the rise and everyone got out and walked the two dozen yards to the crest where they could see the house in the distance. The two cars and a van had stopped near the front of the house. A lot of men were running to surround the house. They were carrying rifles and sub-machine guns. Mark got the binoculars from the truck and studied the newcomers.

"They're not reinforcements, they're attacking the house." His disbelief was shared by the others in the group.

Jim Grady took the glasses from Mark and studied the group in front of the house. "That's Jose Fredo from the west side of Denver. What's he doing laying siege to Don Miland's house? They're rivals but they were never out-and-out enemies."

Mark laughed a graveyard laugh. "I don't think Joe Miland will care about it. He's probably really busy right now."

Suddenly Jack asked, "What about those other two guards we knocked out and the dogs?"

About that time a long bright flare of light indicating a shoulder- launched missile streaked from near the van towards the front door of the house. Just as the missile impacted the front door, the time ran out on the doomsday timer in the ammo room underneath Don Miland's house.

The resultant explosion threw everyone backwards and knocked them down. It also caused the Richter scale at the University of Colorado in Boulder, miles north of Denver, to indicate an earthquake of 4.9 magnitudes.

Sometime later the debris and chunks of dirt stopped falling out of the sky and the ground stopped shaking. The crew found that they could stand up again. Even Jim was amazed at the total destruction. Where there had been eighteen men attacking one house with two outbuildings, there was just burning and smoking debris. Nothing over an inch in height was standing within two thousand feet of ground zero and where the basement had been there was a smoking crater three hundred yards across and probably just as deep. There was no sign of life anywhere on the plain. Anything left was on fire and burning.

As they stood there in awe, Carol pointed down to the left. One of the field guards had the other one by the belt and was moving away from the blast site as quickly as he could. You could even see the dogs near them.

Carol nodded and said, "This looks just like what I always figured Hell would look like. That is just where those jokers belong anyway."

CHAPTER THIRTY-NINE

After cleaning up as much as possible at the house in Littleton, Jim took Carol to a 'Doc in a Box' for some X-rays and an examination to determine the extent of her injuries.

Since everyone was still too wired to sleep, they ate some breakfast and talked about the events of the night. When Jim and Carol returned from their trip to the doctor they all gathered in the living room.

Jim started the conversation off. "Carol has lost two teeth and has a possible concussion. Other than that she has multiple bruises and contusions. We had to show the doctor our badges before he would log the injuries without calling the police."

Jack looked at his teacher. "You still have a badge?"

Jim shrugged his shoulders. "I still function as a reserve officer every now and then."

Mark wanted to go over the raid and what they were going to tell anyone and everyone about it.

Jim held up his hand to stop the multiple conversations that comment started. "Carol and I discussed this while we went to the doctor's office. Our suggestion is that we let Carol tell her people at CBI that her cover was blown. She can certainly prove that she was savagely beaten. The information in those files and her information will completely exonerate Jack and Laura as far as the killing of those two policemen are concerned. Not only that, but the conversations between Don Miland and his police mole were recorded setting up the hit. Don Miland didn't trust anyone. He recorded everything."

"She can say that, in the confusion, when Jose Fredo attacked Don Miland's place, she grabbed the files, which we will give her, and slipped out through an escape tunnel that Joe had bragged about. She can honestly say that she was about three-quarters of a mile away when the explosion took place."

Mark nodded, "That will work for covering up the part we played in Don Miland's demise but what about explaining your use of the police equipment and Jack and Laura's disappearance while the police were attempting to arrest them?"

Carol smiled. "I don't think that they will question those facts when they learn that they have been relieved of two of their worst players in a battle between themselves." She went over to the couch and lugged over the briefcases she had run back to get from the basement. She handed one to Jim Grady and one to Mark. "These are for your efforts in getting rid of that monster and, not incidentally, saving me while you were at it."

Mark opened the briefcase and stared at the stacks of one hundred dollar bills inside. He closed the case and shook his head. "I need a war chest but I don't want to use blood money for it."

Carol laughed. "That's not blood money in the usual sense. That money was for the person who brought Jack to Don Miland. I would say that you definitely brought Jack to him."

Jim asked Carol, "What am I to do with this much money? I don't think the department nor would the IRS approve."

Carol looked at the elderly man for a few seconds. Then she went over and sat down on the couch next to him. She put her hand on his arm. "Can't you use a secret fund to fight crime your way?"

The Sensei looked at Jack and Laura. "Well, student, what would you say that I should do with this moral dilemma?"

Jack thought for a while. "Think about what you have there. That money, in every sense of the word, is God's money. After you discuss it with Him, I think that you will have a definite sense of what to do with some of the money. Sensei, as to the rest of the money, you will make up your own mind, but I would do as the lady says. Put it to good use fighting the type of people that hurt other people to get it."

Jim looked at Mark and an understanding passed between them. Both men put the briefcases down and in turn they each gently shook Carol's hand. Hugging would hurt.

Steve had been half-listening to the conversation and paying the other half of his attention to the television set in the recreation room next door. He said, "Listen to this report on the TV."

Everyone moved into the next room and watched the news. The view being shown was the remains of Don Miland's estate. The announcer's voice was not as steady as normal. ."..what happened here? We have been told little by the police but have received a confidential report from one of our reliable sources that the top two organized crime families in Denver fought a battle here last night and early this morning. As you can see there is little left except a huge crater and bits and pieces of mangled bodies. This reporter wonders if the police know just how powerful the weapons are that these criminals possess. If they can do this to themselves, what in the world could they do to us?" He turned to his left and someone passed him a piece of paper.

The announcer read it and shook his head. He looked back into the camera, "I've just received word that the fight here last night was presumably caused by the murder and despicable mutilation of a young man by Don Miland's gang yesterday. The remains have been identified as the only son of Jose Fredo whose body is reportedly one of those killed here this morning."

"This morning the police arrested a group of people they found unconscious near where the main gate to this mansion used to be. They are being held in the Arapahoe County jail and we should have more information as to who they are later this morning. They have been identified as probably some of Joe Miland's gang. Of Joe Miland himself, the criminal who owned this place, nobody knows if he was in his house during the explosion or not. We will just have to wait for the forensic teams to determine if his DNA is in some of the pieces of humanity lying around here."

Nothing more substantial came out of the report. Carol telephoned her boss and left to meet with him. Steve and Larry had to leave to attend a meeting with a potential buyer of the NovaStar System. The meeting had been arranged for two months and could literally make everyone in the family independently wealthy. Steve quipped on the way out. "Well, the video tapes we got of last night's abortive break-in should sell the buyer."

Larry added, "Especially after we show him the mug sheets Jim gave us on 'Whitey' and his gang of specialists. Those guys were pros."

Mark took his leave with the observation that they were obviously all in God's hands and blessed beyond belief. The fact that they, mostly untrained personnel, could come out of the action last night without any of them being seriously hurt or killed was a result of good planning, capable people and obviously Divine intervention. He shook Jack's hand and hugged Laura. Standing in the doorway with his hands in his pockets he stared at the two of them and Jim Grady. "I want you to know, I've been really glad to know you people. I enjoyed working with you and I hope to do it again soon." He picked up his luggage and walked to his Chevrolet.

As Mark pulled out of the driveway the Sensei turned to Jack."Jack, if you have a minute, I need some advice." They returned to the living room.

Jim Grady took a deep breath and dove in. "I'm not sure I understand what really happened out there last night. I don't know how to explain the obvious power and purity of Jesus. On one hand I thought that I knew what was right and wrong in the universe and how to relate to it. Now I don't and it makes me feel very humble and yet... confused. On the other hand I know what I saw and what the battle was about. My soul was hanging in the balance and Jesus saved it. I need to understand Christ from a new standpoint, as a Christian." How should I approach this matter of religion?"

To Jack it was obvious that the worldly martial arts master had seen the light. Last night he had seen something most people never have an opportunity to experience. Jack was sure it had touched him so thoroughly that he had no doubts as to the fact that God and Satan do exist and that they are in eternal spiritual warfare with humanity in the middle. Jim Grady wanted to know how he could come to truly understand Jesus and God.

Jack sighed, "I too looked for answers from my own mind before I met Alan Throman. None of my own answers satisfied me. I have been indoctrinated in Christianity so quickly and so absolutely, I have total faith in Jesus, but I don't have the answers you are looking for. I would say that Alan can satisfy your need for details. Let me know when you plan to go see him, because Laura and I have the faith but not the understanding. We want to help everyone find Christ. We will go with you and we can all work on our walk with the Lord together."

Jim stood up to take his leave. "I think, personally, that what you two went through and what you did should rate a gold star from the honest people of the world. I know your eyes are now fixed on something far greater. I admire you both for your stand and would be proud to stand with you again, if the need arises."

Jack bowed to his friend and teacher. "Your guidance and support helped make it possible for us to get through this mess and I will never forget it as long as I live. Thank you for my life, my wife's life, and our honor." Jim bowed in return and left the house. Jack and Laura watched him leave.

Jack hugged his wife noticing again how wonderful she was and how very important to his life. "I think I'm going to buy this house from the company and live here. Want to live here with me, lady?"

She smiled "You forget that we don't have a stick of furniture of our own. Nor do we have any clothes, silverware, or anything. Think your credit cards can possibly stand the shopping spree that I am going on?"

Jack groaned, "Oh no. Not until we have a chance to unwind. We are going sailing in the South Seas to get far away from here until the police are convinced we didn't do anything. Since you don't have any bags to pack, let's get our passports out of the bank's safety deposit box and take off."

The couple left the house to retrieve their car and make a trip to the bank. Ten minutes after they left, the phone rang. After four rings it switched automatically to the answering machine. An extremely irritated man's voice sounded throughout the empty house. "Malone. You're dead. You hear me, "Dead!" The call ended and the house returned to silence.

Jack and Laura Malone will return to face new dangers in
"International Crossfire."

If this story has awakened your spirit or moved you to seek the love of Christ and His power for your life, whether you've never accepted Jesus as your Savior or you've fallen away, repeat the following prayer and begin a most wonderful journey into eternal life with Him today.

Father God in heaven, As You said in Your Holy Word, (Romans 10:9) that if we confess the Lord our God and believe in our hearts that God raised Jesus from the dead, we shall be saved.

(The prayer on the next page is a sample prayer when asking Jesus into your heart as your Savior. You can also pray this in your own words.)

Salvation Prayer

Dear God in heaven, I come to you in the name of Jesus. I confess to you that I am a sinner, and I am sorry for my sins and the life that I have lived; I need your forgiveness. I believe that your only begotten Son Jesus Christ shed His precious blood on the cross at Calvary and died for my sins, and I am now willing to turn from my sin.

Right now I confess Jesus as the Lord of my life and my soul. With all my heart, I truly believe that your Holy Spirit raised Jesus from the dead. Today I accept Jesus Christ as my personal Savior and according to Your Word, right now I am saved.

I thank you Jesus, for your unlimited grace which has saved me from my sins. I thank you Jesus that your grace that never leads to license, but rather it always leads to repentance. Therefore Lord Jesus, transform my life so that I may bring glory and honor to you alone and not to myself.

I thank you Lord Jesus, for dying for me at Calvary and giving me eternal life.

Amen.

If you just said this prayer and you meant it with all your heart, believe that you are now saved and have been born again.

You may ask, "Now that I am saved, what do I do next?" First of all you need to get into a spirit-filled, bible-based church that teaches the Scriptures, and you need to study God's Word.

Once you have found a church home, you will want to become water-baptized. By accepting Christ you are baptized in the spirit, but it is through water-baptism that you publically announce your obedience to the Lord Jesus. Water baptism is a symbol of your salvation from the dead. You were dead but now you live, for Jesus Christ has redeemed you for a price! The price was His atoning death on the cross. May God Bless You!